Loved this book!

Romance, mystery, the De

... kept me guessing right u

I have read all of Alexandı

get better and better.

Highly recommend ☺

Stumbled onto these books by sheer fluke and so pleased I did! Easy to read and really great plot and characters. Looking forward to the next April adventure

A very entertaining read, couldn't put it down. Excellent characters, set in the beautiful Derbyshire Dales, an intriguing plot and a bit of romance. This book has it all, highly recommended.

I genuinely did not unravel the plot until the end of the book. April is an engaging heroine with a lovely dog living in beautiful part of the country. The twists and turns keep you hooked and I cant wait for a third instalment in the series.

An April Stanislavski Murder Mystery

MURDER ON HER DOORSTEP

Alexandra Jordan

Copyright © 2020 Alexandra Jordan

All rights reserved.
ISBN: 9798664457582

CHAPTER 1

She finds it sticking out of a bedside drawer. Putting aside her duster, she pulls at it. It's a crumpled page of A4, torn from a refill pad. Not a proper letter at all …

2

Chatsworth, Derbyshire
IT all began with a lovely afternoon walk through the Derbyshire countryside. A November chill clawed at the air as I wrapped my soft cashmere around my neck and stepped away from the car.

The sky in the distance was a deep watermelon pink. Long fingers of orange stretched down to earth like flames. It was a beautiful sunset. At only four o'clock.

Dash, my excitable King Charles spaniel, tugged impatiently at his lead. But I stood my ground, admiring that beautiful sky, the rolling hills, and Chatsworth House in the distance. Gold leaf on the window frames and roof finials reflected the afternoon sun, shining pure and bright like new-bought wedding rings.

Up high and to the left of the House stands the Hunting Tower; to the right the Cascade. Completed in 1701, it's an amazing feature, a manmade waterfall specially designed to entertain the masses, and I love it.

Heading towards the Cascade, we turned right to walk along the bank of the river, the Derwent. The scent of rotting leaves filled the air as I pushed my walking boots through long, clinging grass, and I smiled at the breeze skimming my face.

Just over half an hour later I stopped, hot and breathless and panting even more than Dash, with his lolling tongue and his happy shining eyes. We were quite alone beside the river and it was now completely dark, the only source of light the waxing moon. Pulling out my torch, I tugged on Dash's lead and headed back to the car, back to Edensor, the delightful village owned by the Chatsworth Estate, with its cobalt-blue doors and windows. My Mini convertible was parked on the kerb opposite, just outside the estate's offices.

To avoid walking along the main road, I climbed the grassy bank to Edensor and paused beside a hefty oak tree to catch my breath. The 217 bus drove by, and a couple of small cars, but otherwise all was silent. Hungry now and ready for home, I pulled on Dash's lead. But he resisted. He was sniffing greedily at the ground.

'Come on, Dash,' I said, pulling him away.

But he barked at me in a way I'd never seen before. A single, low bark. Sharp. Fearful. Then he backed slowly away.

My heart was pounding.

There was something there.

'What is it, Dash, sweetie?'

Keeping him close beside me, I used my torch to look around. The tree's lowest branch spread out just above my head and the ground beneath it was piled high with wet, rotting leaves. There was nothing else there.

Placing my free hand against the tree trunk, I balanced on my left leg and poked with the right. But as I pushed away the leaves, I hit something. Something big and heavy and solid.

I shone the torch at it.

A body.

It was a dead body.

My stomach lurched but I controlled it, covering my mouth with my hand.

I'd only revealed his head and shoulders, but the poor guy's shirt, the winged collar type, the kind you wear with a dinner suit, had been ripped open at the neck and was thick with blood. His face had a green tinge to it, there were dark blotches around his throat, and his expression ...

Terrified, I opened my mouth to scream, but made myself stop. Pulling at Dash's lead, I ran. Back to the car.

*

I'd spent the previous weekend in Brussels with Colin, my chap. We'd had a lovely time, but the Christmas season had brought the crowds, and it was busy, noisy, choked with traffic. The queues were horrendous, the streets packed. Non-stop. So that Monday morning, despite sleeping in until ten o'clock, I'd felt exhausted and much too tired to work. What I actually needed was fresh air and exercise.

So I'd unpacked my case and filled the washing machine, then popped into the village for fresh food and milk. After returning home, I made lunch and chatted to Mum on the phone about her forthcoming wedding. We were all so excited - it was going to be an amazing day. Then I did a few other necessities around the house, put my wet clothes into the drier, and drove out to Chatsworth while they tumbled. The drive out was wonderful, the sky a deep blue, the sun low and bright. Winter was definitely here - only four weeks to Christmas. But what a four weeks it was.

I rang the police, of course. Then I texted Sean McGuire, an old friend of mine and senior crime reporter for the Sheffield Star. I have a good knowledge of the Peak District, both its beauty and its intricacies, and Sean had asked me to help with a case before. So I knew he'd be interested in this one.

Twenty minutes later, a DCI Watkins turned up with a crew of coppers and a young WPC called Sonia, her spiky hair dyed a vibrant red. DCI Watkins jotted down the few bits of information I could give him, then crossed the road to organise his crew. WPC Sonia kindly sat in the car with me until Sean arrived.

We watched as the police set up floodlights and streams of yellow tape. Flashes of bright light flickered across the road as they took photos of the body and the ground surrounding it. Cars arrived and went away again. An ambulance arrived and just sat there, waiting.

Finally Sean arrived, his face filling the driver's window. 'You sitting here forever, or are we going to get our hands dirty?'

I was beginning to feel cold, anyway. 'I'm coming.'

So I left Dash in the car with the window slightly open while Sean, PC Sonia and I walked across the road. Sean and I had no authority to approach the body, however, so we just had to stand and watch while two guys in white overalls studied it and took even more photos.

But within minutes a Volvo pulled up and DI Jasper appeared, darting beneath the tape and barking orders to the crew. Sean and I had had dealings with her on our previous case. In plain clothes, slim with short grey hair and pale eyes, she eventually acknowledged our presence, lifted the tape and beckoned us in with latex-covered hands.

'Come on in, you two. Shoe covers are over there, look.' She pointed to a box on the ground behind us and we pulled some on hastily. Luckily, I'd already replaced my muddy walking boots with trainers. 'It's good to see you both. But next time let's just make it coffee, shall we?'

Sean grinned. 'If you say so. What exactly have we got here, then?'

'Sam here from Forensics says a knife attack, two days ago. But bear with me.'

Crouching down, she pulled against the bloodied fabric of the shirt until the wound beneath was exposed, its edges open and raw. As if a small animal had taken a bite. I stepped back, my stomach trying to pull away.

DI Jasper turned. 'You okay, April?'

Hot and sweaty, I nodded. But as she turned back to examine the wound, I did have to walk away. My heart raced. My lungs gasped for breath. Sean followed, placing his arm around me, his voice like warm cocoa.

'Are you up for this, April? I'll take you home if you like.'

Swallowing back my stupid, irrational fear, I looked up at him. I did feel pretty nauseous, but no way was I missing out on this.

'No, no, I'm fine. Thanks. I just need a minute.'

'Okay, if you're sure. We don't want you keeling over.'

We turned back to the scene unfolding before us. A breeze tugged at the edge of DI Jasper's coat, but she held it down as she questioned a young PC.

'So where did the knife get to, PC Cruickshank?'

'DCI Watkins just took it back for Forensics, Ma'am. It's okay, though – we got plenty of photos. He says it's some kind of kitchen knife?'

'Okay. Thanks.' She nodded to us. 'So if you could get this into the papers quickly, Sean, I'd appreciate it. We need to be rattling someone's cage, I think.'

He nodded. 'Of course, Kathryn. First thing tomorrow.' He took hold of my arm. 'But I think we need to get April back now, if that's okay?'

'Of course. Try to get some rest, April – you've had a nasty shock.'

But I protested. 'No, Sean, I want to stay. I need to know what happened.'

'Not a lot to say at the moment,' DI Jasper replied. 'We have a knife attack, probably Saturday, and it most likely happened at night, going on the shirt he's wearing. But we need to comb the area thoroughly and get the body to Forensics before we can make any definite assumptions.'

'I need to get back and write my report, anyway,' said Sean. 'We need to let someone know we've uncovered his dirty little secret. Although how he thought it would stay hidden is a mystery in itself.'

'Indeed,' agreed DI Jasper. 'And don't worry, I'll keep you updated.'

By this time the shock was really setting in and I began to shiver violently. Not helped by the fact I'd eaten so early and was suffering low blood sugar. So I allowed Sean to pull me away, my mind numb, my feet clinging to the soil like glue.

Once we'd crossed the road, however, I began to feel slightly better.

'Kathryn?' I said. 'Kathryn? Since when were you two on first-name terms?'

'Since she finally arrested Emilisa Meadows-Whitworth.'

'Oh? So it was all thanks to you, was it?'

I unlocked the car and opened the door, to be greeted by the sound of Dash yapping.

'Sweetie,' I said, encouraging him to stay on his seat. 'Haven't you been a good boy, sitting there for so long?'

Sean waited while I removed my shoe covers, threw them into the boot, and climbed into the car. Then he shook his head at me.

'And no, it wasn't all down to me, April. You had a hand in the Meadows-Whitworth case too - of course you did. But Kathryn's keen on getting stuff into the papers as soon as. So yes, she does like to butter me up.'

Relieved to be driving away from that awful place, I pushed into first gear and smiled.

'It's fine, Sean, I was only joking. Let me know what happens, yes?'

Sean and I go back a long way. We were at school together; same year, same class, both top in English. He was my very first boyfriend before we went our separate ways, each marrying other people, each divorcing them. We met up again a year ago when he asked me to help find information about a spate of burglaries in Millerstone.

Millerstone. My beautiful village. The inspiration behind Charlotte Bronte's *Jane Eyre*.

It was such a sad case, though. Emilisa Meadows-Whitworth only turned to crime in order to fund her son's rehab fees in London. But what's that old saying? *Before you judge me, walk a mile in my shoes ...*

I think the worst thing about the case was that Emilisa's husband was decidedly wealthy and could easily have paid the fees himself. But he'd disowned their son once he discovered he was a user. Poor Emilisa had to steal, and then kill, in order to get the money.

So Sean's a reporter for the Sheffield Star. I'm an author of romance novels, chick-lit stuff, the kind with pastel colours and swirly girly scrolls on the cover. But they sell. Which means I can afford to live in Millerstone, a stunningly beautiful village on the edge of the Peak District.

Which is how I happened to find that body in the grounds of Edensor. Not quite what you expect when you're out walking your King Charles spaniel puppy on a Monday afternoon. Actually, he wasn't so much a puppy. I got him from an old friend of mine, Louise, who'd decided to emigrate to California to be with her chap. She'd not had Dash long, didn't think it fair to drag him all the way there, so she asked me to take him on. And I have to say he's such a warm, gentle soul, and I wouldn't be without him now. Even though I do have to organise a dog-sitter every other weekend (usually Mum) and my otherwise pristine house is full of dirty towels and brushes and smelly food.

Anyway, I digress. As usual.

Pulling up outside my house, I released Dash from the car. The sky was beautiful that night - so quiet and clear, the moon nearly full, the stars heavy, dazzling. Sighing deeply, I unlocked my front door. To the bleep, bleep of the intruder alarm. It cut into my senses, making me uptight again, and I dashed forward to push in the code.

Turning back to close the door, I picked up the mail I'd ignored earlier. A few letters, nothing important, and a recent edition of the local news rag, the Millerstone Voice. Carrying them through to the kitchen, I threw them onto the table. But as I did so, the magazine fell open at the page advertising a play. *Dangerous Corner*, by J B Priestley. To be performed by Cavendish Amateur Dramatics at Chatsworth House.

I gasped.

The picture, a pen and ink drawing, looked curiously like the man we'd just left, dead on the ground.

'It's the shirt,' I said. 'It has the same collar.'

Dash, who'd been hanging around at the bottom of the stairs, all sleepy and forlorn, suddenly perked up.

I grinned. 'No, Dash, I'm not talking to you. Although - yes - I may as well be.'

My phone bleeped suddenly and I pulled it from my bag. It was Sean.

You get home alright? Just checking you're okay after your nasty shock. Get some sleep and you'll feel better. I'll be up past midnight writing this assignment – suppose that's the nature of the job.

I replied.

Thank goodness I work my own hours! Hope it doesn't take too long. Night night.

There was also a text from Alfie, the director of my local amdram group, the Village Players. I should have been at rehearsal that evening. So I replied, apologising and explaining what had happened. Poor Alfie. Although I'm pretty good at learning my lines, so he wouldn't have worried too much.

I pulled my clothes from the drier and shook them out while Dash had a run around the back garden. My hunger pangs returned suddenly, but it was too late to cook, so I made decaf tea and toast and marmalade, and carried it upstairs with half a bar of Green and Black's tucked beneath my arm.

But then I changed my mind. So much for working my own hours.

I needed to switch off. I couldn't have slept if I'd tried. My head was too full, bursting with awful images that raced ahead of me, that caught at my throat, that threatened to choke me.

I am not good with dead bodies.

So I headed downstairs, back to my office, with Dash following on behind. Soft moonlight filtered through the curtains, books lay open on the desk, and my big blue cardigan had fallen off the chair onto the floor. Lighting some jasmine-scented candles (I'm Aries – I just love candles), I wrapped my cardigan around me and began to write, breaking off small pieces of toast, then chocolate, as I went.

My office is palatial, no expense spared. There's an oak desk, my faithful MacBook, and deep wall to wall carpeting in a dark and mysterious purple. Then there's my chair - a swivel carved from warm oak - and two soft cushions. No phone. No music. No biscuit tin. Just me and my computer. Although I do have a wall that's completely dedicated to books. Reference books, novels, my own first editions, poetry books. Everything I need to help with my writing. Inspiration for when I need it, I suppose.

But it's divine. I can switch off and switch on again with the precision of a light-bulb.

I'd begun a play, a two-parter about a professional theatre company whose director hires prostitutes and brings them back to the theatre after rehearsal. His long-suffering and extremely rich wife is under the impression he makes his actors rehearse and rehearse until he's satisfied with their performances, sometimes until midnight. She does not learn until the second act exactly what it is that does satisfy him. And then she has her revenge.

I hadn't quite decided what the revenge was to be. So I played around with a few ideas until, finally sleepy at two o'clock, I saved my work, blew out the candles, woke up Dash (bless him), and crawled up to bed.

But I was halfway up the stairs when I realised something. I realised that the dead guy under the oak tree might actually have had something to do with the J B Priestley play at Chatsworth. Admittedly, it can take a while for things to filter through to my mind when I'm tired. But that shirt was definitely not the type you'd wear for a leisurely walk through the countryside.

3

Flattening the crumpled letter with the palm of her hand, she reads it over and over again. Three times at first, then another three ...

4

Millerstone, Derbyshire

THE clear night had made for a beautiful Tuesday morning, sunny and fresh. A complete turn-around from the heavy rain of the weekend. I sat in my office until twelve o'clock writing the manuscript my agent Sandy had suggested. It was the usual chick-lit, of course, but set in St Maxime, South of France. A love affair between a dermatologist who performs facelifts on the idle rich, and a pretty waitress from New Jersey. It was rather formulaic, so I was working on some kind of a twist.

Eventually, however, my stomach got the better of me, so I wandered through to the kitchen, switched on Radio Two – Jeremy Vine and the latest Hollywood scandal - and made a lunch of pasta, curried prawns and salad. I read as I ate - *The Guernsey Literary and Potato Peel Pie Society* - a romance set in the Second World War. I found it enchanting, captivating, but even so I kept yawning as the rigours of the previous night began to take their toll.

Placing my dirty pots inside the dishwasher, I stood up to rub my aching back. The previous night was definitely having an effect on me, I decided. I had managed to get to sleep, but I'd tossed and turned so much the duvet had fallen to the floor, waking me up again. I needed time off, time to relax, maybe get some gardening done while the weather was good.

Pulling open the back door, I looked out at my garden, which was green and fresh and sunlit. Then I looked down at the back step, which was not such a pretty sight, with lumps of cat food scattered around and splashes of milk that had gone sour. A local cat, a big ginger with soft white paws, had begun to visit every day, and I'd been leaving out food and milk for him. Both bowls were now empty, so I washed them, and the back step, and put out fresh milk with a bowl of chicken-flavoured Whiskas.

I then fastened up my long hair, spent time clipping back the yew hedge, and filled my terracotta planters with soil. But after an hour or so I could truly feel the result of my late night, so I put down my trowel, made hot tea and sat at the garden table. Placing a large woollen throw around my shoulders, I sat with Dash at my feet, and my book in my hands.

I must have nodded off because when my phone rang I had to shake myself awake. It was Sean again.

'Hi, Sean.'

'Hi there. I'm just wondering if you're free this afternoon at all?'

I nodded at the table. 'Yes. Of course.'

'I'll see you later then,' and he rang off.

Smiling, I went back to my book. So when Sean arrived forty minutes later, I was still in the garden, still wrapped inside my throw, and still reading. The air was becoming quite chilly by now, but I really did need the fresh air. Dash and I had spent a few minutes playing sticks in order to warm up, but he would never catch it, would just pick it up once it had landed and carry it back to me. So I'd given up.

'I thought you must be in the garden - I've been ringing the bell,' Sean said as he approached from the side of the house, a brown paper bag in his hand.

'Sorry, I didn't hear you. What's that?' I looked at the bag questioningly.

He smiled, his deep blue eyes crinkling attractively. 'Vanilla slices. Just fancied them.'

'Thanks, Sean,' I moaned. 'That'll do my waistline a whole lot of good.'

'One won't hurt, will it? It's not like you're fat or anything.' He looked at me appealingly.

I smiled. 'Go on, then. Flatterer.'

'I'll pop the kettle on, shall I?'

'You sure know how to treat a girl.'

As he busied himself in the kitchen I closed my eyes and relaxed, until he returned five minutes later with a tray holding two mugs of steaming tea, and vanilla slices and forks on plates.

'How are you feeling? A bit better?' he asked.

'Much better, thank you. I am a bit tired, but I think I'm still getting over the weekend at Colin's, if I'm honest.'

'He's still working in Brussels, then?'

Yes, I thought. Still working in Brussels. Still working in Brussels with the ex-wife.

'Yep,' I said.

'He'll be coming here this weekend, then?'

'He will. Although I'm not really in the mood to be rushing around again, if I'm honest, and I've got work I need to catch up on.'

'Oh, you'll be fine by then. It's just the shock of last night.' He studied my face. 'You two are alright, aren't you - I mean, since - you know?'

I nodded. 'We're fine, Sean. It's fine. Really.'

The fact is that Sean and I had had a little - I'm not really sure how to describe it - incident? The previous year, it was. Bonfire Night. We'd been celebrating our success at catching Emilisa Meadows-Whitworth, and well, to put it bluntly, I'd woken up in Sean's bed.

Nothing had happened. Absolutely nothing had happened. Sean was curled up on the sofa all night. But - oh dear - not good.

Because I hadn't told Colin. Well, if he would insist on walking around Brussels with the ex-wife, what must he expect?

He worked in IT, and so did she. That's how they first met. So when I discovered she was working in Brussels too - well, you can imagine.

When Colin first took on this contract, we'd agreed to meet up every weekend. I would fly there one weekend; he'd fly here the following weekend. But work was slowly taking over, it didn't always happen. I had deadlines to meet. He had clients to entertain.

So long as he wasn't entertaining *her*.

Sean clicked his fingers. 'Penny for them?'

I blinked. 'Sorry Sean, just feeling a bit fragile today. I did try planting some pansies, but I've not got very far. As you can see.'

My planters stood in a row on the garden path. An open bag of soil and three trays of winter pansies littered the lawn.

'Finding a dead body like that must be a shock to the system. You need to rest up a bit, by the looks of you.'

'I know.' Picking up my fork, I released a corner of my vanilla slice and ate. It was sweet and tangy and delicious. 'Thanks, Sean. This is actually just what I needed.'

'Good. Because we have work to do.'

I grinned. 'There had to be a catch.'

'DI Jasper rang first thing this morning.'

'You mean Kathryn?'

His eyes creased in the sunshine. 'Very funny.'

'And?'

'The dead guy is from Millerstone – not far from you.'

'What? You're joking.'

His face set like stone. 'Unfortunately not. He lives, or did live, on the main road going out towards Grindleford. His wife's a locum pharmacist, works in Sheffield.'

'So where was she when he went missing? How come he was lying there for two days and no-one said anything?'

'New York, apparently. Some seminar or other. She had been ringing him to chat, but when he didn't reply she thought he was busy, seeing to one of his many clients, or out socialising. In fact, he had been to a rehearsal at Chatsworth House that night – they found his car in the car park. They do plays there, you know, with a posh dinner and all that. They have a theatre that dates back to 1820, but it was all painted over, ended up as a sewing room, and they only rediscovered it again a few years ago.'

I smiled. 'I already knew that. And I already knew he was involved in the play.'

'What?'

'I saw a picture advertising it in the local rag. The dead guy was wearing the same shirt, and he *was* killed near Chatsworth. It all seemed to fit.'

'Why didn't you say something earlier?'

'I only saw it when I got home last night, and it was only a thought. I didn't really think I'd found the answer. I was half asleep, to be honest, and it just came into my head. Sorry.'

'No, don't be. But you're in the wrong business – you do know that?'

'Ha! Very funny, Sean. You think I'd rather be looking for dead bodies in the cold than sitting in my lovely warm office, writing glamorous love stories?'

'No. No, I don't think that - that's silly. But you do seem to have a knack for picking up on things.'

'It's my imagination. I just let it run riot and it seems to come up with the answers.'

'Well, it's not to be sniffed at, I say. Well done.'

I smiled. 'Thank you.'

'Anyway, the reason I'm here …'

'To bring me vanilla slices, of course.' I took another bite.

'Well, yes. And to make the tea. But seriously, DI Jasper says she'd like us to help with this case – because you know the area, and because we helped solve that crime last year so beautifully. If we wouldn't mind.'

I groaned. 'You do realise I have a play on the go - I was supposed to be at rehearsal last night and I missed it? Never mind the deadline I have to meet with my book? And a mother who's planning a wedding? And a lover who's living the other side of the North Sea?'

He smiled. 'There you go, then. You must have loads of time on your hands. Relationships take up so much of your time, don't they? So if he's over there and you're over here ...'

'It's alright for you,' I protested. 'You only have the one job to do, and it looks as if you need help with that.'

Smiling, he just sipped his tea. 'So what's this about your mother getting married?'

'It's the engagement party tonight.'

'So who is he, the lucky guy?'

Sean remembered Mum of old, of course. Back in the day, when he had acne and his hair was frizzy with split ends, and she was a glamorous speech therapist walking along hospital corridors in her white coat and high heels.

'He's a musician, actually. A songwriter. He's called Jim Allsop and he lives in that old farmhouse up Sheffield Road.'

'I've heard of him. So how did they meet up? I thought he was a bit of a recluse?'

'My sister Jo does his gardening, and over the years they've become really good friends. Then last year, when we were organising the auction for the Village Players, he agreed to be auctioneer. And well, he and Mum got to chatting, he offered to give her driving lessons, and the rest is history, as they say.'

He beamed. 'That's lovely news, April.'

I had a sudden thought. 'Look, I know you've got work to do, but why don't you come to the party with me? I don't have anyone to take – well, not anyone who's around, anyway.'

'Tonight, did you say?'

'It's at Jim's place, starts at seven-thirty. Just a small gathering, but it should be fun.'

'Tell you what. If you agree to help with this murder enquiry, I'll accompany you to the party.'

I hesitated. I really did have a lot on. But the idea of becoming involved in another murder case was hard to resist. Captivating, in fact.

'Alright, Sean, it's a deal. But if I end up locked in an old shed like last time, there'll be hell to pay.'

Our previous case had ended with my being locked inside a shed by the cannabis farmer. I'd been locked up all night, cold and dark and scared, until the police found me early next morning.

Sean gave me his boyish grin. 'We got you out, didn't we?'

'Only after a night of hell, thinking I'd never be found. So I don't want to go through that again. Okay?'

'I give you my word, April. I promise to look after you, and ne'er an old shed shall cross thy path.'

*

Jim's old farmhouse, with its far-reaching views of Grindleford and Abney, was a razzle dazzle of ageing rock stars, family members and loyal friends. For one night only. People who'd seen Mum and Jim through the good times and the bad. People who really deserved to share their joy. There was Mum's old friend Rita - her carmine red lipstick a constant smile – and Rita's daughter Sofia and little granddaughter Teru, with her beautiful dark skin and huge brown eyes. My sister Jo was also there, with her husband Joe and daughters Vicky, Rebecca and Daisy. Jim's brother Ken and wife Trish were there. And of course Mum was there, her simple diamond ring blazing with light as she poured a chilled Chenin Blanc into lead crystal glasses. Her smile too, was alight, but with sheer happiness. Wearing a demure lime green dress with pearls at her neck, she was a million miles away from the woman she had been - still in her dressing gown at lunchtime, worrying about the cleaner stealing her jewellery. We'd thought they were the early signs of dementia, but they weren't. It was another three syllable word that was the problem. Loneliness.

She waved us in as we arrived. 'Come on in, love. Isn't it a nice big kitchen?'

And it was. A proper farmhouse kitchen. With a huge island made from polished marble in soft grey, and a display cabinet full of *Emma Bridgewater* in black and cream. A small mug announced COFFEE GIVES ME CLARITY & SOMETIMES INSPIRATION. I smiled, thinking how that applied to me, too.

The food looked delicious. Sausage rolls, sandwiches, vol-au-vents, cheese and pineapple on sticks, quiche, blue cheese pizza, various curries and succulent salads. It was all perfect, in fact, even the quiches that are normally soggy and which I usually avoid.

Sean and I helped ourselves to food and wine, carrying it through to the lounge. Here, patio doors filled the whole of one wall, overlooking the moors and the glorious Hope Valley below. Not that we could see it; it was too dark. But we could imagine. Inside the room, three velvet Chesterfields in olive green sat opposite the window, creating a soft rectangle, a large coffee table at its centre. Here, a tall glass vase held a bouquet of pink and white roses, setting off the room perfectly, and I smiled, finally knowing without a doubt that Jim Allsop would make Mum a very happy lady.

His silver hair shoulder-length, his brown eyes smiling, Jim came bouncing towards us.

'April, love – how are you? Welcome to our humble abode.'

'Thanks, Jim, and it's not humble by any means. I love it.' I turned to Sean. 'This is Sean, an old friend of mine. I hope you don't mind me bringing him along.'

'Not at all. I'm very pleased to meet you,' said Jim, shaking hands.

'The wedding's the Saturday before Christmas, then?' said Sean.

Jim smiled happily. 'It is. Not long now. So exciting, but also very humbling. Your mother is a wonderful lady.'

I smiled. 'She's moving in before that, though, isn't she?'

Mum had discussed it with me weeks ago. It hadn't been an easy decision for someone of her generation. But they were nearly married anyway, so why not?

Jim nodded. 'It makes sense. Silly us living in two houses when she could move in with me. And it means I can look after her properly.'

'Well, I've not seen her so happy in years. It is a pity about the driving lessons, though.'

He laughed at that. 'It is. She could have been driving me home when I've had a drink or two. But it wasn't to be, was it? And it did lead to us getting to know each other, so no harm done.'

Jim had offered to give Mum driving lessons when they first met. But after driving out to Castleton and back – a fairly straight and easy run - for six months, she decided driving wasn't for her and gave up. Meanwhile, of course, she and Jim had become firm friends, and then lovers. So sweet.

'So when is she moving in?' I asked.

'Tomorrow. It's all arranged. We've had a couple of offers on the house already, so it shouldn't be long until it's all sold up.'

'But she'll love living here, Jim. It is beautiful.'

'Thank you - it's kind of you to say.'

At that moment Jo waved me over, so I left Jim and Sean to chat.

'He's nice,' she said, smiling and nodding towards Sean.

'It's Sean. He's a friend.'

'Oh - right. The reporter friend.'

I nodded. 'The reporter friend.'

'He's still nice, though. Don't you like him?'

'Of course I like him. But not like that. We really are just friends, and that's how I want it to stay. Come on, I'll introduce you.'

We walked over to the two men, who were chatting about some local band Sean had been to see.

'Sean, this is my sister Jo.'

He held out his hand. 'Hi, Jo. Nice to meet you. I think you were about thirteen the last time we met.'

She laughed. 'What, all fat and spotty and annoying?'

'Not at all. I do remember the pigtails, though.'

'I don't remember you at all. Sorry.'

'No, you wouldn't. You were too engrossed in your new puppy.'

'Bailey?'

'Is that his name?'

'Was. He was a rescue dog – he died a few years later. He was quite old when we got him, and he never seemed to recover properly after that mild stroke he had.'

'Sorry about that,' said Sean.

She smiled. 'Hey - mustn't get miserable, or we'll spoil the party.'

'Come on,' I said. 'Let's get some more wine.'

'If you give it a minute, I'm just about to propose a toast,' said Jim. 'I'll go get the champagne and see where your mum's got to.'

Jim's speech was everything I could have wished for. It filled my heart to see Mum so happy. And we had such a wonderful evening. Laughter, tears, wine and caviar, music and dancing. It ended at twelve o'clock with silent fireworks in the light of the full moon, which were amazing, despite the lack of sound, and I had tears in my eyes when they ended.

Mum was so lucky. Jim was such a lovely man.

So we said our goodbyes and were just leaving when Sean's phone rang.

'It's DI Jasper,' he said. 'Hi there - Sean McGuire speaking.'

The look on his face said it all.

5

The author has used blue pen, the writing slanted slightly to the left, the words anxious, desperate ...

6

Millerstone, Derbyshire

MY phone rang again. But I ignored it. Again.

It had been one of those mornings. I just wanted to hide in the garden, plant my pansies, put food out for Dash and the cat, and ignore the world. I needed to bury my thoughts in self-pity, to wonder why the hell I'd taken my car into the village at that particular time on that particular morning, and what on earth had made me take my car in the first place when I could so easily have walked.

I'd only popped out for milk and a paper, and to order a Christmas tree from the greengrocers. But I was fully aware of the publishing deadline Sandy had set me, the lines I had to learn, and the weekends away that were using up precious hours. So time was of the essence, and that's why I drove instead of walking. However, more haste, less speed, as I was to prove to my cost.

The guy, the idiot who ran into me, had been talking on his phone, hadn't seen the lights change, or my brake lights come on. I'd been driving slowly as well, looking for a parking space, the village overcrowded with visitors eager to buy presents unique to the Peak District.

We exchanged details, of course, and I made sure to take photos with my phone. But I couldn't get over the fact that he didn't seem sorry for running into the back of me. Not one bit. It was as if he did it every day, knew every nook and cranny of a car's bodywork, and wasn't even apologetic. Plus, he smelled weird - kind of yeasty - as if he hadn't washed his clothes in months. Which wouldn't have surprised me, actually. Even Dash was sniffing around him with distaste.

But it took the entire morning to sort everything out. I drove my car into Millerstone Garage, checked out the damage, and left it to be repaired. Luckily, they had room on their calendar. But my poor car, my pride and joy, needed a new rear bumper and some paintwork. About nine hundred pounds' worth.

So I rang the guy who'd run into me, a Carl Smith, to tell him how much it would cost, and that he might want to contact his insurers. He then offered to do the repairs himself. Of course he did. He's in the trade, he said, with a garage out at Gleadless. But I declined, thanking him politely and telling him I'd already arranged everything. I've been taking my car to Millerstone Garage for years, wouldn't trust anyone else, especially not someone idiotic enough to run into the back of me. So in the end I wasted about three hours on that little incident.

So much for deadlines.

I was forced to answer my incessantly-ringing phone, however, because Dash began to howl. So I picked it up, ran into the kitchen away from him, and answered.

'Hi there,' I said. 'April Stanislavski speaking.'

'Morning – it's Kathryn Jasper here. How are you doing, April? Have you recovered from Monday night yet?'

'I'm okay, I think – thank you. Well, apart from crashing my Mini this morning.'

'You're joking. Are you okay? What happened?'

'Some idiot in an Astra ran into me at the lights.'

'A bloke?'

I grinned, despite my frustration. 'A bloke. *Sorry, love,* I mimicked, *I was just talking on the phone. Hands-free, of course, love.*'

She laughed. 'Yeah. I'll bet. But you're alright, aren't you? No injuries or anything?'

I rubbed the base of my spine. 'I'm fine, other than a bit of backache.'

'Arsehole.'

'Too right. But I'll be okay. I think I'm more upset about my car than anything.'

'Well, I might have just the thing to take your mind off it.'

I walked outside, into the sunshine. The ginger cat had cleared both bowls and disappeared.

'Sean's already told me about the guy you found in the river,' I said. 'I was with him when you rang last night.'

'I know. Two deaths in one week, just like that. But look, Sean says you've agreed to help investigate the guy you found in Edensor, and I was wondering if you'd help out with this one too. We need to know if they're linked at all. It's just, with you living in the area?'

I sat down at the garden table, thoughts of impending deadlines and that morning's incident all forgotten. This was exciting stuff.

'Go on.'

'Well, you probably already know the deceased was Felix Porter-Bentley, head forester at Chatsworth House. He died of alcohol poisoning - according to the pathologist, anyway.'

'You sound unconvinced. Surely they won't have got it wrong?'

'It's a difficult one. You see, we've just interviewed some of Felix's work colleagues, and none of them knew him as a drinker. Even at social gatherings, he only ever had a pint or two. He seems a solid type, although no family, apart from a daughter living in Canada, the result of a marriage that dissolved years ago. He has a sister too, and we're trying to trace her. Her last known address was Islington, London, but she's moved.'

'What had the poor guy been drinking, exactly?'

'Whisky. Point five per cent blood alcohol content. Not good.'

'Gosh. Had he been out somewhere special, do we know?'

I noticed I'd just used the *we* word. No backing out now, then ...

'Not that we know of. But that's where you come in, April. We need to know if there's any connection with Lucas Hanssen, the guy you found. Just – with both deaths being the same week and in the same area. Also, Lucas knew one of the Village Players, and I recall you're also a member?'

I nodded. 'Yes. Who is it?'

'Gemma Jameson. Do you know her?'

I nodded. 'I do, yes, of course.'

'Lucas is her lover. Or was.'

A shiver ran through me. Sean had said Lucas was at a rehearsal the night of his death, and Gemma was also a member of Cavendish Amateur Dramatics. In fact, drama was her life. She often rehearsed two plays at the same time. How she remembered the lines of two different characters I shall never know.

'Poor Gemma,' I said. 'I take it she already knows?'

'We've been to see her, just to let her know. We've not interviewed her yet, but we'll need to at some point, once she's over the shock. People aren't always that forthcoming with the police though, so I was hoping ...'

I raced ahead. 'You thought I might get more out of her if I interviewed her?'

'Well, not exactly an interview. I thought maybe you could just call round, express your condolences, have a chat?'

I sighed inwardly. It all sounded very exciting, but I still had that deadline to meet. Sandy would not be happy. I'd just have to cut some corners.

'Okay,' I said. 'I'll do it. So what exactly do you need me to find out?'

'Whatever you can about Lucas Hanssen. His lifestyle, contacts, how he made his money.'

'He's well-off, then?'

'Well, he certainly lives in a nice place. He's self-employed, some kind of financial adviser. So I'm guessing he's - was - pretty good with money. Although his wife's a locum pharmacist, so she'll earn a fair bit, I guess.'

I sighed. Why Gemma had to fall in love with someone who was married, I'll never know. She was so lovely she could have had any man she wanted. None of this was making any sense at all.

'Do you have Gemma's address, DI Jasper?'

'I'll text it through. It's only the other side of Bakewell, so not too far.'

'When do you want me to call round?'

'As soon as. According to Lucas's friends, his wife has no idea there's a mistress. So if he could keep

Gemma a secret, there may be other secrets. But we need as much information as possible, and obviously any connection with Felix Porter-Bentley. And just to let you know – we've diagnosed Lucas's time of death. Between nine and ten o'clock, Saturday night.'

I gasped. 'So he must have left the rehearsal halfway through. In costume?'

'Exactly.'

I nodded at Dash, tickling his ears. 'Okay. I'll get in touch.'

*

I decided to call Gemma the following day, to give her time to come to terms with her loss. Anyway, I had no car until Millerstone Garage had finished with it. And also, I'd agreed to call on Toni, my best friend, once she'd finished work.

Toni and I go back a long way. She's the village hairdresser, brilliant at taming my wavy blonde hair. She lives on the short cobbled street behind the post office in a very nice 1920's bungalow. Mike, her ex, a high-up manager at *Santander*, bought it for her as part of their divorce settlement. He also paid off the business loan on her salon, a small place she and Alistair Bridges, the dentist, share. A generous man, her ex, no doubt about it. They have two kids, Abigail and Jack, and even though Toni does still have some money problems, she's always fun to be with, with her curly red hair and her ready smile. Even though she's on a constant diet. Or tries to be.

So, wrapping myself in my blue duffle coat and scarf, I left the house with Dash at just after five, ambled along Jaggers Lane, and turned left onto the main road. Leaving behind the darkness of the lane, I continued on past the warmly-lit Ashbourne Hotel, originally a centuries' old coaching inn, but now a rather classy five-star. The indescribable aroma of French Onion soup drifting from the kitchens caused my stomach to rumble loudly, but I continued on, my thoughts now on tea and biscuits at Toni's house.

Once outside the house, I pushed open the gate. It's a pleasant property, lit by an old coach-lamp hanging from the wall. The garden to the left of the house is narrow, barely there at all, fenced off from next door by an abelia hedge. But the garden on the other side is lovely - a wide expanse with small, circular flagstones and a weeping willow sheltering the lawn beneath. Walking towards the front door, I turned right and pushed my way through the long, trailing branches of the weeping willow to reach the kitchen door. It was slightly open, so I knocked and pushed gently against it.

'Hi, Toni.'

I stepped inside. The room was warm after the icy wind, and an attractive tub of basil on the nearby windowsill filled the room with its holidays-in-the-sun scent. Toni was at the kitchen table, scrolling through her phone, her hair twitching as she moved.

She looked up and smiled. 'April - hi - come on in.'

She fussed around, hugging me, boiling the kettle, filling a bowl with water for Dash, and bringing out home-made banana cake.

I sat onto one of her pine chairs, recently updated with grey chalk paint. 'You seem very pleased with yourself, missus. What's occurring?'

She smiled, her warm green eyes creasing at the edges. 'It's Mike. He's taking me out.'

'What? Mike-Mike? As in ex-husband Mike?'

'Of course ex-husband Mike.'

'What?' I repeated.

'I know.' Her smile was as wide as the kitchen window.

'What's brought this on, then?' I asked.

Placing the teapot onto the table, she sat down opposite.

'I don't really know, to be honest. He picked the kids up on Saturday as usual, and asked if I'd like to go out next weekend. There's a musical on at the Crucible – My Fair Lady. He's got tickets.'

I smiled. 'Why? Has he no-one else to go with?'

She screwed up her eyes. 'Cheeky. But no, it's not like that. We've been getting on really well just lately. He's changed. A lot.'

'Sorry, I didn't mean it like that. I just didn't think you …'

She walked to the fridge for milk. 'I know. I do know what you mean. And you're right to be suspicious.'

'I'm not suspicious – I just …' But I couldn't find the words. After all, if he'd treated her so abysmally before their divorce, what could have happened to change everything? I was worried for her.

'He really has changed. He's been so lovely with the kids, he's helped out with some of the bills, he wants to take us on holiday next year. All of us.'

'But there's more to a marriage than money and holidays, Toni.'

'I know. But there's still something there, you know? The reason I fell in love with him, married him. He's being kind again, and generous, and he makes me feel good. And I still fancy him like crazy.'

I grinned. 'You weren't saying that three years ago.'

'You want some cake? Abigail made it.'

I nodded. 'Thanks. Just a small piece, though.'

She cut me a slice. 'I won't have any. I need to lose a few pounds.'

I cut off a piece with a fork and bit into it. It was moist and tasty.

'Mm – she's a good little cook.'

'She is. And I don't even know where she gets it from. Probably Mum.'

Toni's mother is a jolly, buxom lady. She lives not far away, this side of Manchester, so is handy for babysitting whenever Toni needs her. She is very good at baking, but her culinary skills are probably the reason Toni has such a weight problem. That, and the overeating problem she'd had since her divorce from Mike.

I put down my fork. 'Look, Toni. You are sure about getting back with Mike, aren't you?'

'I'm not getting back with him. Not yet, anyway. He's just taking me out for the evening, that's all.'

'That's fine, then. No - it's good. But just be careful. Please. You don't want to go through all that again.'

Toni's divorce was the stuff of Hollywood blockbusters. Lies, deceit, tears, smashed crockery, broken dreams. Poor girl. At least mine was cut and dried; he cheated on me so I cheated on him. End of story.

She smiled cheekily. 'I promise to be a good girl and not let him anywhere near my knickers until I'm absolutely sure.'

'One hundred per cent promise?'

'One hundred per cent.' But the smile on her face turned suddenly serious. 'I don't want my kids ending up as delinquents, April. I don't want them going off the rails and experimenting with drugs and stuff.'

'What? What are you talking about, Toni? There's no way Abi and Jack would take drugs.'

Abi and Jack are lovely kids. Thoughtful, caring, extremely verbal, highly intelligent. Abi at fourteen was turning into a real beauty with long dark hair and serious brown eyes. Not quite into the makeup and nails stage, she was a typical teenager with skinny jeans and oversize jumpers. Jack, at eleven, was still a kid with curly red hair and freckles, always making me laugh. So you can imagine why I was puzzled at Toni's remark.

She sat down heavily. 'They need a father figure.'

'Is that what this is all about? But they have a father figure. Mike sees them every other weekend.'

'I know. It's just ...' and she began to cry softly, her hands covering her face.

Dash ran up to her in sympathy. I went to sit beside her.

'Toni - come on now. What is it?'

'It's Fiona. Her kids, Craig and Max - they're in the psychi ward. Drugs. Both of them. Both at the same time. She's taken time off work so she can visit them every day. She's in a right state.'

My stomach turned. 'Oh, my god.'

'It's these universities. They go away as lovely, bright young things, and end up high on cocaine. It's not right, it shouldn't be allowed.'

'So how are they doing? I mean, they will get better, won't they?'

Gulping back her tears, she nodded. 'I hope so. Eventually. But it's messed up their education and it's messed up their bloody lives as well, hasn't it?'

'God, that's awful. Bless them.'

I gave her a tissue from my bag, then found the sugar bowl and put a teaspoonful into her tea.

'Here – drink this.'

But my mind was spinning. It seemed as if the whole world was ruled by drugs. After all, that's why Emilisa Meadows-Whitworth had turned to crime; to support her son's expensive rehab after he'd become hooked on heroin. And at the same time, coincidentally, DI Jasper and I discovered a cannabis farm next door to my mum's house. Just a normal house in a normal street. But they were growing cannabis worth thousands and thousands of pounds.

And those poor children. Because that's what they were – children. The brain doesn't finish developing until the age of twenty-five - an interesting fact. So yes, all those beautiful children are still not fully mature when they leave their cosy homes and their loving parents for the great halls of learning. And then they're taken advantage of. Okay, they think it's fun experimenting with cannabis, drinking themselves stupid, falling into a heap until morning. But sometimes morning doesn't arrive. Sometimes they just never wake up. And if they do, what has all that abuse done to their lovely young bodies, their minds?

The psychiatric ward? Oh, my god.

There had to be something we could do.

7

Soft tears roll down her cheeks as she realises the implication of what she's just read ...

8

Millerstone, Derbyshire

THE French dermatologist, who is becoming more and more creepy by the minute, is to be called Lucien Archambeau. He's already met waitress Emma Russell in the café where she works, and she finds she can't stop thinking about him. They bump into each other again a couple of weeks later, when she's queuing for coffee on the beach. He buys her a coffee, and they get talking. They begin to date. He has a thing for making love in a particularly secluded spot on the beach, and she's happy with that. But a few weeks into their relationship she begins to realise he always takes her to places where they won't be seen. Dark beaches, smoky bars and restaurants, small hotels, all on the outskirts of St Maxime. He never takes her back to his place, although he's been to her apartment a few times, and he's never taken her into the bustling town itself. She questions him about it. Is he married? Is he living with someone? They argue, he becomes angry, and he storms off. She never hears from him again. There's the usual pain and anguish, and bemoaning to her friends.

But I needed to think of an ending. Which for some reason was eluding me. Although it didn't stop me hammering away at my keyboard the first couple of hours that Thursday morning. Still in my pyjamas, I might add.

But at ten o'clock I downed tools, fed the cat, washed and dressed, and took Dash for a walk. I love the fact that I can just pull on my boots and go. Straight into the countryside. No climbing into the car, no polluting the atmosphere, no stressing over where to park. So we headed up the hill and walked briskly through the ice-cold air, up towards Stanage Edge and away from the village. My breath came fast and my pulse raced, and it felt good.

Dash stopped halfway up to relieve himself in the grass, so I looked around while I waited. Such a lovely, lazy scene. The view of the village from here, with its old stone houses and tall church spire, is spectacular. The nearby field, devoid of its usual sheep, was misty, still wet from the overnight rain. Bare trees skirted the edges, their leaves heaped into piles along the roadside. A car, a black sporty type, whizzed past me suddenly, blowing the leaves into the sky. But they settled themselves quickly, and the scene restored its still, calm serenity.

So I continued, trying not to think about my manuscript. Emptying my mind of the scenes I create, letting go of my characters, is sometimes the best way of coming up with new ideas. Instead, I thought about the murders - the Chatsworth murders, I was now calling them. And the more I thought about them, the more I wondered how anyone could leave a rehearsal midway through, and no-one notice. The whole production is there on the page, in black and white. So as soon as someone has a line to say or an entrance to make, they're seen to be missing. So how come nobody noticed? Why did no-one remember him leaving? It was all very strange.

As always on my walk, I looked down towards North Lees Hall. Thought to be the inspiration behind Mr Rochester's house in *Jane Eyre*, it's one of the most beautiful settings for a house ever, I think, with Stanage Edge looking down upon it. Stanage Edge is just about the most impressive gritstone escarpment you'll ever see. Four miles long, it's littered with discarded millstones that have been there since the 1860s, when we began importing white flour from France to replace our boring grey Derbyshire flour. It's a sight to behold, but it amazes me how the millstones were just left, abandoned, like a pile of McDonald's burger wrappers. I often wonder exactly what happened.

Dash and I were just approaching the car park below Stanage Edge when I decided to turn back.

The wind was picking up and my ears ached with the cold. I jogged the first few metres in order to warm up, Dash scampering excitedly ahead, and then slowed to a walk. By the time I reached home, I was ready for a coffee and some lunch. But the extra oxygen must have done something to my brain, because I was firing on all fours, itching to sit down and continue with my story.

So after a salad of camembert and pear, with cherry tomatoes and leaves (delicious), I sat in my office and I wrote. Pages and pages and pages. And I just loved exploring the city of St Maxime. Online, of course. Classy, sophisticated, yet fun and sexy.

So, back to the story.

The waitress pleads with her lover to come back. She says she doesn't mind if he *is* married, she can cope with that. But she loves him and he just has to come back. Weeks later, however, after being snubbed time and again, she accepts the fact that he may be married and is no longer interested in her. However, one night she and her bestie, also from New Jersey (Samantha something?) have one too many drinks, and they decide to investigate further. They discover the location of the dermatologist's house, a palatial manor east of St Maxime and set above the beautiful Madrague beach. So they decide to pay him a visit. But he's in America on business, so the place is completely unoccupied. Slightly terrified, they find they're able to explore the house at will.

And here was the twist I was looking for.

They discover a large, brightly-lit basement, well concealed, disinfectant-clean, and clinical. Exploring further, they find M. Archambeau is using the place to operate on people. But why here and not in his clinic, the incredibly expensive one on Boulevard de l'Esquirou? Could it be he operates on the rich and famous, and they want it kept secret? If that is the case, is there potential here for blackmail? Or is he carrying out procedures that would be classed by the medical profession as illegal, and not to be made public? Upset and undecided, the waitress and her bestie contact the police. But as they uncover more and more detail about M. Archambeau's business dealings, which are indeed strange, the waitress and Tobias Clarke, the investigating officer's son, fall in love.

Suddenly, the doorbell rang, shaking me from my thoughts. It was Andy from the greengrocers with the Christmas tree I'd ordered.

'Thanks, Andy,' I said. 'It's good of you to deliver – saves me a job.'

'No problem at all. Merry Christmas, Miss Stanislavski.'

'Merry Christmas, Andy. Have a good one.'

I spent the next hour bringing down my decorations from the loft and decorating the tree. Bells and baubles, toys and tinsel, twinkling lights, and finally the delicate ivory angel I'd bought the previous Christmas in Brussels. I played a CD of

Christmas carols and drank a small glass of Baileys, as was my habit when decorating the tree. Dash fussed around as if he'd never seen a tree before, and I was slightly worried he might decide to wee against it. So I encouraged him back to my office, but not until I'd checked my phone. Two missed calls from Colin. I rang back.

'Hi there! How are you doing?' I said.

'Thanks for calling back. But I can't talk long - I'm busy, unfortunately - but I was wondering what the plan is for this weekend.'

I grinned. 'Well, you fly over here, we hang around, and then you fly back to Brussels.'

'There's an art exhibition on in Sheffield. You fancy it?'

'Okay, yes, that would be lovely. Although I do have some work to do.'

'That's fine, you can bring it over. Shall we stay at my place? It's empty at the moment, no tenants.'

'Yes, that would be fun. I'll pick you up at the usual time then, shall I?'

We chatted briefly about our week so far, how busy we both were and how much we needed a holiday, then we said our goodbyes. Happily, I made some tea and carried it through to the office.

But I needed to pack. And I needed to pack gorgeous clothes. Something the ex-wife wouldn't look good in. So after writing for an hour, I spent the next two searching through my wardrobe.

My cute Parisian LBD (from that little boutique in the Latin Quarter); we were bound to go out somewhere. Jeans and pale blue tee shirt with chiffon flowery blouse for the art gallery. And my favourite chunky fisherman's sweater in cream, in case it was cold. And of course a complete change for Sunday – jeans and a tee-shirt with pink fluffy jumper? So he'd want to cuddle me? Maybe a walk and a pub lunch?

Colin is lovely, the kind of guy who wouldn't say boo to a goose. Kind, caring, thoughtful. He's not awfully handsome or anything, but he can melt your heart with a wink of the eye. And what eyes – such long, dark lashes. Gorgeous. But that ex-wife was seriously getting in the way. I was convinced he was spending more time with her than with me, and that was really getting to me. *Jealousy, get thee behind me.*

You see, Colin and Natasha, the ex-wife, were IT contractors, both working in Brussels. It was only contract work, but they'd been there just under a year at the time. He worked for J P Morgan and she worked for Axa, just around the corner from J P Morgan's. Much too close for my liking.

I did meet Natasha once, not long after Colin began working there. Tall, slim, long dark hair. Beautiful face with dark eyes and a Roman nose.

For a while there, I did consider going brunette.

She was nice enough, of course, and she did make it plain she only wanted to be friends with Colin. But you never really know, do you? That little spark?

So, having chosen my ultra-seductive clothes – I hoped – I made an oven omelette and salad and sat down to eat, my script open in front of me. I had lines to learn.

*

The Flying Toad is a traditional pub, with hand-pulled beers and leaded windows and warm carpeting. It's named after the famous Toad's Mouth Rock that guards the road into Sheffield. George, the barman, was standing behind the bar, my pint of Guinness already poured. As always.

'What would you do if I asked for a G&T instead?' I asked, handing him a fiver.

George, a relaxed jovial type, had recently grown a trendy beard that actually made him look older rather than younger, but I'd never have told him that.

He smiled as he considered his reply. 'Well, I think I'd just drink the Guinness myself and put it onto my tab like a good chap. Then I'd pour you the most awful G&T you could possibly imagine, so you'd never ask for it again. Confuse me good and proper that would. But I don't think you would. You're a creature of habit, Miss Stanislavski.'

I grinned. 'Oh, thanks, George – lovely compliment, that is.'

Bertie, George's wife, came out of the kitchen at that point. She's the pub's cook, and makes the most delicious made-from-scratch food.

She smiled at me. 'They're all in the back, love. I've just taken the crisps through, but it's not good news in there.'

'Mm, I know all about it. But thanks, Bertie, I'll go on through.'

The bar was fairly empty, other than the few couples who were dining there. So I walked straight through to the back room, to the distinct rumble of lines and stage directions being read out. But a cloud hung over the place, thick and grey and depressing.

Alfie Brighouse, our director, dressed in fluorescent orange tee-shirt and skinny jeans, far too tight for his plump derrière, welcomed me in enthusiastically.

'April, darling. Come on in, sit down. Here, beside me. It's just a line rehearsal tonight, so no rush.'

A talented member of Birmingham Rep for many years, Alfie had gone on to teach drama at our local comprehensive. But now retired, a tall, slightly balding man with a paunch, he devoted himself to the Village Players.

Sitting down, I opened my script hurriedly. 'Sorry I'm late, Alfie.'

'Don't worry, my lovely. You're here now. We've just been discussing Gemma's terrible news. What an absolutely awful thing to happen. Bless her.'

'There's been another one, hasn't there - another death?' said Daniel Oxley, a young barrister from Sheffield. He'd only been with the Village Players a short time, but, handsome with greying hair and deep brown eyes, he was nearly always given the romantic lead.

'They think the second one might be suicide, though,' said Alfie. 'They're saying Gemma's bloke was murdered - a knife or something. Imagine it, though, isn't it just shocking? Makes you wonder whether we should be walking around at night, doesn't it?'

'I've heard a few things about Lucas Hanssen, though,' said Ginnie Thomson, dressed in yellow crop top and baggy jeans. 'Not a nice character, by all accounts.'

'It doesn't mean someone should kill him, does it?' I said. 'Anyway, I'm calling round to see Gemma tomorrow, so I'll try and cheer her up a bit.'

'She shouldn't have been seeing another woman's husband, should she?' murmured Zoe Davies, a plump, anxious, thirty-something bank clerk.

Ginnie rubbed her chin thoughtfully. 'That's not really got anything to do with it, has it, Zoe?'

Alfie stood up then, clapping his hands to gain everyone's attention.

'Now, now, let's have a little humanity here, darlings. None of us is perfect, are we? I mean, just look at me.' Posing as a teapot to signify his innate homosexuality, he twirled round. We laughed and applauded loudly, which is just what he wanted; Alfie is a born performer. So he bowed and curtsied and blew kisses into the air, before sitting back down and turning to me.

'Well, my darling, do give Gemma our love and our sincere condolences. And here, get her some beautiful flowers. It's a terrible thing.' He passed me a twenty pound note.

'Thanks, Alfie. Although what I'll say to her, I have no idea. It's not going to be an easy conversation, is it?'

Taking my hand as I accepted the money, he kissed it. 'I'm sure you'll be wonderful with her, that gorgeous soothing manner of yours.'

I wasn't so sure. It didn't feel right, somehow, gleaning information from a grieving girl. And more to the point, gleaning information to help the police with their enquiries.

'Thanks, Alfie.'

The play we were rehearsing was Lady Windermere's Fan, a brilliant comedy by Oscar Wilde. The plot revolves around Lady Windermere, who suspects her husband of having an affair with another woman. Amidst various twists and turns, it transpires that the other woman is in fact Mrs Erlynne, Lady Windermere's birth mother, who had deserted her family twenty years earlier. But in order to save her daughter's marriage, Mrs Erlynne confesses all, sacrificing herself and her reputation.

Lady Windermere was being played by Ginnie, Lord Windermere by Daniel Oxley. As for myself, I was playing Mrs Erlynne, the scandalous but beautiful mother, and loving every minute of it. The part of Lord Augustus Lorton, a pompous old man in love with Mrs Erlynne, was being played by Percy Wainstone; an ideal part for him with his Winston Churchill figure. His son Luke, who'd only joined us to help with the lighting, was playing Mr Cecil Graham, a young, ambitious politician. He played the part well, obviously a chip off the old block.

Gemma's part of Lady Agatha Carlisle was tonight being read by Marika, a young lady from Helsinki who had never acted before. Having followed her new husband over here, she'd only lived in the Hope Valley for two years. She still carried a strong accent, but otherwise read the part well. Even so, we hoped Gemma would be up to doing the final rehearsals and performances.

I noticed Alfie's long-time partner, Francis, was there tonight, too. Tall and slim, quiet with a shy grin and smiling eyes, he did some kind of engineering design for a living, so was becoming invaluable in the design of our sets.

But our rehearsal became a little stilted, if I'm honest; everyone tired after a busy week at work, everyone shocked at the news. Murder just doesn't happen on our doorstep. As a general rule, it creeps silently and darkly into places like Sheffield or Manchester.

So we were scared. Two murders in one week? What was this evil that had come upon us, threatening our villages, frightening our neighbours, growing like a beanstalk into the very fabric of our society?

Despite our strange mood, however, Alfie as always sent us home with a smile.

'Lines, lines, lines, my darlings. Make them second nature. And Ginnie, do practise that lovely walk of yours. So sexy. So Marilyn Monroe. It just makes the part, darling. They won't be able to resist you.'

Fluttering her eyelashes, Ginnie wiggled her hips salaciously. 'Aww. Thanks, Alfie. You're a real love.'

9

Sitting back, she closes her eyes and pushes a hand through her hair. What is she to do?

10

Millerstone, Derbyshire

I rang Gemma the following day, Friday. There was little else to do, to be honest - the rain was pelting down. So I'd fed Dash and the cat, cocooned myself in the office and worked and worked, only stopping for coffee and biscuits, before finally finishing the first draft of my manuscript. And all before half past two.

So, itching for some exercise, I threw on my waterproofs and took Dash for a very wet and shiny walk up the hill. And that's when I decided to phone Gemma. There was no reply, so I left a message on voicemail. Dash continued to pull me up Coggers Lane, but instead of walking up to Stanage Edge we turned right, onto Birley Lane. This road is long, winding and narrow, and has the most beautiful display of bluebells in the springtime. But it's not easy to navigate if you're driving. There were no cars on this particular afternoon, however, so I could take my time, relax, think about my work, the play, and Mum's wedding, and look forward to the coming weekend.

It would be nice to spend time in the city for a change, I thought. Whirlow isn't really the city, admittedly, but it's not far away. The lovely old trees straddling the pavements there are delightful, as is the nearby Ecclesall Woods. I planned on taking Dash for a lovely Sunday morning walk.

And Colin and I? We needed to get close again. This Brussels job had been coming between us, not only because of the ex-wife, but also because he was always so busy. Yes, he'd worked away before, but there'd always been the opportunity to catch up, to chat. This particular job seemed to be taking all his time. He was barely home before he had to climb into bed. He'd ring me, of course, but it was always rushed, formal, a hasty chat. And our weekends together were the same. Maybe a holiday was what we needed. A nice holiday. We could take some time out, possibly fly down to Nice and drive out to his apartment in St Raphael. A week would be lovely, and long enough at this time of year. Once I'd hit my deadline, of course.

Back home, I wiped Dash's wet fur and paws with an old towel, then rang Gemma again. This time her father answered, instantly passing the phone to her.

'Hi, April,' she said. She sounded faint and helpless and sad.

'I'm so sorry to hear about Lucas,' I said. 'I'm just ringing to see how you are, and if there's anything I can do.'

'Thank you, April, that's really kind. But no, there's not much anyone can do now, is there? It's done, isn't it? And I do have my family here to look after me. But thanks for ringing, anyway.'

'Would you mind if I came over, if it's not too inconvenient? The Players have bought you some flowers and I'd like to bring them round. If that's okay?'

'Oh.'

'I won't stay long, I promise.'

'Well, it's kind of them. Yes, you can come over later if you like.'

'Lovely. Thanks. Would five o'clock be okay?'

'That's fine, yes. I'll see you then.'

As I placed my phone onto the table, I caught sight of myself in the kitchen mirror.

'Just what are you turning into, April Stanislavski? Pestering a grieving girl just to get information for the police?' I turned to Dash. 'But it might help me write crime novels, mightn't it, Dash? Just in case the old chick-lit stuff burns itself out.' Bending down, I stroked his warm head. 'Come on, let's get you a drink.'

Sarah from Millerstone Garage rang at that point. The cost of my car being run into cost just under a thousand pounds by the time they'd finished adding in the labour and the VAT. My poor car. But I'd be claiming it back from the other guy's insurers. And at least no-one was hurt. When I fumed about the idiot who'd run into me, I just reminded myself of that.

So, walking down with Dash to pick up my car, I handed over my debit card.

*

It took over half an hour to drive to Gemma's house. A rather nice house, I was to discover. Originally an ancient cottage with oak beams and squat doors, Blossom Cottage has since had many extensions. All tastefully done, and all beautifully decorated. Gemma's father was an accountant of some kind, and it showed; money talks. Blossom Cottage is set within the most beautiful landscape, with a long wide drive and sturdy trees. Inside, the ground floor is completely open-plan - classy, airy, spacious. French doors open from the dining room onto the garden, but if you turn at an angle of ninety degrees, you're in the lounge, long and lazy and comfortable. With soft, buttermilk leather Chesterfields and original stone walls. Very nice.

George Jameson, a quiet unassuming man of around fifty, led me through the lounge, out along the hallway, and into a small study.

'She's been sitting here all day,' he said, 'but Amber, her sister, has been keeping her company, been cheering her up a bit. Thank the lord for families, I say.'

Gemma was cocooned in the study with a soft pink blanket, a box of tissues, and the TV on. Amber was sitting beside her. As I entered she smiled, said 'Hi,' and left.

Gemma looked up. 'Hi, April. Come and sit down. We were just watching the news, but there's nothing on there yet.'

Kicking off my shoes, I entered her domain. 'It's probably just been kept local for now. I'm so sorry about troubling you, Gemma, but I won't keep you long.'

Her father had remained in the doorway. 'Would you like a coffee or something?' he asked.

I smiled. 'Tea would be lovely - thank you.'

Gemma motioned for me to take her sister's place on the chunky green sofa. Her long dark hair, usually as shiny as an autumn conker, was matted, unwashed and unbrushed. Her eyes looked sore, her cheeks were pale and drawn, and her knees were folded beneath her, covered by the blanket. The room smelled of Vick Rub, an ointment I know is not only good for congestion, but can also be very soothing.

'I'm sorry I missed rehearsal last night,' she began, 'but I've not been in the best of states. It's been just awful.'

I sat down beside her, and she pulled the blanket further around her knees to make room. Then, picking up the remote, she switched off the TV, which had been blaring out a soap of some kind.

'Here,' I said, handing her the bouquet of pink roses I'd bought at the village greengrocers.

'Oh. Thank you,' she said, her voice a husky whisper. 'They're beautiful.' She laid them across her blanket.

'Alfie asked me to get them. He's really worried about you.'

'Oh - he's so lovely.'

'But how are you doing?'

She looked at me hesitantly, not knowing quite where to begin.

'Actually, that's a stupid question,' I said. 'Don't answer. But has there been any news on what happened, exactly?'

'All we know is that Lucas was at rehearsal on Saturday night, and he left still in costume, and no-one even noticed. Which is incredible. I wasn't there - I decided not to do this production, what with work and everything. And I needed a break from rehearsing two plays at the same time.'

I grinned. 'I will never know how you do that. I take my hat off to you.'

'It's easy if you've got the time. But I haven't had, just lately, not with starting this new course, this graphic design course.' Tears filled her eyes. 'But if I'd been there with him, then maybe …'

I placed my hand upon hers in sympathy. 'Don't go there, Gemma. It's really not your fault.'

'But why would you leave to go home without getting changed first? It's so unlike him. I mean, it's automatic, isn't it? You take your costume off and you hang it up. But no-one even noticed he'd gone. Which is unbelievable. I was away last weekend, you see, with a friend in London, so I didn't even know about it - not until I got back on Tuesday.' She paused, out of breath, as if she'd already said the same thing a million times over. She rubbed at her eyes. 'Sorry. I – I just can't believe it. I can't believe it's real. I mean, why would somebody *do* that?'

'Gemma, I know I shouldn't ask this, and I realise you haven't really known Lucas that long. But was he involved in anything? I - I suppose what I'm trying to say is - did he have any vices?'

'You mean like drugs and stuff?' She shook her head vehemently. 'No. Absolutely not. I mean, you're right - I've not been seeing him that long. But I have known him for two years. We've been friends ever since I joined Cavendish Amdram. I'm sure I'd have known if he was into anything like that.'

I sighed softly. I felt bad asking all these questions. But then there was a reprieve as the door opened and Gemma's dad stood there with a tray containing mugs, a teapot, a jug of milk, and a plate of chocolate digestives.

'Here you go, you two. Help yourselves. I'm assuming you don't take sugar.' Placing the tray onto the nearby desk, he came back to stroke Gemma's hair gently. 'Anything you want, darling, just shout. Mum and Amber are outside putting the chickens to bed, but I'll hear you.'

'Thanks, Dad,' she said, softly.

As he left the room, I stood up, poured two cups of perfectly-made tea, and passed one to Gemma.

'Choccie biscuit?' I asked.

She smiled, that extraordinarily pretty smile she has that lights up the stage. 'Thank you. And thanks for coming to see me here. I don't think I can face people at the minute. I'm not even sure I want to keep my part in the play.'

'Alfie said you might feel like that, but you should let him know if you do decide to pull out. Marika played Lady Agatha last night, and it's not a massive part, so she could easily take it on - if that's what you want?'

She blinked hesitantly. 'It's such a nice little part, though. I was enjoying it.'

'Well, have a think, and maybe let Alfie know next week. One way or the other?'

She looked suddenly thoughtful. 'You know, Lucas *was* a bit on the shady side. I mean, he always seemed to have last-minute meetings, things that could never be rearranged. And he'd always light up a ciggie when he was talking about it, as if it made him nervous. Then he'd have to drive out to Sheffield sometimes, but he'd never take me if I wanted to go - said I'd be bored silly.' She shrugged. 'I just thought it was something to do with his wife.' She looked a little shamefaced at that.

I sipped my tea quietly, thoughtfully.

'Do you think he was up to no good, then?' she asked. 'In with the wrong kind of people? Do you think it's that?'

'I really wouldn't like to say. But I do think it's odd he didn't get changed after the dress rehearsal. Don't you?'

She nodded. 'I mean, why would he do that? It's something you do without thinking, isn't it?'

'Unless someone called him away, unless they asked to meet him outside?'

'Urgently? So he wouldn't have time to change?'

My mind was whirring again, my imagination working overtime.

'Did you ever meet up with any of his friends outside the Cavendish Amdram?'

'No. Never. They were our only circle of friends. He was very secretive about our relationship, you see. For obvious reasons. But the amdram people - they knew all about us.'

'Do you think *they* might know something more about him, about his life?'

Suddenly still, she stared at me. 'Why are you so curious about all this, April?'

Blushing, I just had to tell her the truth.

'I – I'm the one who found Lucas. Or rather, Dash did. My dog. We were out walking on Monday night and we found him.'

Her eyes filled with sudden tears. 'Oh, my god - April. That must have been just awful for you. You poor thing.'

'The thing is, if I'm honest - DI Jasper who's handling the investigation - she's asked me to help out. The police need as much help as they can get, and because I know the area and so on, I was able to help with a case last year. DI Jasper wants me to get information from the people who knew Lucas.'

She looked down at her hands. 'Okay?'

'Of course, I'll try and keep it low-key so his wife doesn't find out about you. According to DI Jasper, they've only been married two minutes, so it would be totally devastating for her.'

She looked up. 'Two years, actually. They've been married two years. She was expecting a baby, you see, but then she miscarried after the wedding. Devastated, they were. And nothing's been right since.'

'That's really sad.'

'Yes. It is,' she replied, thoughtfully.

'Actually, Gemma ...'

'Yes?'

'Did Lucas have any connection to Chatsworth House, other than the amateur dramatics? Did he ever mention someone called Felix?'

She shook her head. 'No. Why? Do they think he did it?'

I sighed. 'I suppose you're going to find out sooner or later. He was found dead too, on Tuesday night. But it was alcohol poisoning, and he'd drowned, so it probably has nothing at all to do with Lucas. I'm just checking.'

She shook her head. 'No - no, I've never heard of him. Oh, April ...'

She began to cry again, and I passed her a tissue from my bag.

'I'm so sorry to upset you. But you must understand we need to put the pieces of the jigsaw together. We need to find out who did this thing.'

She wiped her face. 'I know. Poor Lucas.'

'Listen, Gemma, I need to get back home now. And I am sorry to have upset you all over again. But if you think of anything else, please let me know.' I handed her my card.

'Thank you. And thanks for coming over, and for the lovely flowers.'

'It's not a problem.' I went to hug her, and she hugged me back. 'Take care of yourself, and do let Alfie know about the play.'

*

I made sure to set the alarm before leaving the house and picking up Colin. These murders had put me on edge a little, and I was becoming anxious about leaving it unattended, particularly with it being dark for most of the day. But I was so looking forward to spending time with Colin at his place. It had been rented out since he'd begun working in Brussels, so we hadn't spent much time there. But now the tenants had gone, it would be fun to go there again.

The drive to Manchester Airport takes me through Castleton and up Winnats Pass, a ridiculously steep, narrow mountain road that winds up through a steep-sided valley, and which looked amazing as my car headlights picked out its angles and contours. I drove out of Winnats Pass and on, along the A6. The sky was dark but there was little traffic, so the going was easy. After nearly an hour of driving, I parked up inside Terminal 2, left Dash in the car and stepped through to the Arrivals lounge. To find Colin already there.

'April,' he called.

I threw myself into the warmth of him, and we kissed and hugged, then held hands as we made our way back to the car. As he heaved his case into the boot, Dash began to whine, but Colin just grinned, his green eyes crinkling.

'Silly dog. But he's just like me - I can't wait to get home, either. And what I wouldn't do for a nice glass of red.'

'I think that can be arranged, sir. Your place, then?'

Colin drove back to Sheffield, to give me a rest. We discussed the news; the economy, both in Belgium and at home, the government, and the recent deaths in Chatsworth. Then, even closer to home, how his contract was going, and what had happened to my car.

'It's all fixed now, though, as you can see. Although I still need to get my money back. Bloody idiot.'

He pushed up into fifth gear. 'I'm just glad you weren't injured, that's all.'

'And Dash.'

He smiled. 'And Dash. Of course.'

Colin's apartment is situated in an old detached house in Whirlow, an affluent district to the south west of Sheffield. Built in 1910, the kitchen and bedrooms are small, but the lounge/diner is enormous, overlooking a wonderful avenue of matured oaks and the old brick walls of pampered houses. The letting agency had left it in a good state, so I had nothing to do but kick off my shoes, unpack my case, put the milk inside the fridge, and see to Dash while Colin busied himself in the kitchen.

'Okay. Ready,' he called.

I walked through to find lit candles, two glasses of wine, and a large bowl filled with delicious-looking crisps.

'Hand-made,' he said. 'Olive oil and sea salt. I got them in Brussels. They're my new favourite.'

I tried one. 'Mmm - nice.' Licking the salt from my lips, I wondered exactly who it was that had introduced him to these new crisps.

'Come on, let's make ourselves comfy - a film?' he asked, passing me a glass of the Bordeaux.

It was just after ten. A few weeks ago, Colin would have dragged me into the bedroom. Or not even that; he'd have made love to me on the sofa, right there, right then. But no. Not this time.

So we settled onto the sofa to watch The Holiday, a Christmas romcom and a bit silly, but my choice entirely. I needed to feel warm and cosy, and loved.

On the surface, Colin seemed to be the same person he always was - warm and kind and thoughtful.
But something was changing. I knew it.

11

Should she burn the letter? Tell the police? Tell someone?

12

Whirlow, Sheffield

SATURDAY was frosty and bright, with a clear azure-blue sky. And bitterly cold, although it *was* the first week of December. But Sheffield is always two degrees warmer than Millerstone, so at least I could be grateful for that. I was also grateful that I'd changed my mind and left my work at home. Because I needed to switch off, completely. Although my mind did keep switching back to the Chatsworth murder case.

There was one thing that was particularly bugging me. I just couldn't work out why Lucas was wearing his costume, the dress shirt and the suit trousers, when it was just a normal rehearsal. And why did no-one miss him when he left, halfway through rehearsal? And if he *was* called outside by someone, why didn't he just get changed before leaving? Laura, the Village Players' wardrobe mistress, would have had a fit if we'd removed her costumes from the premises.

None of it made any sense at all.

I really did need to switch off, though. Obviously.

So Colin and I wrapped up warm, donned our shades, and left his place to venture into Hillsborough , to the art gallery. My Mini stayed at the apartment so we could drive Colin's Passat. It needed a good airing after just sitting there for two months, the last time he'd driven it. But first, we had cappuccino in a chunky little café just along the road from the art exhibition. They didn't just sell coffee and cake, however; they also sold the cutest hand-knitted mittens, hats and scarves. In shades of mustard, crimson, sky-blue and emerald. The sky-blue I absolutely loved, but to my credit I resisted them all.

So, after a large chocolate-sprinkled cappuccino, we walked the short distance to the exhibition. It turned out to be an art shop, with huge bay windows and rickety wooden flooring that added to its artsy, bohemian feel. The heady scent of glue and paint hit us as we pushed open the door - the result, I guessed, of the picture-framing business they run. Once inside, however, we were warmly greeted by the owner, Meg, a small woman in her forties with long dark hair and black rimmed glasses. She offered us free coffee and cake – a moist gluten-free walnut with a cream filling - but we declined gracefully.

'If you're wanting artwork,' she said in her delicate Scottish accent, 'the exhibition is upstairs. The artists are all Sheffield-based and there are some lovely pictures. Acrylics and oils. Originals and prints. Just let me know if you need to discuss anything.'

Colin nodded. 'Thank you. We will.'

'And there's a jug of home-made lemonade on the side,' she continued.

'She's determined to make us fat,' I murmured as we made our way upstairs.

It was early, there was no-one else around, so we took our time, checking out paintings, wowing over the clay sculptures on display, and trying to envisage exactly what it was Colin was looking for. He wanted something that would cheer up the place, he said – not necessarily a painting, possibly a photograph. He'd never bothered with anything before, he said, but had seen something in Brussels that had truly inspired him.

Stunned, I wondered if it was the ex-wife's place.

But I said nothing, just followed him around while his eyes devoured each picture in turn, assessing it and trying to imagine it hung in his apartment. There was one oil painting that caught his eye, an abstract representing the Peace Gardens in Sheffield city centre. But the colours were cold - greys, lilacs, yellows and black. It was attractive in its own way, but after much consideration we decided it wouldn't look right in the lounge. The room itself was bright and airy; the picture would detract. Dismissing it, we then came across a sign showing us the way to the jewellery exhibition.

'Come on, let's take a look at the jewellery,' he said, pulling me along.

The jewellery was on the second floor, so we made our way up the rickety stairs to a small room, where three chests of drawers painted in white were laden with trays of hand-made pieces. Silver or copper, entwined with beautiful coloured stones. Meg came upstairs at that point, carrying another tray piled high with tiny boxes, but she put it to one side as she spoke.

'They're healing stones,' she explained. 'This gorgeous purple is zinc alloy, representing eternity. The oranges and blues are jasper and agate. The orange represents hope, and the blue represents peace.'

'They're lovely,' I said.

'They're all hand-made, from ethical sources. The stones have been set into leather, or you can get them in rope if you're vegan. I can order them especially. We have some earrings too, and chakra bracelets. Each colour represents each of the seven chakras. The wire itself is copper, which brings luck in love, health and wealth.'

I could do with a bit of luck in love, I thought, picking up a pair. Holding them against my face, I peered into the mirror hanging there.

'I'll pay,' offered Colin, pulling out his wallet.

But I shook my head. It didn't feel right somehow, not any more. Don't ask me why, but I felt the need to spend my own money, not his.

'It's fine,' I said. 'You need your money for when we find that painting. No - I'll leave it – thank you.' I handed them back.

Colin grinned. 'Are you talking about that elusive painting that's only in my head?'

An elusive painting for an elusive guy, I thought.

So we left, empty-handed and a little dispirited.

'Are you okay, April?' asked Colin as we walked to the car. 'It's not like you to refuse the chance of a hand-knitted scarf or new earrings. You'd usually jump at it.'

'I'm fine, Colin - really. Just a bit tired, I think.' Guiltily, I changed the subject. 'So what are we doing about lunch?'

He took hold of my hand as we walked along. 'How about that little place on Sharrow Vale? My treat.'

I really was not in the mood for treats, so I shook my head.

'Actually - it's fine - thanks. Let's just go back.'

Stopping suddenly, he pulled me to him. 'April? What the hell is wrong?'

Tears filled my eyes and I snuggled into his shoulder to hide them.

'April?' he whispered. 'You're worrying me now.'

I pulled away. 'Sorry ...'

He pulled me to the car, opened the passenger door, and helped me inside, his face set like stone. 'We're going back.'

Fastening my seatbelt, I pulled a tissue from my bag. 'Sorry.'

The drive home was awful. I didn't know what I was going to say. How do you say *Are you seeing your ex again? Are you cheating on me? Why have you been so distant, with two minute phone calls, and miniscule texts?*

We pulled up outside the house, having not said another word. Colin unlocked his apartment door to the yapping of Dash in the hallway, his claws clacking against the old quarry tiles. I bent to stroke him.

'Have you missed me, sweetie?'

Colin followed us into the kitchen. 'I'll make veg soup. I bought it yesterday, from the deli in the airport. And I got sourdough and butter as well. I hope that's alright?'

'I'll just take Dash for a quick walk then, if that's okay? I won't be long.'

'You've got ten minutes.'

'Thanks.'

'And April?'

'Yes?' I clipped Dash's lead onto his collar.

'If I've done something to upset you, then I'm really sorry.'

I swallowed back my impending tears. 'I'll just see to Dash,' and I left.

79

The air outside was still cold, but it felt fresh, despite the rush of cars up and down the main road. I walked along Whirlowdale Road and turned left into Ecclesall Woods. Here, Dash stopped for a wee before pulling me further into the trees, away from the traffic and the noise. We tramped over dead leaves and dried twigs for quite a few minutes, until finally we were on our own. Quiet. And calm. I felt as if I could breathe again. I concentrated on my lungs, on the air inside them. Soft clouds. In and out, in and out. Calming me. Strengthening me. Encouraging me to let go.

I bent down to stroke Dash. 'At least I'm not worrying over the Chatsworth murders any more. More urgent things on my mind.'

Dash merely licked my hand in reply.

I stood up. 'Come on, Dash - let's run.'

We ran through the trees, me careful not to twist an ankle on the undulating ground, until, out of breath, we reached a row of semi-detached houses that signalled the edge of the woods. Catching my breath, I knelt to stroke Dash, and he nuzzled into me.

'Lovely boy, aren't you? But come on, sweetie, back home we go. Got to face the music some time.'

I realised suddenly that I'd forgotten all about Colin's soup. I just wasn't hungry, I realised, too upset to eat. But our walk had definitely taken longer than ten minutes.

Colin was fine about it, however. And the soup was delicious. Spicy, yet sweet.

'Thank you,' I murmured, tucking into a huge chunk of sourdough, the butter still melting.

Colin's kitchen table is small, gauche, coated in pink melamine. I've always loved it. Now he was leaning across it, a mug of tea cradled in his hands.

'So come on, then. Talk.'

I've always found it difficult, even though I've been through so many broken relationships. Too many broken relationships. Talking about things. Discussing my feelings. Facing the truth.

My stomach churned and I had to stop eating. 'It's – it's just – it's because …'

Placing his tea onto the table, he walked around, took my hand, and crouched down beside me. His eyes at my level now, he looked into mine, his own gorgeous and green, with those long, long lashes that could sweep me up and keep me there forever.

Usually.

But today I wasn't sure about anything anymore. I'd had so many men lie to me, betray me, use me.

'Just spit it out. Please, April. Are you finishing with me? Is that what you're saying?'

What a quaint word. Finishing. These days we're more likely to call it dumping. I smiled down at him. Such a kind man, really.

So I blurted it out. 'You're seeing your ex again, aren't you? Tell me the truth.'

His face was a picture. As if he didn't know whether to laugh or cry.

Dropping my hand he stood up and backed away. 'What?'

I felt sick. 'Be honest with me, Colin. Please.'

He shook his head violently. 'April, you're the only one for me – you must know that. What, all the travelling I have to do, the hours I have to waste, just to come and see you? Why would I do that if you weren't so precious to me?'

'I do the same,' I retorted.

Taking my hand again, he looked me in the eyes. 'April. I love you.'

*

If I said the rest of the weekend was spent making love, going for long walks, cuddling in front of the TV, I'd be lying. But it did feel better. I felt better.

But I must have this innate self-destruct button. Why else would I mistrust someone so wonderful and so caring? Someone who'd go to the ends of the earth for me? I sometimes think I don't deserve to be happy.

Crazy. A crazy weekend.

We spent Saturday evening at the Green Dragon, Colin's local pub, throwing darts and playing pool and drinking beer. So my LBD from Paris lay untouched in the wardrobe, but I didn't mind. We ate veggie burger, chips and peas, followed by chocolate Guinness cake, two of my most favourite ingredients rolled into one. And we had a good time, laughing and joking with the other punters. But we were so tired after our busy day we just collapsed into bed afterwards and slept.

On Sunday morning we walked through the woods with Dash, afterwards leaving him at Colin's so we could walk out to Hunters Bar and eat. La Griglia is a tiny bistro, billowing with gusts of warm parmesan and garlic and teeming with polite Italian waiters. I chose a small pasta dish made with tagliarini and truffles, which was delicious.

Colin looked up from his pizza. 'So how about a little shopping? Just to prove you're still the same old April who thinks nothing to spending three hundred quid on a silk shirt?'

I had to laugh. The memories.

Yes, Colin had been there after my disastrous trip to France with an ex, a serial proposer who'd thought nothing of taking me on the most boring holiday ever, then having the cheek to propose to me. I managed to escape his awful clutches by booking a ridiculously expensive taxi, landing in Paris with hours to spare before the next train to St Pancras, and then of course shopping in *Le Printemps*, the local department store. I spent nearly three hundred euros on a pale pink shirt in shantung silk. And did I care? No. Not one bit.

'Okay. You win,' I said. 'I'd love to go shopping with you. But what about your flight?'

He grinned. 'I've changed it. I did it online while you were out with Dash. At no small charge, I might add. I'm flying back tomorrow morning now. I've emailed work.'

Confused, I shook my head. 'What? I don't understand.'

'I'm staying over at your place, so we can spend a bit longer together. If that's okay with you?'

I smiled. 'Okay. I'll just powder my nose, then we'll get down to some serious shopping, shall we?'

We walked along Sharrow Vale Road, past trendy, bijou, boutiques and cafés, their coloured bulbs lighting up the windows and their pine trees taking up the pavements. We found a shop that smelled of roses and sold Italian linens and alpaca woollens. There was a gorgeous crew neck sweater hanging right there, right in the window. Pale blue and beautiful. So I went inside and tried it on. It was made of alpaca wool and lambswool, and was so beautifully soft and warm I didn't want to take it off. So the young assistant, congratulating me upon my choice, placed my old pink fluffy jumper inside a paper carrier for me to take home.

'There - job done,' said Colin, smiling and taking my arm.

'It feels amazing,' I agreed, snuggling up to him. 'Thank you.'

We headed along the road, ostensibly to visit the antiques shop. Colin wanted an old clock for his mantelpiece as the other one had stopped working. But as we passed *The One and Only*, a picture framing shop, Colin paused. There was a display of paintings, summer scenes of Sheffield, all reduced for the winter season, and one had caught his eye. A print of Porter Brook Falls in Endcliffe Park, a park that happened to be not too far from Colin's apartment. The stream in the picture was flat and smooth, with overhanging trees reflected in the water. And the silver-grey stepping stones were portrayed from an angle that made them appear huge, all-encompassing. A simple black frame set off the picture beautifully, giving it a stark simplicity.

'It makes you feel as if you could just dip your toes into the water,' I murmured.

'And to think Endcliffe Park is only two miles outside the city centre,' Colin said. 'It's beautiful, April. It's exactly what I'm looking for.'

Grabbing my arm, he pushed against the door.

We hung the painting in the lounge, above Colin's chunky brown leather sofa. It was perfect.

'It's lovely, Colin. So come on, then - what made you decide to put a proper picture up here? I thought your taste was more of the Blur and Madonna poster kind.'

I was jokingly referring to his apartment in St Raphael. Mum, Jo and I had been there for a holiday the previous year, and it was like a teenage boy's dream, with groupie posters stuck to the walls and ceilings.

'Very funny. That's my retreat, the place no-one else is supposed to see, where I can just go and chill whenever I want.' He grinned. 'I regret letting you go now.'

'Is that why you've never taken me there yourself?'

He patted at the sofa, encouraging me to sit down beneath the picture.

'I never thought you'd want to go with me, that you like more exciting places.'

I had to think about that one. It's true I like to visit interesting countries; Hong Kong, New Zealand, Japan, the USA. But I think I like European countries the best. Italy, Greece, France, Austria.

'Well, of course I do. But I'd also love to visit St Raphael again, and to see the apartment through your eyes. One day?'

He stood up. 'How about next year, in the spring? That time of year is amazing. No traffic, hardly any people, and lovely food that's made just for the French.'

'You mean no trashy fast food?'

'I mean all the restaurant owners who cater for the rowdy tourists have left, closed up, gone home for the winter.'

I sighed deeply. 'That sounds lovely. When?'

'I'll see what time I can get off work, shall I?'

'A rhetorical question, I think.'

Pulling me to him, he kissed me deeply.

13

With trembling fingers, she folds up the letter, carries it through to her own room, and pushes it to the bottom of her red leather handbag ...

14

Millerstone, Derbyshire

COLIN pulled me to him before stepping into the busy Departures lounge. It was six in the morning and I felt drained.

'I'll let you know about the holiday. And stop worrying. I love you.'

'What – even when I've got no makeup on and feel like an empty duvet cover?'

'Yes. Silly.'

'I love you too, then,' I murmured, snuggling into him, 'so let me know when you get there.'

'I will. And thank you for an amazing evening.'

My drive home was uneventful, but was I glad to see Dash again. He'd gone back to sleep after his initial wee in the garden, so we'd left him there. But I was so ready for coffee and a long walk.

'Right, Dash, it's just me and you now. So let's have breakfast, then a nice wander outside, shall we?'

Our walk took us up towards Stanage Edge, our usual haunt. The cold air was exhilarating, the grass frosted, frozen, like candied angelica with a dusting of icing sugar. Once at the top of the hill, however, I suddenly fancied cappuccino and cake. That's the trouble with getting up so early - the body craves sugar. Well, my body does anyway. So instead of going home, we turned right to walk down into the village.

But then my phone rang. Pulling it from my pocket, I saw it was Toni.

'Hi, Toni. Are you okay? It's early.'

'I know. Sorry. I hope you don't mind.'

'No, it's fine. I've been up since half four, anyway. I had to take Colin to the airport. Is anything wrong?'

'No, nothing's wrong. I just thought we should have a catch-up, that's all. And I've got some news.'

My mind raced ahead. No, I thought. She's letting Mike move in again. No - it's way too soon.

'What is it?' I asked.

'It's complicated. I'll tell you when I see you, because I have a favour to ask.'

'I'm just heading into the village now, as it happens. What time do you start work?'

'My first client's at ten, but Mandy's opening up shop, so it'll be fine.'

'I'll pop round now then, shall I?'

'That'd be lovely. I'll put the kettle on.'

Toni had made fresh coffee by the time I arrived. Not quite my frothy cappuccino, but still very welcoming.

'I've got some mince pies if you fancy one? I put holly shapes on the top. I think they look quite yummy.'

So we sat at her kitchen table with a plateful of sugar-dusted mince pies before us, and discussed the weekend's events. Me and Colin. Toni and Mike. But there was other news.

'I'm setting up a protest group.'

So that was her news.

'What?' I said, astounded.

Honestly, Toni was the last person I'd have expected to be setting up a protest group. Unless it was a protest against the amount of tax she had to pay. Or the cost of school uniform.

'Me and Fiona and Penny,' she said. 'We've decided to set up a campaign against universities allowing their students to take drugs. We're calling it MAUD – Mums Against University Drugs.'

'What?' I repeated.

She looked offended. 'Please stop saying that, April. No, really, honestly, it's not a joke. We're serious. We're setting up a Facebook group to get other mums involved, and Fiona's putting it on Twitter, and Instagram for the young ones.'

'But no-one actually allows students to take drugs as such, do they?'

'No, but they don't discourage them, either. Fiona says there's nothing in universities to help kids, to advise them.' She gesticulated wildly with her hands. 'Because, let's face it, they're only babies when they get there, and they're all so naïve. But they just leave them to their own devices, bless them.'

I smiled. 'Gosh, Toni, I'm proud of you. So what exactly are you going to do?'

'We're going to put posters up. Halls of residence, shops, cafés, takeaways, libraries. Everywhere, in fact. I mean, they do have self-help groups for addicts, obviously. But they need someone to tell them about the dangers before they actually start taking the stuff - the *real* dangers.'

'You mean psychosis and mental illness and so on?'

'Exactly what I mean.'

'That's amazing, Toni. Good for you. So is there anything I can do to help?'

'Would you, April? That'd be fantastic.'

'So how much do you think you'll need?'

I was thinking in terms of paying towards expenses and so on. But Toni had other ideas.

'Oh, no, no. It's not about the money, it's about the publicity. You're quite well-known, aren't you, and you'd be able to talk about it, to let people know?'

Given my current workload, what with the manuscript I was writing, the play I was trying to write, the work I was doing for Sean and DI Jasper, and the rehearsals I was attending, my stomach dropped to the floor.

But I just smiled and said, 'Okay, that's fine. I take it you already have something in mind, so just let me know when and where – yes?'

'Thanks, April, that's so sweet. You're an angel.'

*

I pushed open the heavy cobalt-blue door. The room inside was vast, high-ceilinged, but scuffed and shoddy, bearing in mind it was being used by the Cavendish Amateur Dramatics company, the crème de la crème around these parts. I was surprised. So even though they have the use of that amazing theatre at Chatsworth House, they only have an old outbuilding at the rear of the House for rehearsal.

Lily Tylershaw, the company's new director, welcomed me in with open arms. Young and nimble, clothed in a short black cotton dress and leggings, she just oozed confidence. I imagined her to have studied dramatic art at some posh college in London or somewhere - the type to have rich parents who would encourage it, even though there was little chance of gaining lucrative work.

There again, I could have been wrong. That supposition may just have been the result of my overactive imagination, running wild again.

Lily put out her hand to greet me. 'April, come on in. It's lovely to meet.'

The scent of mossy, oaky perfume surrounded me as we shook hands.

'It's good to meet you, too. And thanks for agreeing to see me – I know you're busy at the moment.'

I sat back into the chair she offered me, a Colonial design in walnut with a forest green leather seat. Her director's chair, I guessed. In fact, as I looked around, I realised the whole room was a mock-up of a film studio. There were pencilled set designs on the walls, photos of costumes, rehearsal schedules, cast lists, and a huge montage of flyers from previous performances.

'You're so right,' she replied. 'As I said on the phone, it's the main dress rehearsal tonight and I need to get over there as soon as. My mother is doing the honours until I get there, but I promised her I wouldn't be long. She was stage manager at the Aldwych in London for a time, you know?' Pulling up another chair, a modern tubular one this time, she sat opposite me, and smiled. 'Would you like a drink before we start?'

I shook my head. 'No - thank you - I'm fine.'

'I don't have much time, but I know we need to discuss Lucas, bless him.'

I shook my head miserably. 'Such an awful thing to have happened.'

'It is. I've had to get someone to take on his role, too. Such a pig, actually. But the show must go on, as they say. And I'm sure you'll understand - you're a member of the Village Players in Millerstone, aren't you?'

I smiled. 'For my sins.'

'So how long have you been involved with the theatre?'

I had to think about that one. I looked up at the ceiling thoughtfully, suddenly noticing long flowing cobwebs in the far right-hand corner. So the famous and impeccable Chatsworth cleaners didn't clean this room as well as the ones inside the house, then.

I turned to Lily. 'I only began acting after I moved to Millerstone fourteen years ago. If I'm honest, I only moved there to escape a disastrous marriage, but it was the best thing I've ever done. I went to one of the Village Players' performances and ended up chatting to Toni, who's now a good friend of mine. She does their hair and makeup, and she talked me into joining. So I did. Although I do write novels for a living, so the dramatic arts quite interest me, anyway.'

Her cheeks dimpled. 'Lovely. So what genre are you?'

I shrugged. 'Just chick-lit, really. Mills and Boon-type stuff.'

'So you enjoy it, the acting?'

'Of course. Otherwise I wouldn't do it.'

'Well, if you ever want to spread your wings, we're always on the lookout for new talent.'

I nodded. 'Thank you. That's very kind of you.'

She folded her hands onto her lap primly. 'So - you're a writer. Is this why you're looking into Lucas's death?'

'Actually no, it has absolutely nothing to do with my work. But DI Jasper from Sheffield Police is on the case, and she's asked me to help out. I know the area, I helped her solve a case last year, but she's also asked me because - because I'm the one who found the body. I'm the one who found Lucas.'

A vision of his dead body filled my head and I began to tremble.

Lily stood up quickly, folding her hands in prayer. 'You *do* need that drink. We have some brandy in the kitchen - medicinal purposes. So bear with,' and she returned after only a minute with two glasses. 'I've added a little water, and not too much brandy, so we can still drive. But here.'

Embarrassed at my stupidity, my weakness, I accepted it and drank it back. 'Thank you. Sorry - I'm obviously not over the shock yet.'

'No, don't be. I can't imagine what it must have been like. How absolutely awful for you.'

'I was out with Dash, my dog, walking, having a nice time, enjoying the fresh air. It's Dash who found him, actually. Hidden beneath some leaves. How on earth anyone could think they'd get away with it, I have no idea. He was bound to have been discovered at some point.'

Downing her brandy, she looked at me thoughtfully. 'Well, maybe it was someone who thought they'd be completely above suspicion. Someone who considers themselves above the law?'

'Like a policeman, you mean?'

'Or a barrister, or an MP, or even a child? Who knows?'

'It makes you wonder how on earth the police track these people down.'

'Analysis. Deduction. Information. Which is why you're here, I guess.'

I nodded. 'Yes.'

'So you want to know all about Lucas Hanssen ...'

*

Meeting Lily made me late for my own rehearsal, but it was the only time she'd had free before their production began that week. I literally ran into the Flying Toad.

'Deep breath,' said George, handing me my Guinness. 'I thought I'd have to drink it myself - thought you weren't coming.'

'Thanks, George.' I pulled a fiver from my purse.

'Are you alright?' he asked, anxiously.

I nodded. 'I'm fine, honestly.'

He handed me my change. 'Go on then – they'll be waiting for you.'

The pub was heaving, despite it being a Monday night. People huddled together nursing their drinks;

waiters rushing in and out of the kitchen; underdressed women in high heels loitering beside the bar with tinsel around their necks; men playing darts in the corner. I had to force my way through to the back room.

The table and chairs had already been moved to one side so that Act Two could be rehearsed. This is the act that introduces Mrs Erlynne to Lady Windermere. The Duchess of Berwick, Lady Agatha, Lord and Lady Windermere, their butler Parker, and their guests, were already on stage, so to speak. Laura, our wonderful and very talented wardrobe mistress, having in an earlier career made two wedding dresses for *Emmerdale*, was sitting with a script in her hand instead of the usual needle and thread. She'd obviously been asked to read in for me.

'Gosh I'm really sorry, Alfie. Sorry, everyone,' I cried, pulling my own script from my bag.

Alfie looked across. 'It's okay, lovely. Laura was going to read in. So long as you're okay, that's the main thing. I did try ringing.'

'I'm so sorry. I had some business to attend to and it had to be tonight, unfortunately. I got here as fast as I could.'

The room was becoming noisy, so Alfie clapped his hands.

'Right. Can we please continue, ladies and gentlemen?' He paused for dramatic effect. 'And of course, any others present.'

There was a giggle from Ginnie in the corner.

'So - page eleven,' he continued.

My character wasn't needed at that point, so I could relax for a few minutes. Taking a deep breath, I tried to still my mind, allowing me to mull over the conversation I'd just had with Lily.

It would seem that Lucas Hanssen was a bit of a philanderer.

And how did Lily know this? Because she'd been the subject of his attention for quite a few months. But she'd resisted him, she said, wasn't interested in a married man with a head as big as the Himalayas.

So what about poor Gemma, I thought? And his poor wife?

I was beginning to feel less and less sorry for Lucas Hanssen by the minute.

But there were other things to think about. For instance, why was he wearing that dress shirt on the Saturday, when the dress rehearsal was tonight? Lily did say they do the usual thing of wearing costume for the technical rehearsal too, which is traditionally the night before the dress rehearsal. But on the night of Lucas's death, it had just been a normal rehearsal. No costume required.

And why was Lucas on his way to Edensor when, from the estimated time of death, it would appear the rehearsal was still ongoing? Yet no-one had missed him. No-one had alerted the police.

I needed to speak to Gemma again. And DI Jasper. And the wife.

But Alfie's voice cut across my thoughts. 'April, my darling – do you wish to play Mrs Erlynne tonight or not? You do seem to be somewhere else at the moment?'

Flustered, I jumped up and stood in place, down left. 'Oh god - sorry, Alfie – a bit tired, I think. I will concentrate, promise.'

'Sorry, darling, but the show must go on. I know you have other things on your mind, but we all have our trials, you know. Just think of poor Mrs Erlynne and the trials she has. And allow this part to take your mind off your other problems, darling. That's the reason we have our theatricals, my dear.'

He was right. I really did need to switch off.

So, pointing my nose into the air and putting on some amazing airs and graces, I took on the character of Mrs Erlynne, birth mother of Lady Windermere.

I put out my hand. 'How do you do again, Lord Windermere?'

*

I left my car outside the Flying Toad and walked home, the brandy and the pint of Guinness on the borderline of being over the limit. But I was just unlocking the front door when my phone rang. Kicking the door shut behind me (not easy with Dash fussing around), I answered it and pushed the buttons of the intruder alarm, all at the same time.

It was DI Jasper.

'Good evening, April. I hope you're well?'

'Yes, yes, I'm fine – thank you.'

What now, I thought?

'I'm just ringing with an update, actually. Strictly confidential, but just to let you know that the knife used on Lucas was a stainless steel paring knife, nine centimetres long.'

I was a little confused. 'Okay, but does that actually help? Everyone owns a paring knife, don't they?'

'They do. And there are no fingerprints because they were wearing gloves, so the killing was most probably pre-meditated. Now that *does* help.'

'Or it could just have been a very cold evening.'

'Well, let's assume otherwise for now, shall we? The shirt, by the way, was definitely part of the costume for the play, as were the trousers. And no-one has any idea why he was wearing costume, because it wasn't a dress or a technical rehearsal, and they've no idea why he left the rehearsal still wearing it.'

'You've interviewed the other cast members, then?'

'The majority of them, yes. They're not all available, unfortunately. It's their production this week and they've been too busy building the set. But we will catch up with them.'

'Yes, of course.'

'But look, April, the real reason I'm ringing – I've just made an appointment to see Lucas's wife, Katie.

And I wondered if you'd mind coming along. As a chaperone, a friendly face.'

'Yes - no problem,' I said, kneeling down and stroking Dash, who was fussing.

'Fantastic, brilliant. Thank you. Is seven o'clock on Wednesday okay for you?'

'That'll be fine, I'm sure.'

'Good. I'll pick you up at quarter to, then.'

As the call ended, I pushed open the kitchen door to allow Dash to reach his water.

'Manuscript?' I murmured. 'What manuscript?'

15

The letter is well-hidden. She can think about it for days.

16

Millerstone, Derbyshire

I awoke the following morning to the sound of heavy banging on my front door and Dash yelping at me to get up. Forcing my feet to the floor, I pulled on my dressing gown (the grey silk one, a present from Colin) and rushed downstairs. But as I switched on the light, the banging stopped. Yawning, I checked the hall clock; nearly half past five. What on earth would someone want with me at this time of day?

Peering through the glass, I saw a figure, a woman's figure, about the same height as myself. Dash stood guard beside me, so I pulled back the door slowly, nervously.

'Yes? Can I help?'

She just stood there, arms folded, her tired brown eyes staring at me as if she owned the place.

'You've got to let me in. I've been travelling most of the night. I'm Felix's sister.'

'Felix?' I repeated, sleepily.

'Felix Porter-Bentley. I'm his sister, Felicity.'

The name was ringing bells, and I searched my memory banks. Of course - the head forester at Chatsworth. The *deceased* head forester at Chatsworth.

Why on earth was his sister here? Glancing behind her, I saw a car parked beneath the street light. It was dark, angular, old-fashioned-looking.

Why I believed what she'd just said, I have no idea. But there was no reason not to. So, pulling back the door further, I welcomed her in.

'Come on in, then. You must be exhausted.'

'Thanks.' She entered, her boots dirty, scuffed, her clothes shabby. Asking her to remove her boots, I took her through to the kitchen.

'Come through and sit down, Felicity. It's a bit cold in here, but I'll put the heating on.' I pressed the switch on the wall. 'Would you like a hot drink - some tea or coffee?'

Sitting down gratefully, she pulled off her parka and pushed it onto the table. Beneath it, she wore a red woollen jumper with a brown calf-length skirt, both of which had definitely seen better days.

'Coffee, please - thanks. And call me Fliss.'

I detected a faint American accent that peaked my interest. Exactly how far had she travelled?

'Milk, sugar, cream?'

'Cream, please, no sugar.'

'I have some whisky, if you'd like? Warm you up a bit?'

She smiled, her face worn and tired. 'In the coffee?'

'Yes.'

'What – like Irish coffee?'

I nodded, showing her the bottle. 'Just like Irish coffee.'

'That'd be good. Thanks.'

That accent ...

'Where are you from?' I asked.

'Jackson, Wyoming - originally.'

I made coffee, stirred in the whisky, and added some double cream from the fridge. 'Here you go.' Removing her coat from the table, I placed the mug in front of her.

'Thanks so much. Actually, could I please use the bathroom?'

'Of course. Just through the door, on the left there, next to the office.'

Switching on Radio Two as background noise, I made myself a cuppa. Decaf. I intended going straight back to bed after this woman had gone.

But once she'd returned, I noticed a change in her, almost as if she mistrusted me. She was anxious, alert, almost paranoid, looking around, watching my face.

I stifled a yawn. 'So why have you come to see me, particularly? And please tell me you haven't come all the way from Wyoming.'

She cupped her hands around the coffee. 'I haven't lived in Wyoming for years. I live in Fishguard now - Pembrokeshire - and I've come to see you because you're one of the guys investigating my brother's death.'

Shocked, I sat upright. 'No. I'm not. Who on earth told you that?'

On the defensive now, her every sentence became a question. 'Someone McGuire? A reporter? He rang to get information on my brother? He said you're helping investigate his death? That it could be murder?'

The room became even colder, and I shivered.

'No. You've got it wrong. He's got it wrong. I'm investigating a murder, yes, but at the moment I haven't even begun to look into your brother's death. And if I had, I certainly wouldn't be discussing it with you.'

She looked at me defiantly. 'Why not? I'm his sister.'

I breathed in deeply. 'Look - before we discuss this any further, can I ask what's so urgent? It's nearly six o'clock in the morning and you've dragged me out of bed for no reason.'

'I need to know what happened, who murdered him. He's all I have left ...' and she burst into tears.

Consoling her for a few minutes, I then insisted we move to the lounge, where I took time to light the wood burner. Making sure she was comfortable, I went back to the kitchen to let Dash out and feed him and the cat, then made more coffee, with toast and marmalade. Eventually, cosy and warm, Fliss Porter-Bentley told me her story.

She and Felix were born and raised in the States, in Wyoming. Their father worked for the Yellowstone National Park, and this is where Felix learned his trade, watching his father at work. Their mother was a stay-at-home mum, gentle but firm, never still, taking care of the kids, the house, and the local community. When both parents died in quick succession, Felix and Fliss were only in their twenties. But they became homeless suddenly, their house being a perk of their father's job. And there was no family to help out, other than an aunt in Montreal. So, uprooted and unsettled, they decided to leave the US and travel. Fliss spent years in Naples, Strasbourg and Athens before finally settling in London. She moved to Wales after being made redundant, and had lived in Fishguard for the past three years. Felix had married, produced a daughter, divorced, and then spent time honing his trade before coming to England to find work at the Chatsworth estate. He'd been head forester there for over five years.

'He's a hard worker, you know, just like Daddy. He'd work twenty-four seven if it needed it.'

'Do you know why anyone would want to kill him, Fliss?'

She was becoming emotional again, so I passed her the tissue box. Wiping her nose, she shook her head.

'You see - that's just what I don't understand. They're saying he was drunk, intoxicated, that it was alcohol poisoning. But he didn't drink that much – unless it was to celebrate something – and even then not *that* much. He was sensible. Unlike me.'

I ignored that comment, even though my curiosity was aroused. 'So when did you last see Felix?'

'A couple years ago. He invited me over here for his birthday. Oh, god …'

This time the tears were long-lasting and I just had to sit and wait it out. But I did wonder how she'd be able to help us if she hadn't seen Felix for two years. She'd have no idea of his mental state, or of any other problems he may have had.

'Sorry if I've upset you,' I murmured.

'No - it's fine. I'm sorry. I just can't believe I'll never see him again. It's taking some sinking in.'

'It's not easy, I know it isn't. But if you can help us get to the bottom of why he died, that would make us all feel a whole lot better.'

*

Eventually, I persuaded Fliss to get some sleep. I drew the curtains together in the spare room and settled her down with warm milk and a hot water bottle. She was exhausted, bless her. She did insist on finding a local B&B, so we booked her in for that night, but she really needed a daytime nap.

Downstairs, I made more coffee and sat at the kitchen table. I needed to speak to Sean. Yawning loudly, I picked up my phone and called.

'Hi, April,' he said. 'How's things?'

'Fine. Except I have Felix Porter-Bentley's sister staying with me. Apparently, you gave her my name.'

'Did I? Oh, yes - I did. Sorry about that. But what's she doing at your place? I only needed a few bits of information.'

'She wants to know what we know.'

'Is it okay if I come over?'

'She's asleep.'

'I won't keep her long, I promise.'

I spent an hour in my office, catching up on work and eating lunch, even though I was much too tired for food. But I forced it down. Egg mayo salad with green beans, sauerkraut and beetroot, and granary toast. Not very exciting, but necessary.

Once Sean arrived, however, I coaxed Fliss out of bed and down to the lounge. She said she wasn't hungry, either, but I made fresh coffee and warmed the croissants Sean brought with him. Ever the thoughtful enhancer of the waistline is Sean.

I pushed a mug of coffee into Fliss's hands. 'Are you feeling any better?'

Pulling her messy hair back from her face, she smiled. 'I'm much better - thanks.' She nodded towards the window. 'You have a lovely view here. It was dark when I arrived – I couldn't see it.'

I looked out at the hills. The wide grassy peaks were dotted with sheep as usual, but today they were edged with a seamless blanket of soft grey cloud. That's the wonderful thing about where I live - the scene changes every day.

I smiled. 'Thank you. I like it.'

She did look brighter after her sleep, and was in a way quite attractive, with sparkling eyes and an engaging smile. I guessed she was around her late-thirties, about seven years younger than me - but her long mousey hair, her bird-like edginess, and the lines around her mouth made her appear much older.

I introduced Sean. 'This is Sean McGuire, the reporter you spoke to – from the Sheffield Star. He'd like to ask you some questions.'

Sean pulled out his notebook and turned the page. 'Hi there. It's nice to meet you, face to face. I do hope you're alright talking about this - I realise it's all very upsetting for you.'

She nodded. 'If I can help at all, then that's just fine.'

'Thank you. I have a list of questions here, so I'll start from the top - if that's alright?'

'Fire away.'

'So – what did your brother do when he wasn't working? Did he have any hobbies? Were there any women? Did he have any extra-curricular earnings that you're aware of?'

She sighed heavily. 'You asked me all this on the phone.'

'I know, I know. But sometimes it takes a while for people to remember things. And when you're upset it's not easy, people putting you on the spot, asking stuff out of the blue like that.'

She sighed again. 'Okay, yeah. Well, as far as I know Felix didn't have a girl. The last one was a couple years ago, but they split after an argument. It was over something stupidly trivial – a gift he bought her or something. But it all blew up, and that's all I know. As for hobbies, I think his job was his hobby, and that's the truth. I suppose he did a little shooting now and again, but that was something he did for a living anyhow.' She shook her head, sadly. 'No, I doubt he had time for hobbies. If his job was anything like Daddy's, it was full-on.'

'So what about money? Did he have a certain lifestyle he needed to keep up? Did he gamble at all, sell stuff? Was there anything he shouldn't have been doing?'

She shot a glance that could have melted ice, and again shook her head. 'No. Definitely not. Nothing illegal. Not Felix.'

Sean scribbled a few notes. 'Okay. Thanks for that.'

'Could he have turned to drink after he split with this girl two years ago, and no-one realised?' I asked.

She looked up, and I saw she'd begun to cry again. 'I suppose. It's possible.'

'Right,' I said. 'So let's assume he *was* out drinking that night. How come no-one saw him? And how did he end up in the river?'

'You don't have to be out drinking – he could just have taken himself off with a bottle, drunk too much, and fallen in,' said Sean.

'But you think there may be a link to this other murder – you said so,' cried Fliss.

'No,' I said. 'It's a possibility. They happened the same week, that's all, and they were both found in the same area.'

'So what happened to the other guy?'

'Knifed,' said Sean, brutally.

'Oh, my god ...'

'Yes. Awful,' I said.

'And they still don't know who did it?'

Sean looked up. 'That's why we're investigating your brother, to see if there's a connection.'

'So who was the other guy? Did he know Felix?' she asked.

I shrugged. 'He was local, a financial adviser. Into amateur dramatics. Which is what he was doing when he was killed.'

'What – he was killed while he was up on stage?'

'No, he was at a rehearsal. For some reason he left without changing out of his costume, and he was found dead a mile away, two days later.'

'Where was it then, this rehearsal?'

'Chatsworth House.'

She turned pale. 'So he could have known Felix? They could have met at Chatsworth House?'

Sean nodded. 'It is possible. It's also possible Lucas was Felix's financial adviser. The police are looking into it as we speak.'

*

Fliss and Sean stayed at my house well into the evening. Fliss took a hot shower, and we ate a meal of mushroom pasta bake with stir-fried mangetout and carrots. Over dinner, we talked about Felix's life, his marriage, and his daughter Juniper, now aged eighteen and living in Canada. After her parents split up, Juniper and her mother went to live in Ontario. Fliss had no idea where she was living now, but had been able to message her through a mutual friend, briefly informing her of her father's death.

'A cute kid,' she said. 'I only met her a few times after they moved, but she always came across as the sensitive type. So like her dad.'

'If Felix is that sensitive, he may well have turned to drink, then - you know, when his relationship ended,' I said.

She looked confused. 'I honestly don't know. It's possible, I guess. It's just, he thought more about his work than that. He was real conscientious. No way would he have turned up for work crazily overhung. And he might have been needed at any time, y'know? Even through the weekend.'

'So what do you do for a living?' asked Sean.

'I have a gift shop. It's a little thing, just a hut. Mostly local stuff, but also some made in China tat.' She shrugged. 'It brings in the punters.'

'So where were you on the night of Saturday, the twenty-fourth of November?' asked Sean.

Shocked, I stared at him. 'Sean?'

'Just a formality, April. We need to check everything, don't we, leave no stone unturned?'

'I know, but ...' I protested.

'Fliss?' he said, turning to her.

Embarrassed, I stood up to draw the lounge curtains across. It had been dark for hours, but suddenly ice-cold air was penetrating the glass. Turning, I noticed Fliss feeling just as awkward. She stammered out her reply.

'Well - I - I was at home. I'd had a delivery and I was working through the paperwork. It needs to be all ready for Christmas. But - I thought you said Felix was found last Tuesday?'

'He was,' said Sean. 'But the other guy, Lucas, was killed on the Saturday. I just need to see if there's any connection.'

She studied her hands carefully. 'I see.'

'I'm not accusing you or anything. I just need to tick boxes, that's all.'

She nodded. 'Yeah. I know.'

'And where were you last Tuesday?'

She looked up. 'Again, I was in the shop. I don't have any assistants or anything, so it's all down to me.'

I was still standing at the window. 'Shall I make us a drink?'

Fliss shook her head. 'No, nothing for me, thanks. I guess I'm still pretty tired from last night. I'll get along to my guest house, if that's okay?'

I noticed her accent had become stronger; she was obviously quite upset.

'No – that's fine – no problem. I'll give you the directions. It's not far.'

*

It was nine o'clock. Sean was still around. I needed to take Dash for a walk and pick up my car from the Flying Toad, but first I rustled up a quick gin and tonic for us both.

'Poor Dash,' I said. 'He's been neglected all day. I think we both need to stretch our legs.'

Sean downed his drink. 'Would you mind if I came along, too? I could do with the fresh air.'

So, wrapping ourselves in coats, scarves and gloves, we went out, the three of us. We walked down the hill towards the village, past the life-size Nativity scene, along the main road with its brightly lit Christmas trees, then up, towards the Parish church. It was very dark here, but Sean had brought his heavy torch from the car, so we picked our way carefully up the hill. At the top, we paused to sit down on the wooden bench that sits just outside the graveyard. Dash, having had his fill of exercise, waited patiently.

Sean was looking very thoughtful.

'What?' I said.

'You know, she's just the right height for the stabbing.'

'What? Who?'

'Fliss. She's just about the right height, don't you think? The knife came in from below Lucas's chest.'

'I didn't know that.'

'Well, some things need to be kept quiet until we have the full story.'

'So you think she might have come over, killed Lucas for some reason, then got her brother so drunk he fell into the river?'

He shrugged. 'Could be.'

And I thought *I* was the one with the overactive imagination.

'It is strange she hadn't seen him for two years,' I said.

'You didn't tell me that.'

'Well, some things need to be kept quiet until we have the full story.'

'Haha. Very funny.'

Warm from the walk, I undid my scarf a little. ''Two whole years. It's not like they were at opposite ends of the world, is it? Do you think there might have been some family issues going on?'

'Possibly.'

'Or some kind of weird love thing. Lucas Hanssen was a bit of a philanderer, by all accounts.'

'You didn't tell me that, either.'

17

Eventually, the house empty, she pulls out the letter and carries it down to the kitchen …

18

Millerstone, Derbyshire

DASH and I were halfway up the road to Stanage Edge when my phone rang. I swiped at the touchscreen. It was DI Jasper.

'Hi - April here.'

'Sorry to disturb you, April, but I understand you've had Felix Porter-Bentley's sister round at your place?'

'Good morning to you as well, DI Jasper. But it's half past eight in the morning. Don't you ever sleep?'

She laughed. 'Not when there are murderers sneaking around, I don't. No - Sean rang me earlier, filled me in on the detail, so I had no choice but to get out of bed.'

'He doesn't sleep either, then. Obviously.'

'I'm assuming Fliss is still at the guest house in Millerstone? So where is this place, exactly?'

'It's the one on Station Road. It's a smallish place, but you'll see the sign easily enough. On the left, opposite the station.'

'Do you think she'd be up for a chat?'

'I think she'll be hanging around for a while, anyway. She'll have funeral arrangements to make, poor girl.'

'I'll give her a call, then.'

'Do you have her number?'

'Yes thanks. And - April?'

'Yes?'

'Any gut feelings on this one?'

I looked around thoughtfully. The sky was now layered in hues of red and orange, a yellow ball hanging at its heart. I paused to admire. I never stop pausing to admire.

As for my gut feeling - I'm never quite sure about that one. Is it gut feeling, or just a writer's overactive imagination?

'Sorry, no, not at the moment. But there are still plenty of questions to be answered, so maybe I just need a bit more information.'

'Well, I've spoken to Felix's mates at Chatsworth now, and they've verified the findings from Forensics. He was definitely a user. Cannabis, cocaine. They'd share in his habit sometimes, although they're still insisting he didn't drink – other than a pint at the local sometimes. And, apart from the odd get-together at work, he usually kept himself to himself. But they did have the feeling he was seeing someone, a woman.'

'Okay?'

'We've actually got CCTV of them at the local pub, the Elm Tree, but you can only see the back of her head - dark hair – that's all we've got. But it's going back to July, so it's a while ago.'

'And we've no idea who she is?'

'Not a cat in hell's chance. We could do with her coming forward, so Sean's on the job now, putting out feelers as we speak.'

'Do we know who was supplying Felix with these drugs?'

'I'm kind of thinking it might be Lucas. But that's only my gut instinct.'

'Gemma said Lucas didn't do drugs, although she did say he had secret meetings and wouldn't tell her what they were. She just thought it had something to do with his wife.'

'I take it you're still okay with calling round at Katie Hanssen's tonight?'

'Of course, yes. I said I would.'

'We're not to say anything about Gemma, so be careful. We've agreed to keep her out of the picture for now - his poor wife's got enough on her plate.'

'I know. But then so has Gemma.'

'Yes.' She went quiet. 'This whole thing's a bloody mess, isn't it?'

'I know.'

'So I'll pick you up later, then.'

Ringing off, I pulled on Dash's lead, turned round, and headed for home.

'Sorry, Dash, sweetie – it's breakfast-time.'

I really did need to get some work done.

*

Mum rang just as I was finishing the nineteenth chapter of the second draft of my manuscript. It was definitely getting there and I was feeling good about it, as always when nearing completion of a project.

I'd left my phone in the kitchen as usual, but had just gone through to make tea and to let Dash out.

'Hi Mum, you must be psychic. How are you?'

'I'm okay, thanks, love. But why psychic?'

'Because I've been in my office nearly all day, and as soon as I walk through to the kitchen, you ring me.'

'Ha! I always said I had eyes in the back of my head, didn't I?'

I laughed. 'That's true, actually. So what can I do for you on this lovely day?'

'I just wondered what you're doing this weekend, love. Jim's off to do a charity gig in Birmingham, and I thought maybe I'd have a look round at wedding dresses.'

'Well, it's about time. When did you say the wedding was?'

She laughed. 'I know - the Saturday before Christmas. Not long, is it? But we've been so busy making arrangements, and sorting out the house and estate agents and everything.'

'I'm only joking, Mum, but you do need to get a move-on. And I suppose you'll need some help choosing this dress?'

'Well, if you're not too busy. I've asked Jo as well, of course. We could have a lovely day out.'

Mum's wedding was to be a small affair with family and close friends. There really wasn't much time left at all, but I'd been so busy with work I hadn't even considered her not having chosen a dress. Which is very unlike me. Shit, I hadn't even thought about what *I* was going to wear.

But now my mind was shooting off in all directions. It was my weekend to fly to Brussels, and I'd already told Colin I'd need to take some work with me. Which had completely scuppered his plans for a drive out to Antwerp. He'd been wanting to take me there for a while, and it was particularly beautiful over Christmas, he said. So what would he say now, when I told him I was taking time out to shop for Mum's wedding dress? It didn't look good, did it? But I had no choice; I couldn't let my mum down.

'It's fine, Mum. I'll be there. What time shall I come over?'

'Well, I thought maybe ten o'clock? Then we could have coffee, and lunch somewhere nice. It'll be fun having a girls' day out.'

So it was all agreed. But I was absolutely dreading the phone call to Colin.

I rang him later, in between his work proper and his work overtime, and explained all.

'So there's no point in my coming over to your place, then?' he said.

I felt truly wretched. 'Not really, no. I'll be with Mum all day Saturday, and I really need to get down to some work on Sunday - I need to get this manuscript on its way. I'm so sorry, Colin.'

'Oh, well. I'll find something to do. I might still drive out to Antwerp, maybe do some Christmas shopping.'

'I could always come over next weekend?'

'That'd be lovely. And it really doesn't matter about seeing Antwerp if you've got work to do. I just thought it would be nice to have a drive out.'

'It would be nice, but I'll see how I'm getting on.'

'Okay. I need to find you a Christmas present, anyway. But what do you buy the girl who's got everything?'

I felt even worse. 'I'm so sorry, Colin.'

'No, it's fine. Choosing your mother's wedding dress is important. I understand.'

*

Lucas Hanssen's wife lived in a lovely old house on the main road out of Millerstone, past David Mellor's famous cutlery factory, and out towards Grindleford. Stone-built and steeped in character, the garden was bursting with Japanese Maple trees, their red leaves still ablaze with colour, despite it being December. It was dark when we arrived, but the garden was lit by soft exterior lighting placed discreetly along the edge of the house.

Pulling onto the long gravelled driveway, DI Jasper parked up behind a white BMW, shiny and new and expensive. Leading the way to the front door, a dark, shiny Georgian type with brass fittings, she rang the bell.

'Here we go.'

It was Katie Hanssen's mother who answered the door, her short dark hair and rose-pink suit giving her the air of an elegant secretary, or maybe an air hostess. She shook hands with DI Jasper.

'Carol Bainbrooke. We spoke on the phone,' she said, before acknowledging my presence. 'And you must be April. Pleased to meet you.'

We shook hands, and she offered to take our coats.

'Come on in. Katie's just in the small dining room – she's not been feeling too good at all. Has there been any more news?'

DI Jasper shook her head. 'No. Sorry. We'll let you know, of course, as soon as we hear anything.'

She nodded. 'We'll cut through the banqueting room, then – just through here. Would you like some tea, biscuits?' She was leading us through the most magnificent room I've ever seen. Smelling of warm polished oak, it was appropriately named, with its stone flooring and its panelled walls. The long, highly polished, refectory table was completely bare, apart from an enormous glass hurricane lamp, a lit candle flickering away inside. A long cabinet rested against the wall, seemingly untouched, and I guessed this room was definitely used for entertaining. Nice.

The small dining room, which was in fact pretty huge by anyone else's standards, was reached via a short hallway, and was much more informal. Books and newspapers had been piled to one side of the circular table, making room for the worn leather coasters that had been scattered around. Carol introduced us, poured the tea she'd already made, and left us with her daughter.

Katie turned to greet us, her face pale, her eyes red and swollen. She was sitting at the table reading, her shoulders hunched, her arms wrapped around her chest protectively, and a soft grey cardigan thrown around her shoulders. Slim, petite, with long dark hair and large blue eyes, she was clearly very upset over the death of her husband; she had to keep pausing when speaking in order to compose herself.

'We're having a baby,' she said, smiling painfully. 'I'm two months' gone.'

DI Jasper and I sat at the table, not far from the tea-tray. I reached out to Katie's hand protectively.

'I'm so sorry, Mrs Hanssen.'

She nodded, her lips trembling. 'Katie – please.'

DI Jasper spoke softly. 'I can't imagine how you must be feeling. It's such a tragedy. But April and I are here so we can take away as much information as possible. We need to find out who did this. And I know my team have already been to see you, and Forensics have been round ...'

Clutching at her cardigan, Katie moaned loudly. 'God, that was awful. They've even taken his laptop. All our pictures.'

'I know. And I'm sorry, and we will get them back to you as soon as possible. But what April and I would like to do is glean a little more information, in more intricate detail, about Lucas, about the kind of man he was, the people he knew - that sort of thing.'

Picking up the plate of slim and expensive-looking biscuits that sat before us, I offered one to Katie.

'Here. You need to eat. Especially if you're eating for two.'

'Thank you.' Taking one, she bit into it, her fingers pale and delicate.

'So could we start with the names of Lucas's friends?' said DI Jasper, pulling an iPad from her bag.

*

The Wheatsheaf Hotel in Baslow is an old coaching house, built in the 18th Century. We chose to go there because it was out of the way, no prying eyes and no awkward questions.

Sean turned up just after we arrived. The time was nine o'clock and the pub was teeming with people, celebrating Christmas, hugging loved ones, or just catching up on the day's news.

I got the first round in. Guinness for myself and Sean, white wine for DI Jasper. Then we found a table in the corner, not far from the log fire. The cracking of the wood and the flickering flames were a welcome distraction from the conversation we were about to have.

'How on earth anyone could cheat on that lovely lady, I have no idea,' I began in earnest. 'He had everything anyone could wish for. An absolutely amazing home, an incredibly beautiful wife, and a baby on the way.'

Sean grinned. 'How old is she then, this wife?'

'She's way above your league,' warned DI Jasper, pulling her phone from her bag. 'Don't even think about it, McGuire.'

He laughed. 'So come on then – tell me – what have we found out? Anything?'

I sipped my Guinness thoughtfully. 'Okay. For a start, Katie has no idea Lucas had been cheating on her with Gemma Jameson. Madly in love they were, or so she thought. And secondly …'

DI Jasper looked up. 'Secondly, Forensics has just found some kind of a link with Felix Porter-Bentley. Something to do with a car? DCI Watkins has just messaged me.'

Sean turned. 'Really?'

'Really. I'm to call in first thing tomorrow.'

'Well, that is good news,' he said.

I wasn't so sure about that. 'We still need to determine whether or not Felix actually killed Lucas.'

'And who killed Felix. Assuming he was forced to drink all that booze,' said DI Jasper.

'What a great way to go,' said Sean, grinning and holding up his pint.

DI Jasper pulled out her iPad, found the list of names she'd made whilst talking to Katie Hanssen, and glanced through it. 'We still have people to speak to. There are a couple of amdram guys, and some of Lucas's work colleagues who were away when we did the first interviews. I've got a couple of sergeants on the job.'

I looked at her thoughtfully. 'The second thing I was going to say was that Lucas's wife is adamant he wasn't into drugs. According to her, he abhorred the stuff, would never even take it, never mind deal in it.'

'So there was nothing illegal going on?' asked Sean. 'Nothing to help him make a few extra bob? I find that hard to believe, somehow.'

'His wife's a locum pharmacist and he was a financial adviser. That'd make you enough money, wouldn't it?' said DI Jasper.

'That house was rather superb,' I insisted. 'But they might have been given money by the parents or something – you know, they might be helping out. Her mother was very well-groomed, wasn't she?'

'She was,' she agreed. 'So let's assume he wasn't out to make money from drugs. What other connection might there be with Felix?'

'How tall was Felix - do you know?' I asked.

DI Jasper consulted her iPad. 'Five ten. Why?'

'Was he taller or shorter than Lucas?'

She turned to her notes again. 'Lucas was taller by a couple of inches – not much. But Felix was much broader and heavier, according to these stats.'

'I've been thinking about that one,' said Sean. 'Lucas could actually have been pushed down, or the attacker might have fallen over during the fight. So their height doesn't really have to come into it.'

I yawned; the fire and the Guinness were making me sleepy. 'So what if Lucas Hanssen had agreed some kind of a deal with Felix?' I said. 'Possibly something to do with this car? And what if he wanted to pull out of the deal for some reason, and it got nasty?'

'So it was done in temper?' asked Sean.

'But then who killed Felix, and why?' I asked.

'You mean who forced him to drink enough to cause alcohol poisoning? Assuming that's what happened?' said DI Jasper.

'What if there was someone bigger in the picture?' I said. 'A gang of some kind? And they got Felix to kill Lucas, then himself? Or they forced the drink down him?'

'April, you know that overactive imagination of yours?' said Sean.

I smiled. 'Sorry.'

'I really don't think the Derbyshire Dales Street Gang exists,' he said.

DI Jasper stared at him. 'You'd be surprised. Anyway, we need to discuss Fliss. When I saw her this afternoon, she was genuinely upset, and I don't think she had any involvement in the murder. But we're getting the Dyfed Powys Police to check out her story, just to be sure. Quietly, of course.'

'What is it you're looking into?' I asked.

'We need to know how she got the money for the business she runs, for a start. She won't have got that much redundancy money if she'd only been at that place in London a few years.'

Sean nodded. 'Well, as she said, it's only a small hut she runs. She buys and sells from day to day, so she doesn't really need that much money. And she lives behind the shop, so her living costs are cut to the minimum by the sound of it. Although she was struggling, because prior to that she'd been sharing an apartment with another girl.'

I had a sudden thought. 'What happened with Gemma? You went to see her as well, didn't you?'

DI Jasper nodded. 'I was curious about the baby, but she had no idea Katie was pregnant. Lucas had never mentioned it. And we've checked her alibi. She was definitely in London with a friend the weekend of the murder. We've seen hotel bills, theatre receipts, the lot.'

'And you really believe she didn't know about the baby?' asked Sean. 'A woman scorned and all that?'

'Yes,' she said. 'I believe her. But what's happening with finding Felix's lady-friend? Is there any luck on that score?'

He shook his head. 'I've placed an article asking for her to come forward, in confidence, obviously. I mean, she may be married or something. But there's been nothing yet.'

DI Jasper pushed back her chair. 'I'm hungry. Crisps, anyone?'

19

She pulls a box of Bryant & May Extra-long matches from the drawer. Striking one, she calmly watches as the flame leaps up ...

20

Millerstone, Derbyshire

IT was still the first week of December, but what a beautiful day. Bright yellow sunshine, frost sparkling on the lawn, the soil beneath as hard as brick.

I was outside, planting my pansies. Finally. It took just under forty minutes to do the lot, planting three pansies into each planter. But come the spring, my back garden was going to look adorable.

I was clearing excess clumps of soil from the lawn and tidying up when my phone rang. Dash, who'd had a pleasant early morning walk and was fast asleep in the sunshine, woke up and came running over.

It was Sean. Answering it, I slouched against the garden table, allowing the weak sunshine to bathe my back.

'Just letting you know DI Jasper has rung,' he said. 'It's about the link between Lucas and Felix.'

I stood up straight. 'Okay?'

'The police found a V5 document in the glovebox of Felix's car. It was only issued a few weeks ago, so they decided to follow it up. Turns out the previous owner part-exchanged the car with a dealership in Sheffield. Interestingly, Lucas Hanssen is one of the dealership's company directors. Now it's a Mitsubishi Shogun, worth about £22,000, and the car Felix part-exchanged was worth around £10,000. So he should have paid £12,000 towards the Mitsubishi. The weird thing is that there's no trace of any payment having been made. The police have been able to access all relevant bank accounts – Felix, Lucas, Lucas's wife – both private and business accounts, including the car business. But nothing. So the question is - where did the money get to? Why didn't the car dealership put it into their account? Where did it go?'

My mind was working overtime. 'I have no idea, Sean. But they've obviously found a link between the two guys. And that's a step in the right direction. Well done, Sheffield Police.'

'We're not out of the woods yet, though. We still need to determine exactly where that money went, and why these men died.'

'Do you think it *was* some kind of gangland killing?'

'I don't know, April. And until we do, I for one am making no assumptions.'

'You're right to do so. I don't suppose DI Jasper would appreciate gangland killings being splashed all over the Sheffield Star.'

*

Having tidied up the garden and arranged my planters in their rightful positions around the edge of the patio, I left food and milk for the cat and went inside to make a much-needed coffee. It was only as I was fetching a clean tea towel from the drawer that I realised Dash was sniffing around in the hallway, growling and baring his teeth. I stroked his head to calm him.

'What's wrong, Dash? This isn't like you?'

Suddenly uneasy, I realised I could smell some kind of scent; flowery, cheap. I checked the front door, pulling at the handle.

'Damn it – no ...'

I'd forgotten to lock it after returning from our walk. So I'd been in the back garden all that time while the front door was unlocked.

So I locked the door, left Dash in the kitchen, and checked each of the rooms; the lounge, the office, the cloakroom, and the bedrooms upstairs. There was nothing. Nothing had been moved and nothing had been taken.

Stupidly and in desperation, I ran outside to check the road for unusual cars, for movement - anything untoward, in fact. But again, there was nothing.

'What an absolute idiot ...'

Angry with myself, I made the coffee, hot and fresh and strong, and sat with it in the kitchen, contemplating what had just happened. It was possible Dash had made a mistake, but it wasn't like him. And anyway, I was sure I'd been able to smell perfume. No, Dash was a pleasant, placid dog, not taken to growling for no reason. I was convinced someone had been inside the house.

I rang Sean back.

'Someone has just been inside the house.' The words hit me hard, and my hands began to tremble.

'What? Your house?'

'Yes, my house.'

'Shit. Have you rung the police?'

'They can't do anything. There's nothing missing or anything, it's just ...'

'You should ring them, April. Now. There might be fingerprints.'

'Possibly. But I have a feeling they knew what they were doing.'

'Even so, you need to report it.'

'I will. I just need to calm down first. But they must have been straight in and out. I was in the back garden – I'd left the front door unlocked.'

'Oh, April.'

'I know. Stupid. I wouldn't even have known if it hadn't been for Dash sniffing around.'

'You want me to come over?'

'I'll be fine. I've got a rehearsal tonight, anyway. I need to get some work done, then go through my lines.'

'You will report it to the police, then?'

'Yes, yes, I will. Promise.'

*

The station clerk took the details, but as I'd correctly guessed, there was nothing they could do. After all, nothing had been damaged or stolen, so there was no real urgency. Besides, the police had enough on their hands without me bothering them. But I'd promised to report it, so I did.

I tried my very best to get some work done that afternoon, but it wasn't easy. My head was all over the place. Apart from the fact that someone had been inside my house, I was confused about the deaths of Lucas and Felix. Nothing seemed to make sense. Nothing at all.

Suddenly, I needed a run.

So I dug out my old Nike running shoes from the pantry floor and put them on. They felt just like old friends, so comfortable they might have been soft leather gloves. Fastening Dash's long lead to my wrist and donning my head-torch, I set the intruder alarm and locked up the house securely. My joggers and sweatshirt did little to protect me against the icy cold wind, but I knew I'd warm up once I got started.

So I ran.

And I ran.

I ran all the way up Coggers Lane, past Birley Lane, and on for another ten minutes, then slowed down to a speed-walk. By the time we'd reached the car park below Stanage Edge, both Dash and I were gasping for breath. But boy, did it feel good.

Turning back, I walked quickly. But as the sweat I'd produced dried off, I began to shiver. Rubbing my arms to warm them, I reached the house, unlocked the door and disabled the alarm. Inside the privacy of my bathroom, I stripped off and stood beneath a hot shower. I was there for ages, just warming myself up. After drying off with a soft towel, I put a little heat rub containing eucalyptus oil onto my shoulders and knees and massaged it in. It felt amazing.

Poor Dash slept in the kitchen while I thawed out, but I didn't neglect him. Finally dressed in fresh comfy clothes, I washed him too, then dried him off with the hairdryer, even though he hates it.

Warm and cosy now, I sat reading my lines in the lounge, a cup of hot tea and a chocolate ginger biscuit to one side, while Dash slept on his big cushion. Spoilt dog. But, very sleepy myself, I was just beginning to nod off when the phone rang.

It was Sandy, my agent. An amazing woman. She worked for a couple of tabloids in her youth, but now, married and affluent, she runs a small agency for a select list of clients, myself being one of them. I just happened to get lucky, I guess. She was only just setting up in business, eager for new authors, when I sent her my very first synopsis. She's a sweet lady if you're on the right side of her, but if you cross her, beware. So you can imagine my horror when she rang to enquire how I was getting on with my manuscript, bearing in mind the deadline for its proofreading was January the twentieth – only forty-five days to go.

So I blabbed on about how I'd found this dead body, and how the police had needed me for their enquiries, and how much time it had all taken.

'I have actually finished the MS, Sandy. I'm just on the second draft now. So I'll get there, I promise, don't worry about it.'

'It's just that I haven't heard from you, darling. You're usually filling me in on everything.'

'I know. I'm sorry, but I have been incredibly busy.'

'Well, remember that deadline is set in stone, as always. It has to be on the shelves by June, all ready for the holiday market. No two ways about it.'

'I know, Sandy.'

'Darling, if you're needing some help, you just let me know. Send me your first draft, if you like, and I'll take a look.'

'I'll be fine,' I insisted. 'I'll work through the night if I have to. I won't let you down, I promise.'

'I know, my darling. But if you do need me, I'm here. Ciao for now.'

It's a scary thing, publishing a book. Even now. Because I always worry; what if they don't like it?

What if my readers don't like it? What then? But Sandy's always so confident about these things, has every faith in me. I just needed to get my finger out and finish the job.

So I immediately went through to my office. The time was five o'clock and I needed to get in at least an hour before I ate. Even then, I sat with my home-made sweet potato soup on my desk. A girl's gotta do what a girl's gotta do. Can't disappoint the punters. Or Sandy.

*

I stopped work at seven and changed into my new red velvet skirt and lilac sweater. Navy tights and ankle boots completed the look, which I knew was quite dazzling. But hey. It put a smile on my face.

George was there as usual, a pint of Guinness in hand, and compliments galore.

'Yes, siree! Nice outfit, April. Been shopping?'

I laughed. 'Actually, I've not had time to go shopping. I bought it online a few weeks back.'

'Well, you look a million dollars.'

So I did my Miss Piggy impersonation. 'What – moi? You are so very kind.'

This made George laugh so much he let me off the price of my drink. Result.

The rehearsal was good fun, and very productive. Daniel had already learnt his lines, even though Lord Windermere is quite a big part. And Luke, as Mr Cecil Graham, was amazing and set for a much bigger part in the next play, I had no doubt.

Alfie was adorable, as usual. 'April, please don't lean over so much - that skirt of yours, darling,' and 'Daniel, sweetie, be a love and say that line again.'

But the thing that surprised me most as I walked through the door was Gemma. She was just sitting there, a script in her hand, busy with her lines.

I spoke to her during the break over a cup of tea and a jaffa cake.

'It's lovely to see you back again, Gemma. How are you feeling?'

'I thought it'd be better to just come in and get it over with,' she said. 'And I'm hoping it'll take my mind off things. I've really not been sleeping well.'

'You poor thing. But you can always ring me, you know – for a chat.'

'Thanks, April. I just feel really bad about it all.'

'Listen. It's not your fault. None of this is your fault.'

'I honestly thought their marriage was over. Otherwise I'd never have …'

She looked close to tears, so I changed the subject.

'I met Lily Tylershaw,' I said. 'She was very impressed with your performance in Gaslight last year. Said you were amazing.'

Her face lit up. 'Did she? Thank you. Yes, I really enjoyed that part. Felt like I could get my teeth into it. But then, Lily's a brilliant director, and the costumes were amazing. Velvets and silks and – mind you, that awful old wig I had to wear was pretty disgusting.'

I smiled, having worn some awful old wigs myself. 'Itchy? Flea-infested?'

She laughed. 'It was horrendous.'

'So how *do* you do two plays at the same time? Don't you get confused?'

She smiled. 'Well, it's just like learning a poem or something, isn't it? The lines just kind of follow on from each other, don't they?'

'I suppose so. I don't think I could do it, though.'

'You're a good actress,' she insisted.

Alfie was clapping his hands for rehearsal to start again.

'Thank you,' I said.

'I just wish I'd agreed to do Dangerous Corner …' she began.

I hugged her in an effort to stem the tears.

'Look,' I said. 'We need to get back to rehearsal now. Why don't we meet up some time, go for a coffee or something?'

'Actually – I think I'll go home now. I might take a few days off, get away somewhere. Amber has suggested we drive out to Norfolk together - rent a little cottage - somewhere to chill. But we could meet up when I get back?'

'Okay. Just ring me when you're ready. And take care.'

She apologised to Alfie and left promptly. Alfie understood, of course.

'Bless her,' he said. 'What a state. What a bloody awful state.'

'She just needs time,' I said. 'Poor girl.'

'Do they know yet who did it?' asked Francis.

'No,' I replied.

'Well, I tell you what - I've been locking my door extra carefully just lately,' said Alfie. 'You don't know who's lurking around outside.'

'There was someone inside my house today,' I said quietly. 'I don't want it broadcast, but I left the front door unlocked while I was in the back garden. And I could swear someone had been inside the house.'

Alfie's hand went to his mouth in horror. 'No. Oh, darling, how absolutely dreadful for you. Are you alright?'

I nodded. 'I'm fine. I'd just like to know who it was, that's all.'

'Goodness me. What a thing.'

'I know, I know. But no-one was hurt, and nothing was stolen. And I've learnt my lesson.'

'What about Dash, your gorgeous young pup? Didn't he see him, chew his leg or something?'

'No. He was fast asleep in the garden with me. '

'Oh, dear. Well, listen, darling, if you ever need to talk about it, you just let me know. Any time.'

'Thanks, Alfie. And – Alfie?'

'Yes?'

'I'm not here next Thursday. It's Mum's hen night and we're going to see My Fair Lady at the Crucible.'

He pressed his hands together in admiration. 'Oh, I just love that musical. Do have a lovely time, and tell me all about it.' He winked. 'And yes, I will allow you time off on Thursday, my darling.'

'Thanks, Alfie, I appreciate it.' I blew him a kiss.

'You are irresistible. But make sure you keep on top of those lines.'

I smiled. 'Thanks, Alfie. I will.'

The rehearsal was a success on the whole. We were a little distracted by Gemma leaving when she did, but otherwise it went well and Alfie was pleased.

'Books down by the end of the month, darlings. You'll have time over Christmas to work on your lines. But we've only another two rehearsals, then we break up. So well done, and thank you, everyone. You were all absolutely amazing.'

Exhausted, I drove home to find Dash behind the door, whining and anxious. Unsettled, I checked every window and every door before I went to bed.

But I had great difficulty sleeping.

21

The flame is appealing, cleansing even. But she can't bring herself to do it. It's too final …

22

Millerstone, Derbyshire

TODAY was my hairdressing day, and even when I have a million and one things to do, I make sure to keep my appointments. Well, a girl has to look after herself, doesn't she?

My hair is long and wavy, and blonde. Well, not really blonde, if I'm honest. Highlighted is the word. Years ago it would have been called bleached. But that has certain connotations that are probably inappropriate for someone of my age and standing. Although it still reminds me of a bloody Norwegian prostitute when I've just had it done. So the first thing I do when I leave the hairdressers is to go home and stand beneath a hot shower. It soon sorts it out.

So yes, today I was to have it highlighted. With style. I was so looking forward to just sitting for two and a half hours, magazine in one hand, coffee in the other, and Mandy, Toni's assistant, attending to my every need. Bliss.

Toni's shop is on Station Road, just round the corner from the Ashbourne Hotel and along from the Flying Toad. Station Road is so-called because it leads to the railway station, one of the great advantages of living in Millerstone. Especially when we have piles of snow and no way of driving anywhere.

The shop that's now the hairdressers has been a shop in the village since the 1960's. Its door, a deep moss green, was in dire need of refurbishment, but it did have a certain charm. As I pushed against it, the scent of hairspray and coffee hit me like a wave of Madagascan vanilla.

Toni was busy, drying the hair of a teenage girl. A classy teenage girl, with long, shiny hair and immaculate clothing. She's the daughter of a local MP, which I know for a fact as I've interviewed him for one of my novels – a nice guy.

'Hi, April. Cuppa?' called Toni, shouting over the noise of the hairdryer.

I grinned. 'Why else do you think I come here to have my hair done?'

'Because you enjoy my company, of course. Tea or coffee?'

'Coffee, please. Milk, no sugar.'

Mandy, Toni's assistant, her thick auburn hair fastened into a stylish plait, took my coat and patted the chair beside Toni.

'Here, sit down. I'll put the kettle on. We've got chocolate lollies if you want one?'

I smiled. 'I know. It's your Friday treat.'

'You want one, then?' she said.

'Actually, I'll resist, thank you.' Picking up a copy of Vogue magazine from the rack, I sat down and laid it out in front of the huge illuminated mirror.

'I've been trying to ring you all morning,' said Toni.

'Sorry - I've been writing.'

'It's the guy from the BBC,' she continued. 'They want us to do an article on Look North.'

I stopped reading. 'What?'

'It's on Monday - they want to interview us.'

'What?' I repeated.

She switched off the hairdryer. 'In Leeds.'

'Leeds? On Monday?'

'It's to do with MAUD. They want me, you, Fiona and Penny. They want the works, what we're going to be doing, what it's all about, how it originated, and so on. We need to publicise it, get it out there, and you did say you'd help us.'

'You've not given me much notice,' I grumbled. 'I've got loads to do, and I've not even started my Christmas shopping yet.'

'Well then, you could do it in Leeds while we're there. They have some lovely shops.'

That's true, I thought. I could kill two birds with one stone. I really didn't have time for Christmas shopping, though. Or an interview. But that was selfish of me; this thing needed publicity. I'd just have to do it.

'Okay, fine. It's fine. I'll ask Mum to look after Dash for a couple of days – I'm sure she won't mind. So how are we getting there?'

'Train. We're catching the 9.45 to Leeds. The train home is 6.45. Is that okay with you? It's exciting, though, isn't it?' Shrugging her shoulders, she smiled at me over the girl's head.

I had a sudden thought. 'Actually, would it be okay if I stayed over until the Tuesday? I could get all my shopping done in one fell swoop. I've got my outfit for the wedding to buy as well. I was going to wear something I already have, but …'

'But seeing as you're going to be in Leeds anyway, you might as well take the opportunity. And why not? It's not a problem. I'd come with you, but I've got clients booked in. And the kids to see to, of course.'

'Okay. It's okay. Let's do it. I'll have to tell Alfie I can't make rehearsal – again – but he'll be fine about it. It's all for a good cause.'

*

Now I would never tell Toni this, but as I've said before, whenever I have my hair done I go straight home to wash it. Otherwise it looks awful. But it's the cut that's important, not the styling. So of course, as soon as I left Toni's shop, I walked home along Station Road, crossed over to the cottages on Downing Row (built to house the pin and needle workers from the old mill), walked up Jaggers Lane, then home. It was cold and dark, so I could pull up my hood without looking ridiculous. I really, really, didn't want anyone to see me.

Dash greeted me with a look that said *What? Who?* so I dived quickly beneath the shower. It was hot and steamy, and wonderful. But I'd only just finished in the bathroom and dressed myself in joggers and tee-shirt when the doorbell rang.

It was Sean. And I was standing there at half five in the afternoon with a towel wrapped around my head and no makeup.

'Going somewhere?' he asked.

'Sorry, Sean, I've just been in the shower. I've had my hair cut.'

He frowned. 'Sorry?'

'Come on in, it's freezing. Then I'll explain.'

He stepped inside, to the honour of Dash licking his shoes.

'Dash!' I exclaimed, shooing him away. 'Sorry.'

'It's okay. I think I spilled tea on them earlier. He's probably licking the milk off.'

I grinned. 'Right. Well, if you come through to the kitchen, you can make us both a cuppa while I dry my hair.'

'Sorry to drop in like this, April, but I've just been to report on a burglary in Bamford. Thought I'd pop in on my way home.'

'It's fine. I just need to dry my hair, that's all. Won't be long, I promise.'

'What were you saying about having it cut?'

'I've just been to Toni's place. But I hate it when it's just been done, so I come home and wash it. But don't ever tell her. Please.'

Holding out his hand, he grinned. 'How much?'

I pushed it away. 'The kettle's there, Sean McGuire,' I said, pointing to it. 'You know where everything is. I'll be two minutes.'

Ten minutes later, I returned, complete with gorgeous newly-highlighted hair and makeup. I felt like a million dollars.

'Wow,' said Sean. 'You certainly brush up well.'

I smiled. 'Thank you, kind sir.'

'So what were your plans for this evening? A cosy night in?'

Alarm bells rang. 'Why? What's happened?'

'Tea first?'

I sat at the table. 'Please.'

He poured two cups and passed me one.

'So what is it, then? What's wrong?' I asked.

'It's Fliss. The police have traced a payment into her account. Two years ago. It would appear Felix lent her the princely sum of one hundred thousand pounds.'

'Wow. That's an awful lot of money to lend someone, even if she is your sister.'

'So she lied to us. Looks like she did borrow money from Felix to buy the business. She's been paying him back at five hundred a month – the police checked her account. At least she was until last June. Then the payments stopped.'

I went cold. 'Oh, no …'

'We're not saying she killed him, there's no evidence. We're just saying it needs further investigation.'

'It's not looking good, though, is it?'

He shook his head. 'No. It's not.'

I thought about it. 'She doesn't seem the type to murder anyone. And besides, where does Lucas come into all this?'

'We're thinking along the lines of Lucas lending money to Felix – some kind of financial deal. Then Fliss stops paying, so Felix can't provide the payments, and somewhere along the line it gets messy.'

I stood up. 'I was thinking about going to see her anyway, see how she's bearing up. I'm assuming she's still at the guest house?'

'I was hoping you'd say that. Yes, she's staying on to organise funeral arrangements once they've released the body. Looks like she's closed up the shop for Christmas.'

My stomach suddenly rumbled, and I placed my hand upon my abdomen.

'Shall we eat first? I'm hungry.'

'Tell you what – let's see if we can call round now. I'll ring her. Then we can eat at the Flying Toad. My treat.'

I smiled. 'That'd be lovely - thanks. I'll just take Dash round the block while you speak to her.'

'Don't be long. I'm starving, too.'

I'm convinced Dash understands every word I say. He ran up to me even before I'd pulled his lead from the hall cupboard.

'Come on, sweetie.' I fastened on his lead, grabbed my coat and torch, and left.

After a fairly still afternoon, the wind was getting up, sending the piles of leaves from the roadside high into the air. Dash and I walked quickly up towards Stanage Edge. The trees bordering Coggers Lane rustled as we walked past, despite the lack of leaves. Dash stopped for a wee against one, and we carried on our way.

But all the while my thoughts were churning. I couldn't believe that someone like Fliss (even though I'd only just met her, admittedly) could murder her own brother. She was so upset about it all. And why would she wake me up at half five in the morning if she had something to hide? Was she more devious than I gave her credit for? Was she playing the grieving sister so we wouldn't suspect her? But how awful, if she had killed him, if she had forced him to drink that much alcohol. And did she kill Lucas, too? Or did Felix kill Lucas, round on his sister because it was her fault, and then she forced him to get drunk to the point of alcohol poisoning? But then, how on earth do you force someone to drink themselves to death?

This whole thing was eating me up, so I stopped walking, took a deep breath to calm myself, and turned around. Just at that moment, Colin rang.

'Hi, stranger,' he said.

I smiled. 'Hi, you.'

'You didn't ring me last night. I tried you, but you didn't pick up.'

I felt really bad. 'I'm so sorry, Colin - I forgot. I had a visitor, completely unexpected. She's the sister of one of the murdered guys we're investigating. She arrived very early and stayed really late, and I was exhausted by the time she went. I'm so sorry. How are you, anyway – you had a good day?'

We chatted about work, and about the investigation, and about the coming weekend, but the wind was becoming so noisy we had difficulty hearing one another.

'Look, I'll call you tomorrow night, shall I?' he said.

'Okay. Lovely. Have a good day, then.'

'You too. I hope your Mum finds just what she's looking for.'

I grinned. 'Oh – she will.'

He laughed. 'Love you. Night night.'

'Night. Love you, too.'

So Dash and I continued home, the wind raging across the fields, the air icy and full of scattered twigs and leaves.

The door opened as we approached the house. Sean had been looking out for us.

'I've rung Fliss and she's fine to see us this evening,' he said. 'How was your walk?'

'Windy. Colin rang me for a chat, but we could barely hear each other.' I pulled off my walking boots. 'I just need to settle Dash, then we can go.'

So I wiped his paws, broke some biscuits into his bowl, gave him some water, and patted his head gently.

'There you go, Dash. We're just off out for the evening, so you be a good boy, yes?'

But he licked my hand, his eyes huge and brown and appealing.

'I'm sorry, Dash. I'll take you for another quick walk when I get back, promise.'

So Sean and I walked into the village, past the pub and Toni's shop, then along, turning left towards the station. The guest house is opposite the railway station, handy for visitors to the area. It's built of manufactured stone, with pebbledash above the windows and exterior lights on the driveway. There's space for only two or three cars, and I noticed Fliss's car parked there as we walked up to the door.

The landlady was welcoming, said Fliss had told her to expect us, and showed us into the dining room, which was devoid of guests. Although I could smell food cooking - something spicy, cumin and coriander. Indian food, maybe. My stomach rumbled again.

'I'm Pam,' said the landlady, who was tall and slim with grey, stringy hair. 'Can I get you a drink? Tea or coffee?'

I sat down on the chair she offered. 'Tea would be lovely. Thank you.'

'Not for me, thank you,' said Sean.

'I'll just let Fliss know you're here,' she said, and left.

I looked around. It was a typical guest house with small oak tables and wheel-backed chairs. The walls had been papered, but the far one had been covered in the same manufactured stone as the exterior. A small millstone had been placed at its centre to create a feature. It was of its time, and I wasn't overly impressed, but just as I was wondering how I myself would design a guest house in Millerstone, Fliss entered the room.

Dressed in a short grey jumper, jeans and trainers, her long hair had been trimmed since last time we'd met, making her look a little less dishevelled. I stood up to greet her.

'Hi, Fliss. How are you?'

Tears filled her eyes. 'I've been to see his body today. It was awful.'

I patted the chair beside mine. 'Come on, sit down.'

She sat, and at that moment Pam returned with two mugs of tea.

'Here you go, my love,' and she looked at Fliss compassionately.

'Thank you,' I said, feeling really bad about being here. The poor woman had just lost her brother and we were here to interrogate her. I looked to Sean for assistance and he picked up the baton.

'I'm really sorry about your brother, Fliss, but we do need to ask you a few questions. I know it's not easy ...'

She nodded. 'It's okay. I understand.'

'Thank you.'

I sighed, wondering what the hell I was doing there. Surely this was a police matter?

But then suddenly I knew what I was doing there. I was there to help Fliss cope, to make it less painful than being dragged to a police station and questioned by complete strangers. Passing her a mug of tea, I smiled encouragingly.

'So what we need to understand,' said Sean, 'is why you didn't tell us about the money Felix lent you. And where he got the money from in the first place.'

She looked hot, embarrassed, and her accent intensified. 'Sorry. I'm sorry I didn't tell you about the money. Yes, Felix lent me it to me so I could buy the business. But I *was* paying him back.'

It was my turn, and I spoke gently. 'But you stopped paying him after a while, didn't you?'

She looked shamefaced. 'Yes. I got into a few problems – couldn't pay the rent, couldn't pay the council tax. That's why I left my flat and went to live behind the shop. But Felix understood, he said it was fine, that it could wait. He was very kind like that.'

I stared at the millstone behind her. None of this was making any sense. She loved her brother; there was no way she'd have killed him.

'Fliss, do you know how Felix got the money in the first place?' asked Sean.

'He told me he had it saved up, that it was in the bank. Why?'

'You remember we told you there was another death, that same week?'

'Yes?'

'He was Lucas Hanssen, a financial adviser. He could very well have arranged a loan for Felix.'

She looked shocked. 'What? You mean - Felix didn't have the money?'

'That is something we're looking into,' said Sean. 'But we need to check the facts before we go making assumptions.'

She looked down at her hands. 'Okay.'

'You say you were working in the shop the week Lucas and Felix died?'

She looked up. 'Yes. Of course.'

'So why were you able to use a VISA credit card at the Tesco's in Aberystwyth on the Monday, the day before Felix died?'

23

There must be someone she can talk to. Someone who will understand …

24

Millerstone, Derbyshire

SATURDAY morning. I woke early, left food for the cat, took Dash for a walk, then showered and dressed, ready for our big day out. The choosing of Mum's wedding dress. Gosh - how scary was that?

Jo was pulling up in her new Ford Mondeo as I arrived at Jim's. She'd put together a posy of mistletoe, Christmas roses and hyacinths, and surprised Mum with it as she pulled open the door.

'Oh – Josie love,' she cried. 'They're beautiful. Thank you.'

Jo hugged her. 'Happy Christmas, Mum.'

'I'll just put them in some water before we go. Oh, but I'm getting so excited.'

Jim was in the kitchen as we walked in. 'What a lovely bouquet. But come on now, you three get off and I'll find a vase for them.'

I stared at Mum. She looked amazing. Fresh new hairdo, shoulder-length with auburn colouring; burnt orange lipstick; a brown teddy bear coat with brown leather gloves and boots, and a handbag to match. Being with Jim had taken twenty years off her.

'Looks like you've been shopping already, Mum,' said Jo, admiringly.

'What – this old thing?' she said, smiling and twirling around.

Taking my arm, Jo pulled me towards the door. 'Come on, April. I don't think she needs our help.'

Mum burst out laughing. 'Just a minute, young lady. I seem to remember spending weeks looking for your dress when you got married. And I've only got one day, so let's not waste it.'

Jim pulled open the front door for us. 'I've got a train to catch, so I'll be seeing you tomorrow night, love.'

Standing on her toes, Mum kissed him. 'Have a lovely time, darling.'

Jim's pine trees swayed violently as we gathered outside. After a calmer night, the wind was definitely picking up again, rushing across the moors and sending clouds skittering through the sky.

'You too,' Jim called as we walked away. 'You've got a key, haven't you?'

'I've got two,' she said, holding down her coat in the wind. 'I think this storm's taking hold, so you be careful.'

'Winter weddings,' murmured Jo. 'We'll be needing Afghan coats and wellie boots at this rate.'

But we had an amazing day, and I hadn't seen Mum look so happy in years. We began with coffee in John Lewis and ended with the most gorgeous dress you could imagine. Cream silk, calf-length, with a lace over-bodice and long lace sleeves. Mum chose a small fur stole in the same colour, cream velvet high heels and bag, and a woollen felt hat to match.

'Mum – you look a million dollars,' said Jo, once Mum had finished trying everything on.

'It's not like in my day, you know,' said Mum. 'You had to hunt round for everything then. Shoes in the shoe shop, hats in the hat shop. It wasn't all in one place like it is now.'

I smiled. 'It's called progress, Mum.'

Sudden tears filled her eyes. 'Oh, but I can remember your father's face as I walked down the aisle. And my dad, nervous as anything ...'

I blinked back my own tears as memories came flooding back. The wedding photo on the lounge wall, just behind the sofa at home. Jo and I being careful not to knock it while we bounced up and down on the cushions. Mum having to rearrange it afterwards, tut-tutting and telling us off. And when Dad came in from work, he'd sit beneath it and watch the telly. But first he'd get washed and changed, and eat his dinner at the table. He was a tall chappie, my dad, solid, with a kind face, always smiling, always happy and grateful to be alive - his words. And he made me feel the same. So even though fate can, and often does, dump some awful stuff at my door, I'm still happy to be here.

My dad was a builder by trade, specialising in renovation and refurbishment. He travelled the country, but more often than not worked within a sixty mile radius, so he could come home at night to be with Mum. He died at the age of fifty-five, bless him; a heart attack. And they were in love right until the very end. I remember, he'd bring a huge bunch of red roses home on a Friday night. Every week. Never missed. Marks and Spencer's they were - only the best. And Mum would have his dinner ready, and they'd canoodle in the kitchen while she dished up.

'I still miss him, you know,' she said. 'Even though I'm with Jim now.'

I smiled. 'I think Dad would approve of Jim. I think he'd be glad to see you so happy, Mum.'

Wiping her eyes, she nodded. 'I know.'

'Come on,' said Jo, excitedly. 'We need to get back – the girls will be waiting for us.'

We left Mum's dress at the shop as it needed taking in a little. But the shoes, the fur stole, the hat and the bag all came with us as we trundled back to the car.

*

Jo's cottage is small but delightful, nestling as it does into the hillside next door to Hartleton primary school, and smelling as it does of rose oil, Jo's passion. Her husband Joe is the head teacher next door, so only has to tumble out of bed each morning with a lick and a spit before work. Nice.

They have three girls and Henry, their Old English sheepdog. And how Jo manages to run the house, look after the girls, and work as a busy landscape gardener, I'll never know. Vicky is the eldest, Rebecca the middle child, and Daisy the youngest. The younger two still attended the primary school next door, but Vicky now went to the local secondary school. Having to catch the bus each morning was a big deal for her at first, but then she loved it. *I get to chill with my friends before school, Auntie April.*

Joe is tall, well-built, rugged. He loves Jo to distraction, and their home is always happy, always filled with fun. He'd taken the girls swimming at the outdoor pool in Millerstone that afternoon. It is heated, but even so I would have thought twice about it - that wind was freezing. So when we arrived at the house, there they all were, their hair still wet, eating pizza and watching telly in the sitting room. Some film about teenage witches.

'Mum,' called Daisy as we walked through the door. 'We're having pizza.'

'Shhhh,' said Vicky. 'I'm watching.'

Joe stood up. 'Come on in, I'll put the kettle on. Have you eaten?'

'We have,' said Jo, sitting into the armchair he'd just vacated. 'We had fish and chips, Mum's favourite. And I honestly couldn't eat another thing.'

Vicky stood up and promptly sat down on the floor beside Henry. 'Gran, come and sit down. Auntie April, you can take Daisy's chair. She's being much too noisy, anyway.'

I smiled. 'Thank you, Vicky. But it's okay - I can sit on the floor beside you and Henry.'

Mum sat onto the couch and I squeezed myself in between Vicky and Henry. The girls were all engrossed, so not much talking went on until Joe returned with tea and biscuits.

'Come on, let's switch it off now. You can watch it on catch-up.'

'Aw, Dad,' moaned Vicky, twisting her long hair with her fingers.

'Now, come on - we don't see Gran and Auntie April that often, do we? So let's make the most of it. You can watch that silly old film any time.'

'It's not a silly old film.'

Leaning forward, Mum stroked Vicky's hair. 'He's right, my darling. You really should treasure your family. We won't be here forever, you know.'

My heartstrings pulled tight, and I felt a wave of emotion. Hardly able to speak, I managed to murmur, 'Don't talk like that, Mum.'

She stared at me as I sat cross-legged on the floor. 'We've all got to die some time, April. So we need to make the most of it while we're here.'

Jo grinned. 'You're certainly doing that, Mum.' She looked up at Joe, who was passing cups of tea round. 'You should see Mum's outfit. She looks just adorable.'

'Good enough for a dog's dinner,' said Mum. 'Eeh - do you remember your dad used to say that? You look good enough for a dog's dinner, he'd say.'

My throat constricting again, I smiled up at her, remembering how in love she and Dad were; how inconsolable she was when he died. Dad. A typical Yorkshireman. Mum always said it was his Yorkshire sense of humour that had attracted her. Then she'd start laughing and say, 'Well, I didn't marry him for his money, that's for sure.' They were always laughing, Mum and Dad, rarely had a cross word.

I'd never had that kind of love. Even with Colin I wasn't sure. I wasn't sure I trusted him; not enough to let him into my heart, anyway. Not enough to commit to forever and ever. Maybe I would never trust anyone again. Not after Jeremy, not after my one and only disaster of a marriage. Once bitten, twice shy, as they say.

God, I hate that saying.

*

Sunday morning was cool and calm. No wind. No rain. The calm before the storm, as I was to discover. Dash and I were out walking. Down Coggers Lane, right onto Jaggers Lane, then down, onto Castleton Road, the main road that takes you out to Bamford. I thought we'd visit the garden centre, have a look round, stop for coffee and then wander home. A nice, relaxing morning.

And as I walked, I thought about the Look North interview. I really needed to make a few notes, decide what to wear, what I should say. I'd already researched information on what to wear for television. Apparently, grey or navy work best as they're seen as safe and understated. So maybe my silver grey trouser suit, I thought. But that's pretty boring. Unless I wear my pink blouse with the ruffles underneath, jazz it up a little. But no, I decided. This was a serious subject. We needed to look honest, dependable. We needed people to listen.

The grey suit it was then, with a white shirt. That should be fine. It was Giorgio Armani.

It was while I was drinking my cappuccino in Bamford Garden Centre that I got the call. From Mum, in a state. Jim had hurt his leg and was in A&E, having an x-ray. He was going to have a problem coming home on the train.

'You couldn't give us a lift, could you, love?'

I nodded at the phone. 'Of course, Mum. I just need to get home – it'll take me about half an hour, then I'll come and pick you up. Okay?'

'Okay. Thanks, love.'

'And Mum, don't worry. He'll be fine.'

I practically ran home with Dash racing ahead of me, as happy as anything. But I needed a quick shower after all that running, so I showered and changed, filled a bottle with water, and jumped into the car with Dash fastened in behind me.

Mum was all ready to go when I arrived. She'd been crying, so I hugged her and helped her into the car.

'It's Dudley Road Hospital. Here, I've written down the postcode.' She passed me a post-it-note and I put the details into my satnav.

'So how did it happen?' I asked, pushing into first gear.

'The most stupid thing. He'd had his breakfast and everything, and was just coming downstairs with his case when he tripped and fell. He must have twisted his knee or something, because it's his fibula that's broken, just below his knee. He's on crutches.'

I headed out of Millerstone, up Sheffield Road, past Toad's Mouth Rock, and out towards Sheffield and the M1. We had to pull in at Trowell Services near Nottingham, so Mum could use the loo, and so we could buy egg mayo butties in M&S. We were just heading back to the car when my phone rang. It was Sean.

'Sorry to disturb you on a Sunday, April.'

'It's fine, Sean – but what's wrong?'

'We've finally got Felix's medical report. He was taking prescribed meds for high blood pressure. But as well as that, they're saying he suffered from non-alcoholic fatty liver disease.'

I'll confess I was slightly confused. 'Okay - so what's that telling us?'

'It's telling us that he would have been advised not to drink alcohol to excess. It would have told us that he can't have drunk all that whisky on purpose.'

I went cold. I pressed the key fob to allow Mum into the car. I just needed a minute. 'So are you thinking what I think you're thinking?'

'If you mean did Fliss know about his medical history – then yes, I would have thought so. Wouldn't you?'

'It's also possible someone else knew. He might have given that as an excuse for not drinking. You know, *I can't drink, mate – I've got this medical thing going on.* Male ego and all that.'

Sean laughed. 'It is possible, I suppose. But Fliss must definitely have known about it.'

'I know, I know. But can you really see someone as petite as Fliss forcing alcohol down her brother's mouth? He wasn't exactly a lightweight, was he?'

'No-one's saying she forced him to drink it. It might just have been a dare. Or a taunt of some kind – sibling rivalry or something.'

'So what's next on the agenda?'

'We get more information. About her, and about the loan.'

I sighed. 'Okay.'

'You don't have to do this, April, not if you don't want to.'

Opening my car door, I climbed in. 'No. It's fine. It's just – I have to get Mum to Birmingham – Jim's hurt his leg. Then I need to drive home, and then I've got to go to Leeds tomorrow. I'm on the telly - I'll explain later - and I'm staying over, so I'll be there all day Tuesday as well.'

'Look, it's fine. I'll manage. I'll do as much digging as I can. And I'll call you on Wednesday with my findings, so we can dig together. How about that?'

'What's DI Jasper up to, then? Can't she help?'

'She's just been put onto another case – missing teenage girl. But she's keeping me up to date. A guy called Josh Rao has taken over, but he's not too keen on us rookies, as he calls us, dealing with things.'

'Oh, dear. What do we do, then?'

'We carry on, and we stay in touch with DI Jasper, just as we were.'

'Okay. That's fine. I'll see you Wednesday, then.'

Mum looked at me guiltily. 'Sorry, April. Have you got things you should be doing?'

'No, Mum. The only thing I have to do right now is look after my mum. I need to get her to the hospital to see her lovely new fiancé, make sure he's alright, and bring her home. The other stuff can sort itself out.'

Tears filled her eyes. I could tell even without taking my eyes off the road.

'You're a real treasure, April - do you know that?'

I grinned. 'Take after Dad, don't I?'

*

I hate hospitals. The smell reminds me of death, of walking through the long, lonely corridors to find Dad, dead upon arrival. As they say.

It was so completely unexpected. Mum found him in the bedroom, flat out on the floor. She thought at first he'd slipped, bashed his head, knocked himself out. Then when she couldn't wake him, she knew. She just knew. Poor Mum. There was absolutely nothing she could have done. But every time she looks back, she feels that awful, gnawing, sense of guilt. Was it the food she'd been feeding him? Could she have spotted the signs sooner, made him get regular check-ups? Worst of all, had he been shouting for her and she'd not heard him?

Awful, terrible, thoughts.

I think back to the last time I saw Dad, to the last time we hugged, the last time I saw him smile. If only I'd known, I'd have hugged him for longer. If only I'd known, I'd never have let him go. If only I'd known, I'd have told him how much I loved him, how I would always love him.

Too late now. All too late.

I slipped my arm through Mum's as we followed the nurse.

'Just through here,' she said. 'He's been discharged. You just need to collect some painkillers from the pharmacy, then you can go.' She handed Mum a prescription on crisp, green paper.

'Thanks,' said Mum, gratefully.

Jim turned as we walked into the room. His eyes were puffy, he looked miserable, and he was obviously feeling very sorry for himself. The bed he sat on was basic, with two large pillows but no blankets, and there was a TV blaring out; some kind of documentary. He switched it off using the remote.

'Load of rubbish. Can't wait to get out of this place.'

Mum hugged him. 'Well, that's why we've come to take you home, darling. Can you stand up alright?'

Jim pulled two crutches from the side of the bed and swung his legs around. 'With a little help from my friends, I can.'

I grinned. 'It's about drugs, you know.'

'What is?' Mum asked, innocently.

'The song. With a Little Help from my Friends. It was about drugs.'

'Was it? Well, I never knew that.' She smiled. 'You learn something new every day.'

'Drugs,' I said, grimly. 'They have a lot to answer for.'

25

But who would understand? Who on earth can she trust?

26

Leeds, Yorkshire

THE train to Leeds was quite relaxing, really. We had a fifteen minute wait in Sheffield, where we bought Costa coffee and discussed the ice-cold metal seats we had to sit on in the waiting room. Finally deciding they were not fit for purpose and must have been designed by someone who wears very thick coats, or someone who never used trains. But the rest of the journey was spent mainly in thoughtful reflection. Toni's not really the type for thoughtful reflection, to be honest, but I think she was feeling quite nervous now we were actually on our way.

    I'd not met Fiona and Penny before, so, having introduced ourselves and discussed roughly what we were going to talk about, we fell into a kind of sleepy companionship. I'd learned that Fiona was a science teacher at a comprehensive school in

Chesterfield, that she was recently divorced, and that her kids were now out of the psychiatric ward, but still needed some serious medication. She just hoped they'd be well enough to go back to uni after the Christmas holidays. Fiona is lovely, tall and slim and quiet, although you could see the stress was taking its toll - she looked tired and kind of distracted. Penny, on the other hand, is more like Toni, doesn't mind what anyone thinks, and is outspoken with a crude sense of humour. But she did make us laugh. She wore an enormous fake fur in black, with black leather boots, a black skirt suit and a cream blouse. Penny lives in Millerstone, not far from Toni's, and I had seen her around occasionally. She's the type who likes to get involved in whatever's going on. Charity events, film nights, school plays. Her children were still at the primary school, so she didn't work, but she did manage to do the books for her husband's building business.

 The train was a few minutes late, but we still had time to visit the Ladies and brush up. A dash of lipstick, a flick of the hair, and a squirt of Chanel.

 'April, I don't know why you bother,' murmured Toni as we stared into the mirror.

 'What?' I replied, taken aback.

 'You always look perfect. Why are you bothering to titivate yourself?'

 I laughed. 'Well, it's very nice of you to say so.'

 'It's true.'

'It is not. To quote the words of Dolly Parton, it costs a lorra lorra money to look this cheap.'

She giggled. 'That's not just Dolly Parton. That's a cross between Cilla Black and Dolly Parton. *Lorra lorra laughs.* Do you remember?'

'I'm surprised you can remember Cilla Black.'

'What? No. I loved her on Blind Date. I used to get home from my apprenticeship on a Saturday night, throw my bag onto the settee, and watch it while I ate my dinner. Brilliant, she was.'

'I used to watch it, too,' said Penny. 'Saturday night, while Mum made dinner.'

Anxiously, Fiona pulled a notepad from her rucksack. 'Look, I know we've discussed everything already, and I know you've made some notes, April, but I've brought this. It's a list of things we mustn't forget. About what the doctors have said, about how awful our lives have become, and how drugs can affect our kids for years, even after they've left uni. It's really important we get everything out there. They've only given us five minutes.' She gave it to me, but I passed it to Penny.

'You're the best person to act as spokesperson, Penny,' I said.

But she stared at me, aghast. 'But I thought you were the public speaker, being a writer and all that?'

'Not really. I write - I'm not really the type to stand up in public. I just invent stories. That's what I am – a storyteller.'

She looked upset. 'But I thought …'

I felt really bad then, so I took the notepad back. 'No, it's okay, I'll do it. I need to get myself together, though, read through it. Otherwise I'll be way too nervous.'

She smiled. 'Thanks, April.'

So I glanced briefly through the notes Fiona had made, and actually did feel so much better about the whole thing – she'd explained everything in a way that described the way she'd been feeling exactly, how she'd brought up her boys well, and what lovely kids they were. But she'd also made notes on the long-term psychological implications of taking recreational drugs, and how they had affected Craig and Max. So we left the station in a slightly happier frame of mind, making our way to St Peter's Square, to the BBC Studios, which was a big round glass building and not quite as imposing as I'd imagined.

Inside, the receptionist took our coats and led us into the Look North studio. Now that bit of the day was scary, if I'm honest. There were two huge black cameras, lots of production crew, and the producer, who introduced himself as Todd Blackwell. He had a soft London accent, and was smartly dressed with a shirt and tie.

The presenter, the person who was to interview us, introduced himself as Paul from Leeds, and was very chatty, making us feel much more relaxed and ready to do some work.

'But first let me introduce you to Bo, our lovely makeup lady. She'll just add a few touches so you don't look too pale on screen. If that's okay?'

'Lead me on,' said Toni.

Bo, who was Danish and very beautiful with two pencils criss-crossed through her piled-up hair, showed us into the makeup room. A long mirror set between two rows of lightbulbs illuminated a line of soft leather chairs, and we sat there, two at a time.

I watched as Bo messed with Toni's hair, teasing her red curls into place with a tail-comb.

'She's a hairdresser,' I warned, smiling. 'Don't let her know you can make it look any better than she does, whatever you do.'

'It's fine,' said Toni. 'I fancy some new ideas.'

'There's not a lot we can do with such curly hair,' said Bo, 'except make it ultra-shiny for the cameras.'

She sprayed some kind of product onto Toni's hair, all the while teasing and rearranging the curls.

'There,' she said, standing back.

'Gosh. That looks lovely,' said Toni, staring at herself. 'What is that stuff?'

'It's quite expensive,' said Bo, 'but it is worth it. Here - you can keep this one.' She handed Toni the tin.

Toni was so awestruck I thought at first she was going to refuse. But after a slight hesitation, she accepted.

'Thank you. Thank you so much. Wow.'

Bo then brushed powder onto Toni's face and applied blusher and lipstick.

'There. You'll do nicely,' she said. 'Right - next one, please.'

We each had our hair and makeup done until, thirty minutes later, we were ready to go. As I straightened my jacket before the mirror, sudden butterflies began to play in my stomach and I felt quite sick. But I just smiled at the others.

'Are we ready for this, guys?'

*

The interview had gone well. Todd Blackwell was an angel, sitting across from us encouragingly, letting us retake if we stammered or if there was a gap in the conversation or we'd made a mistake. So patient. And Bo would fuss around, powdering our noses and retouching our lipstick between each take. Then afterwards we watched the rushes, as they call them, and I have to admit we came across very well. Poised, intelligent, but with understanding and compassion. Plus, we managed to get our point across without being overemotional - particularly Fiona, who was obviously upset about her own children. Excited, we agreed that the production was just what we had wanted it to be. So, once Todd had shaken our hands and wished us luck with the campaign, we thanked everyone and left.

'Right. Food,' said Toni, heading towards the shops. 'I am starving.'

We were all hungry; it had been a tiring morning. So we found a bar called The Alchemist where we ordered rubbishy but tasty fast food, followed by large cappuccinos.

'Come on,' I said. 'Let's do some shopping before you all head home, and then it's back to my hotel for G&Ts. On me.'

'Only one for me, though,' said Fiona. 'I'll be driving home from the train.'

'One's enough, isn't it?' I said. 'It's just a little celebration. Because we all did brilliantly, didn't we?'

So we set out for the Victoria Quarter, a lovely place with high ceilings and stained glass, and the most amazing architecture. It's a whole Victorian street, but in the heart of Leeds, all enclosed by a modern glass covering. There were shops like Harvey Nichols, Vivienne Westwood and John Lewis, with real Christmas trees, and decorations, and vintage lanterns in beautiful colours.

'Wow. How the other half live,' murmured Toni. 'I bet I can't afford one thing in Harvey Nics.'

She could, though. A Le Creuset silicone spoon in pale blue.

'Just what I need,' she said. 'Those wooden ones make my teeth go all funny.'

So we headed back to my hotel for G&Ts with petits fours, which were fun, and which gave an appropriate ending to the day. The hotel I'd chosen was beautiful; traditional and rather expensive. But I was worth it. Anyway, I placed the bill on my Expenses list, citing research for my next book.

Three G&Ts later I waved the girls off, promising to stay in touch, and all of us agreeing to watch Look North on catch-up. But after they'd gone and I went up to my room, I felt slightly lost and empty. I changed into jeans and a sweater, then rang Colin for a chat, but there was no reply. So I texted.

Had a fab day. Now on my own in some fancy hotel. Wish you were here. Love you. xxx

Again, there was no reply.

So, settling into my room, I took a small bottle of Oaked Chardonnay from the bar and sat on the huge bed, trying to make the TV work. Twenty minutes later, and despite my best efforts, I still wasn't able to access BBC iPlayer. So I gave up; I could easily watch it at home.

Bored now, I rang Sean to see if there was any more news on the case. And there was.

'DI Jasper says Fliss's story about her being at a friend's party in Aberystwyth checks out,' said Sean. 'She used her VISA card in Tesco's to buy wine and nibbles. And the friend seems genuine – they worked in London together before Fliss moved to Wales. Although she had no idea Fliss even had a brother.'

'That doesn't prove anything, really. They could have driven over to Chatsworth together,' I said, miserably. 'But I'll take it. So where do we go from here?'

'Back to the drawing board. Although there are two or three amdram people we've not yet interviewed. They could know something about Lucas's death, and that in turn may have led to Felix's. Who's to say he didn't see something that night, and had to be got rid of?'

'That has occurred to me. After all, he was head forester. He could have been hanging around anywhere, couldn't he? Did we ever trace the girl he was with, the one on CCTV?'

'No. There's CCTV of his car driving along the Pilsley road, and there's a passenger. But it's too dark, so even if they zoom in there's nothing there. Other than that, we have no idea.'

'And she's not come forward?'

'No. Which is slightly worrying, I must admit.'

'Maybe she's married or something, doesn't want to get found out? Especially now he's dead and there's no future for her.'

'That's true.'

A thought suddenly occurred, a sudden thought that seemed to make everything else make sense.

'Sean ...'

'Yes?'

'You don't think Fliss takes drugs, do you?'

'What? Why?'

'It's just something Fiona said in the interview this morning. '

'Okay?'

'She said she realised her son Max was on something because he'd sometimes be clenching his teeth, and he'd get thirsty and a bit twitchy. She was so worried she'd begun to wonder if he had diabetes or something.'

'And your point is?'

'You're a reporter. Didn't you notice? Fliss was like a little fluttery bird, clenching her teeth, twitchy, kind of paranoid. I just wondered if ...'

'So you think she might have bought them from Felix?'

'Either that, or he was just giving them to her. Even though she said she hadn't seen him in years.'

'Gosh. That's a biggie. Tell you what – I'll have a word with DI Jasper, see if she can do a bit of digging.'

'Thanks, Sean. It's just a hunch, that's all.'

'No – you're good at hunches. As I've said before. So what was your telly interview about, then?'

I smiled. 'We were discussing the MAUD project Toni's involved in – it was on Look North tonight.'

'Excellent. I'll watch it on catch-up, then.'

'I've not managed to see it myself yet. I can't get the telly to work properly. Bloody hotels.'

'Why don't you ask Reception?'

'I can watch it when I get home. It'll be more fun at home, anyway. It's a bit maudlin here. Everything's too grand and pristine.'

'I would have thought you'd like grand and pristine.'

I grinned. 'Obviously not. I must be getting old and set in my ways.'

'You, Miss April Stanislavski?'

'On that bombshell, Sean, I'm going. I'm starving and there's a very nice restaurant downstairs. And I've had way too much to drink, so I need to pig out.'

'Sounds delicious. Have a lovely evening, then.'

*

The clock showed twenty past eight as I made my way down to the restaurant. I'd showered and changed into a dress and heels. The colour, a warm teal blue, suited me, and I felt good. But even so, I've never become used to eating out on my own. I had considered room service, of course, but it was too late to order by the time I thought about it. Besides, the restaurant looked so inviting with its low-hanging lanterns and the small candles flickering inside purple glass bowls.

The most delicious aroma – something like red wine cooked with mushrooms - filled my senses as I entered the room. The waiter, dressed in white with a black frock-coat, looked about fourteen years old, but he kindly found me a table at the edge of the room near the window. Once seated, I ordered another G&T to calm my nerves before settling down to check out the menu. Which was decidedly pricey. But oh, so worth it. I chose a starter of Mediterranean Stuffed Peppers, then a main course of Spiced Cauliflower Roast, then Pavlova with raspberries and blueberries for dessert. I really needed to soak up the alcohol.

It was all scrumptious, and as the waiter came to collect my dessert plate, I asked him to pass my compliments to the chef. But I was just ordering an espresso from him when, out of the corner of my eye, I noticed someone approaching my table. So I thanked the waiter, who nodded and left.

I looked up to find Todd Blackwell, the Look North producer, smiling down at me. He'd changed and was now wearing jeans and a blue cotton shirt.

'Hi,' I said.

'All on your own?' he asked.

I nodded. 'I'm staying over so I can get some shopping done.'

He indicated the empty seat opposite. 'Mind if I join you?'

'No – it's fine. I've just ordered coffee. Would you like some?'

'I was thinking about a glass of wine myself. I've already had coffee. Should I order a bottle and we can share?'

I'll confess I was slightly flattered. I'd never been chatted up by a TV producer before. Also, I found him incredibly attractive physically, with his smiling blue eyes and his dark wavy hair. But I was still very wary.

'It's up to you,' I replied, 'but I've already had a bit to drink - we've been celebrating with G&Ts - so maybe I shouldn't have any more.'

He sat down. 'Fair enough. I can always ask them to save it for tomorrow if I don't finish it.'

'Are you staying here, then?'

He nodded. 'I'm up from London, just filling in for someone for a couple of weeks.'

'Oh.'

My espresso arrived, and Todd ordered a bottle of chilled Pinot Grigio, organic if possible.

I smiled. 'So what do you do at home in London?'

'Documentaries mainly, and that's my preference if I'm honest. But I also get pulled in to do news programmes – like BBC Look North.'

'Don't you mind being away from home?'

He shrugged. 'There's nothing to keep me there, really. I'm divorced, there are no children, and there's no-one else on the horizon just at the minute. So I'm a free agent.'

The waiter brought over the wine at that point, with two glasses. He poured some for Todd and awaited his acceptance before pouring more.

Todd took a sip. 'Lovely. Thank you.'

The waiter filled both glasses, then left.

Todd indicated my glass. 'Sorry about that. You don't have to drink it.'

'It's okay – he wasn't to know.'

'So, tell me about yourself. You're a novelist, I understand?'

'I am. And I know - you've never heard of me.'

'I have heard of you, actually. But I've never read you.'

I smiled. 'There's a first time for everything.'

His smile was infectious. I could feel tiny bubbles forming in the pit of my stomach.

'My thoughts entirely,' he said.

27

She can't trust the police, that's for sure. They would reach exactly the same conclusion ...

28

Leeds, Yorkshire
IGNORANCE of the law is no defence; we all know that. Nor is being completely and utterly intoxicated. *But in my defence, your honour, I'd had way too much to drink. That's okay, isn't it? Your honour?*

So, even though I hadn't actually broken the law as such - because Colin and I weren't married – I'd still broken the unwritten rule. You don't sleep with someone else when you're already in a relationship. Not when you wish to continue said relationship.

Looking back now, though, I can see where I was coming from.

Firstly, I was highly suspicious of Colin's activities over in Brussels, especially with the ex-wife hanging around. Secondly, I wasn't sure I believed him when he said he loved me. And thirdly, he hadn't rung me over the weekend, as promised.

But when I woke up in bed, naked, with Todd beside me, I was panic-stricken, distraught, couldn't believe what I'd done, what had happened.

Sitting up, I looked around warily. An empty wine bottle was perched on the edge of the hotel's dresser, its huge mirror reflecting the white chandelier hanging above the bed. *The scene of the crime.* I looked at Todd, fast asleep, oblivious to the destruction he'd caused, the two wine goblets on the cabinet next to him, and the empty condom packet. *Irrefutable evidence, your honour.*

I groaned loudly.

Todd stirred, opening his eyes. 'What?'

Grabbing my dress from the floor, I covered myself and dived for the bathroom.

'April?'

'Just getting a shower,' I called.

Turning on the shower, I dived beneath it. The water was steaming hot and powerful. I turned around slowly, praying it would wash away the scent. After-shave. Sweat. Sex.

'Oh, my god. Shit, shit, shit,' I whispered, soaping myself vigorously. 'Oh, my god.'

Parts of the evening were coming back to me. Pictures, colours, words. Feelings. We'd talked well into the night, drunk the entire bottle of organic Pinot Grigio, ordered another, and come up to my room to finish it off.

'Shit,' I repeated.

I heard a noise. Todd was pushing open the door. 'You okay, April? Not feeling sick?'

'No – I'm fine. Thanks. Won't be long.'

Actually, I am feeling sick, I realised. Only - not because of the wine.

Luckily, I'd hung my jeans and sweater up in the bathroom before going to dinner the previous night, so I was able to get myself ready before having to face Todd again.

Eventually, dressed with full makeup and nearly dry hair, I took a deep breath and opened the door.

Todd was sitting on the bed, dressed and busily checking his phone. He looked up.

'It was a mistake, wasn't it?' he said.

'No. It's fine. It takes two to tango.'

He looked sad suddenly.

'Sorry,' I said.

'No - *I'm* sorry. Not married, are you?'

I shook my head. 'No.'

'Thank goodness for that. That would have been a disaster.'

'But I am in a relationship. A fairly long-term relationship.'

He rubbed his forehead in embarrassment. 'Oh - sorry. I'm really sorry.'

'As I said, it takes two. I should have refused you, I should have said no.'

'You weren't really in a state to be thinking about saying anything. But there was no wedding ring, you were here on your own – I thought you were single. I'm truly sorry.'

I waved my hand around aimlessly. 'Stop apologising. It's fine.'

He stood up. 'Look – I need to get changed and get to work …'

'It's fine. You go. I'll be okay. I'm going to shop, shop, shop. My mum's getting married soon and I'm choosing my outfit.'

He nodded, as if this explained everything. 'Right. Yes. You mentioned that last night.'

'Did I? Sorry …'

'No. It's okay. I'm very happy for her.'

'She's had two wonderful relationships, and I can't even keep hold of one …'

Walking over, he took me in his arms. 'You're lovely. Don't let anyone ever tell you otherwise.'

'Thank you,' I said.

So how do I manage to mess up every relationship I ever begin? I thought.

Kissing me gently on the cheek, he made to leave.

'Here – take these with you?' I grabbed the wine glasses and empty bottle and pushed them at him. 'Please?'

He took them. 'Not a word shall leave my lips, April.'

And he left.

Sorry tears rolled down my cheeks, but I brushed them away.

*

Breakfast was a two-stage affair. I had the croissants and coffee the hotel offered me, dunking the croissants piece by piece into my extra-large cappuccino - the Parisian way. But then, after leaving my case with Reception, I needed more. So I braved the ice-cold wind and ordered a cooked veggie breakfast from the Vintage Tearooms on the edge of St Peter's Square. It was warm and cosy in there, and I had finally begun to relax a little when my phone buzzed. Colin.

Sorry didn't ring over the weekend, darling. Had a great time in Antwerp, but missed you. Then I had work to catch up on - that new system again. Arse of a job! How was your weekend? Love you. Speak soon. xxx

Oh - my - god.

No, I thought. I can't do this. I have to end it.

The veggie breakfast I'd just eaten began to congeal in my stomach, and I felt sick. Gulping down my tea, I paid my bill and left.

Outside, the cold wind was freezing the pavements white, and the Christmas decorations hanging above the streets were swinging precariously, to and fro. Pulling my scarf around my face, I braved the cold before diving into Harvey Nics. It was warm and welcoming in there, highly perfumed, and I was able to shake off my melancholy and spend the next two hours browsing.

Retail therapy is all well and good, but it doesn't really take away the problem, does it? It doesn't make it all disappear – *poof* and it's gone?

No.

I did look through some really gorgeous clothing. Silk, cashmere, suede, merino wool; soft, squashy leather boots and handbags. All of it lovely, but I really was not in the mood. So I found the Ladies, locked myself into a cubicle, sat down on the loo, and had a good cry. Quietly. Continuously. I had some makeup in my bag, could easily do some repair work. So I just let it come. I sobbed and sobbed and sobbed. I really didn't think I would ever stop.

Ten minutes later, however, I did stop. I wiped my eyes, blew hard on my nose, and unlatched the door. To find a long queue and some very strange glances. But did I care? No. I felt a whole lot better. So I washed my hands, reapplied my makeup, and left.

The Harvey Nics restaurant wasn't far away, so I queued up and bought roasted carrot soup and a cup of tea, and sat at a corner table. I wanted to be alone, but I also needed to talk. So I pulled out my phone and rang Toni.

'Hi, April,' she said. 'What's up? Have you run out of money already?'

I smiled. 'No. No, I've not really bought anything yet. I'm not quite in the mood.' More tears threatened.

She laughed. 'What? Do my ears deceive me? April Stanislavski in the centre of Leeds and not in the mood to shop?'

'I know ...'

The line went quiet. Then I heard a soft, 'What is it?'

'Oh god, Toni,' and I began to cry.

'April, what's happened?'

'That producer. Todd.'

'Yes?'

'He was at the hotel. We – we …'

'What?' she screamed.

'I know, I know. It – it just seemed to happen. We were drunk …'

Another silence, then, 'Are you serious? What about Colin?'

I couldn't speak.

'I guess you haven't told him?'

I shook my head. 'No.'

'Oh, my god …'

'I know.'

'So just what do you intend doing?'

'I don't know, Toni. Shit. Shit, shit, shit.'

'Listen. Get out there, get your damned shopping done, then come over here and we'll talk.'

'Okay.'

'And wipe your face. You must look a bloody mess.'

I grinned. 'I do. And I've only just redone my makeup after crying in the loos.'

'Looks like another trip to the Ladies, then.'

'Toni?'

'What?'

'Thank you.'

I ate as much of the soup as I could stomach, and returned to the Ladies to sort out my face. I did look a bloody mess. Toni was right.

So the afternoon was spent shopping. I bought *Jo Malone* for Jo, Vicky and Toni; crisp cotton shirts by *Monsoon* for Rebecca and Daisy; *Clarins* fragrance for Joe and Sean, and a beautiful cashmere cardigan in pale lemon for Mum. And as for Colin – well, there was every chance I wouldn't still be seeing him by the time Christmas came around, but I still bought a soft woollen sweater in navy blue and some *Dior Sauvage*, his favourite.

I stopped for some much needed coffee, then wandered along to the Headrow, a busy shopping area. There was a young man outside Greggs, the sandwich shop, surrounded by a crowd of people. He was balancing, his arms stretched out, sometimes wobbling and sometimes looking down, as if he was walking a tightrope. But he wasn't. He was on the pavement. On the pavement, and high as a kite.

I paused briefly, wondering if I should get someone out to him. A paramedic, or the police, maybe. But that would only get him into trouble, I decided. So I carried on walking, guiltily. Sadly.

So it wasn't just university students who needed our help.

The next couple of hours I spent on myself. A blue sweater, a pair of soft leather shoes in bronze, and an outfit for Mum's wedding in a delicate shade of pink. The dress was chiffon, the jacket cashmere, the

Jimmy Choo shoes and bag suede, and the hat a delicate frou-frou of sinamay and chiffon.

It was five o'clock by the time I'd finished. So, carrying my bags, I made my way back to the hotel. My call to Toni had made me feel a little better, but even so the scene of my crime hit me with a thud.

How could I have cheated on Colin? Why would someone do that? He didn't deserve that.

Did he?

I asked the girl on Reception to order a taxi to take me to the station. I then asked for my suitcase, which I'd left with her earlier.

'Certainly, Miss Stanislavski. I won't be a minute,' and she hurried off.

She returned quickly and I was surprised to see not just my suitcase, but a small teddy bear, wrapped in cellophane with a red velvet bow.

'This has been left for you, madam.'

Shocked, I accepted it and thanked her with a five pound note.

Tired now, I sat back into the leather sofa and examined my gift. It was a girl bear, with a tartan ribbon wrapped around her head, and big eyes that looked out appealingly. I had no choice but to remove the cellophane. She was beautiful, made from long fluffy mohair in a greenie brown colour. So soft. So expensive. And there was a card fastened to her leg.

This is Mavis. She so reminded me of you I just had to buy her. I am truly sorry, and if there's anything I can do to make things better, call me. Todd xxx

His mobile number seemed to be an afterthought, scribbled hastily at the bottom. As if he wasn't quite sure.

I asked the girl at Reception to dispose of the cellophane, and I returned to my case to await my taxi. I cuddled the bear as I contemplated my predicament.

As far as I could see, I could do one of two things.

I could come clean and admit my transgression, citing the aforementioned reasons (mistrust, doubt, lack of phone calls) for my folly. I would be distraught, in tears, begging forgiveness, until he either gave in or threw me out.

Or I could accuse him of not caring enough to ring when he'd promised to do so, of being thoughtless and abrupt with me, and of sleeping with the ex-wife (possibly). Then I would admit to cheating on him, but only because I thought we were over.

But.

There was always that third alternative.

I could dump him. Then I wouldn't have to admit to anything.

Soft tears filled my eyes, and I hugged Mavis even closer.

'Your taxi's here, Miss Stanislavski,' said a voice behind me.

I nodded unhappily. 'Thank you.'

*

The train was just leaving Grindleford, the last stop before Millerstone, when I began to panic. Home. Where Colin and I spent our time, where we'd got to know each other, where we'd fallen in love. How could I continue with us now? How could I pretend everything was alright when it wasn't?

But then, wasn't I suspicious of him? Didn't I think *he* was cheating on me? Weren't we doing the same thing, each behind the other's back? Didn't we both have our stories to tell?

Pulling my phone from my bag, I texted Toni.

Nearly home – you still okay to talk?

Her reply came quickly.

No probs. I'll put the kettle on. Or something stronger?

I replied.

I'm driving. But okay - a small one - I need it.

I'd parked my car at the station, knowing I'd have a case and some shopping to carry home. So now I drove to Toni's and parked up outside, hiding my bags inside the boot. Toni had left the kitchen door slightly open, so there was no need to knock.

'Hello,' I called.

Toni was behind the door, folding up some tea towels. Her hair was wrapped in a thin turban, obviously hiding some kind of lotion. Her hair is lovely, but it must take some looking after.

'Can't cope with messy kitchens,' she said, smiling. 'But it's okay, we can talk. The kids are fast asleep. It's these Christmas shows they're doing in school – knock them out for the count.'

'Bless them,' I said, closing the door behind me. I placed my handbag onto the table and sat down with a groan.

'So come on, then – let's have it,' she said, passing me a glass of white wine. 'Here's one I prepared earlier.'

'Oh, Toni,' I said, and burst into tears.

Placing her arms around me, she murmured, 'Come on now – there'll be a way round it. There always is.'

But I shook my head vehemently. 'No. Not this time.'

'So – answer me this. If you're so in love with Colin, how come you were able to jump into bed with Todd?'

'I was pissed, Toni. Completely pissed. You should never have left me on my own.'

She stood back, shocked. 'What?'

'I should have come home with you. But no, I had to stay in Leeds and do some bloody shopping, didn't I? And it's not like I've actually got time to go shopping, is it? I have a million and one things to do, and I decide to go shopping.'

'You still need to take time out sometimes, you know. So stop beating yourself up, will you? It's done, it can't be undone. You just need to come clean.'

I jumped up. 'What? No way. No. We'd be finished. That would be it. Over.'

'So what do you suggest, then?'

'I don't know. I either dump him, or we just carry on as if nothing's happened.'

She sat down, crossing her arms. 'Right. So that would work, then.'

Tears rolled down my cheeks. 'I have to dump him.'

'What a mess.'

I looked around the kitchen. It seemed different, somehow. There was a vase of pink lilies on the windowsill, and another, huge, vase of red roses to one side of the Kenwood.

'Who bought the flowers?' I asked. 'They're gorgeous.'

She smiled happily. 'Mike.'

I shouldn't have been surprised, although I was. 'Oh. Right.'

'I got home from work on Saturday and the house was full of them. There are three vases in the lounge. Luckily, he brought vases as well as flowers. Or I'd have been using old jugs and milk cartons.'

'So it's definitely back on, then?'

She nodded. 'It was the anniversary of the day we met.'

I sipped my wine. 'That's sweet. I'm pleased for you.'

'Oh god, April. I'm so sorry about you and Colin. I really hope you get it sorted.'

'Thanks. Me too.'

She removed the turban from her hair, letting it fall, still wet, around her shoulders. 'We've had calls, you know, to the number they gave out on Look North. Lots of people wanting to help. It's unbelievable.'

I felt a great sense of relief. At least I could do something right.

'That's just brilliant, Toni. So what happens next?'

'We get organised. We print off posters and distribute them to our volunteers. They each have their own area, so it will be their responsibility to deliver.'

'What about lobby groups? What's happening with that?'

'Fiona is on the case as we speak. She's sending a petition to Downing Street.'

'That's fantastic. Good luck with it.'

'Which reminds me – have you heard about that ecstasy haul they've found?'

I was so tired her words didn't register at first. But then my ears pricked up.

'Ecstasy? Where?'

'Somewhere out near Bakewell, it is. Monyash?'

'Monyash? Do they know who it belongs to?'

'No idea. I only heard about it today from old Patsy Williams – she was in having her hair permed. It's all over the village, though.'

I put down my empty glass. 'Thank you for the wine, Toni, and for listening when I've been such a bloody idiot. But I need to collect Dash from Mum's and get myself home. And you need to go and rinse your hair.'

But first I needed to check in with Sean.

Monyash? A village much too close to Chatsworth for my liking.

29

But would they? Would the police reach the same conclusion? Just how would they treat this letter?

30

Millerstone, Derbyshire

I slept at Mum's place that night. After leaving Toni, I'd picked up Dash and driven home to find my intruder alarm wailing and the neighbours out in force. Ralph, my next-door-but-one neighbour, was standing guard at the front door, chest out, stomach in, both arms crossed.

My heart missed a beat. After the day I'd had, this could *not* be happening. Leaving Dash in the car, I ran up to Frances, my next-door neighbour. An icy rain had begun, and she was huddled inside her black padded coat chatting to Pam, Ralph's wife. As I approached, she put out her arms to hug me.

'Oh, April - such an awful thing. We've rung the police already, and they're on their way. But we didn't see anyone, and there were no strange vans around or anything. They must have just walked off down the road from what we can make out. I'm so sorry, pet.'

I returned the hug, but inside I was feeling quite sick. What was this – the universe turning my world upside down and emptying out its contents? All in one fell swoop?

'Thanks, Frances,' I said, 'but I'd better get the alarm.'

The racket it was making was incessant, piercing, and much too loud. Covering my ears, I pushed open the front door and ran through.

Ralph followed. 'I have checked the house, love – I used the spare key you gave us. It's empty, there's no-one about. They got in through the window at the side there – your study, I think?'

My office. 'Oh, my god.'

He saw the look on my face. 'Your computer's still there – they didn't touch that. But the place is in a bit of a mess.'

I went inside, pressed my code into the alarm, and stepped back, welcoming the silence. Then I pushed open my office door and stepped inside. The window on the far wall had been forced and my books, my precious book collection, had been thrown willy-nilly onto the floor, like scraps of unwanted garbage. I looked around, but couldn't tell if anything was missing. My Macbook, however, was completely untouched and I thanked God, silently.

What an idiot, I thought. What an idiot. For some reason I hadn't backed up my most recent work onto the external hard-disk, and would have had it all to do again. I'd been so busy delving into other people's lives and going shopping and doing other, unmentionable, things, I hadn't even had the time or the wisdom to back up my work.

My oak swivel chair had also been thrown to the ground. Picking it up with both hands I replaced the cushions. My cardigan had been dumped onto an empty book-shelf and both sleeves hung lazily down. In a daze, I pulled it away and was carrying it to the door, intending to place it into the washing machine, when Ralph appeared.

'The police said not to touch anything. Fingerprints and all that.'

I dropped it to the floor. 'Oh. Sorry.'

He smiled. 'Do you want to come and stay at ours, once the police have been?'

I shook my head. 'No. No, I need to stay.'

He held out his hands sympathetically. 'Look – you're in shock. Why don't you come and wait outside with us? I don't think they'll be long.'

Again, I shook my head. What else had the bastards done? What had they taken? Was this anything to do with the murder investigation?

'Thanks, Ralph. I just need to check the rest of the house.'

'Okay. But try not to touch anything,' and he left to return to the others.

I moved around in a daze. First to the lounge, then the cloakroom, then the kitchen. Nothing, and all my spare keys were where they should be. Everything was fine. So I moved upstairs, my mind whirling irrationally. But again, nothing. The sense of relief was something I find hard to describe. It was like being lifted up off the floor and placed upon a cloud.

So it was just my office they'd attacked. Or maybe once the alarm had triggered, they'd run off before they could do more damage. Thank goodness for intruder alarms.

I went back outside, pulled my coat and scarf from the car, made sure Dash was alright (he was actually fast asleep), then went to stand beside the others. Most of them had gone home, but Frances, Ralph and Pam were still there.

'Shall I make you a nice cup of tea, pet?' asked Frances. 'We can't use your kitchen, so I'll pop back to mine. Won't take a minute.'

I nodded gratefully. 'Please, Frances - that'd be lovely - thanks.'

Frances had lived on our street for the past thirty years, knew all the ins and outs of the village; knew everyone's names, their occupations, their weaknesses and their strengths. But her husband Doug hadn't been very well recently – some kind of lung infection – and she'd been at a loose end without him. But she was coping, and I'd often stop and chat if she was pottering about in the garden.

So, glad to be doing something worthwhile, she smiled and rushed off, her coat hood bouncing up and down. 'Won't take me long …'

The police arrived twenty minutes later, a man and a woman. They checked the house while we stood around, and then took photos of the damage.

The WPC came out to me while the other PC made the window secure.

'They've only forced the one window,' she said. 'But PC Whiley has managed to push it back and make it secure. I'd get someone out to check it over tomorrow, though. And we need to get Fingerprints out. But we can't do that until tomorrow, either, so it's best you stay somewhere else tonight.' She looked around. 'Maybe one of these lovely neighbours?'

But I shook my head. 'No, it's fine. I can stay with my mum. Thank you.'

She gave me her card. 'Okay, if you're sure. But any problems, this is my number. You need to check everything and make sure nothing was taken – keys, cards, anything they can use. But we'll get off in a minute, Miss Stanislavski, so make sure you get a good night's sleep.'

'I did report someone entering the house last Thursday, you know.'

'Did you?' She made a note in her handbook. 'Did we investigate it?'

'There didn't seem much point, really. It was just that I was in the back garden, and they came in through the front door. I'd not locked it - stupidly.'

She scribbled it down. 'Was anything taken?'

'No. I think we disturbed them – me and Dash, my dog.'

'Okay, I've noted it down. Thank you.'

And so it was that I drove back to Mum's, told her and Jim the whole story, and went to bed in that beautiful farmhouse. But I hardly slept a wink.

*

The following morning, I got up, weak and exhausted, my throat sore and my eyes red. I visited the bathroom and Mum, having heard me, brought in a cup of tea.

Sitting back onto the pink chaise longue that sat beneath the bay window, with the rain lashing down outside, she sighed loudly.

'So what's wrong, love? And I don't just mean the house being broken into, although that's bad enough. Have you and Colin had a fallout?'

I looked at her, cautiously. 'Why?'

'Well, normally you'd be ringing him, moaning about what's happened, looking for sympathy. But you haven't. Not as far as I can tell, anyway.'

I felt myself blushing hotly. 'I – I didn't even think about ringing him, to be honest. I was too exhausted. But I will – I'll ring him later, once I'm out of bed.'

Folding her arms across her chest, she nodded. 'Okay. So you're both fine, then?'

I hated lying to her, but I just couldn't face her disapproval, not then. So I nodded and said, 'Yes. We're fine.'

She stood up. 'Okay. Well, let me know if you need to talk. But you sound like you're getting a cold, love, so take it easy this morning. And we'll be coming along to the house with you later on.'

Holding back my tears, I swallowed hard. 'Thanks, Mum.'

But I didn't ring Colin. I couldn't face talking to him – not just yet. So I texted.

Don't panic, but I was burgled last night. Me and Dash are fine – we were at Toni's when it happened and police are investigating. Sorry didn't ring last night but now you know why. Staying at Mum's for now. How are you? Speak soon. xxx

His reply came quickly.

Oh god! You okay? Was up til midnight working, and no better today. Will try and call later. And see you at the weekend, yes? Take it easy. xxx

The police rang at eleven thirty to say the fingerprints guy was on his way. Mum, Jim, Dash and I braved the rain and climbed into the Mini.

The rain turned to sleet as we drove to my house, and there was already a dusting of snow covering the hills in the distance.

'Isn't it pretty?' said Mum.

'It is,' I agreed. 'I just hope it's not washing away any evidence.'

The fingerprints guy, a tall Welshman with a large face and large hands, introduced himself as Elliott Wilkinson. I unlocked the front door for him, and we waited in the kitchen while he dusted the office. He checked the other rooms as well, but found nothing.

'It looks like the perpetrator forced his way in through the study window, threw a few things around, then left when the alarm got too much for him. Luckily, the sounder is just outside that room, or he'd have carried on with it.'

'It is quite piercing,' I agreed. 'But I forgot to tell you – he knocked the chair over and I picked it up. And the cushions. Sorry.'

'It's fine, Miss Stanislavski. I've dusted it all, but they were wearing gloves, I'm afraid. Pre-meditated, I should think.'

'Can we make you a cup of tea?' asked Mum, politely. 'I take it we can touch things now?'

He nodded. 'Yes, of course, love. And thanks for the offer, but I need to get back before the snow settles. I've another house to check before I go back - out Totley way.'

'Well, thank you for coming out,' I said. 'What happens now?'

'You need to check the place, let us know if anything's missing, then report it to your insurers. And if you find anything unusual, anything that shouldn't be here - again, let us know.'

Mum showed Elliott to the door while I prepared tea and biscuits. But when she returned, she looked quite upset.

'What's wrong, Mum?' I asked.

She sat down at the table. 'Oh, I don't know. All this upset. Jim's leg, and your burglary. What's next, that's what I want to know? I was feeling so happy.'

Guilty tears pricked the backs of my eyes. 'Oh, Mum - don't.

Jim walked in at that point, his arm around one of his crutches. 'What's going on here, love?'

'Mum's upset about your leg, and about the burglary.'

He went straight over, sat beside her, and hugged her.

'Now then, we'll have no maudlin, my soon-to-be Mrs Allsop. What's done is done, and we just need to get on with it. Doctor says my leg'll be fine for the wedding. And April here is alive and well, and we have some wonderful times to look forward to. So we'll have no more tears. You got that?'

Tearful suddenly at his innate kindness, I stifled a sob. Mum didn't hear me, but Jim did, and he came over to where I was making the tea.

'Now then, love, I can do that. You go and sit yourself down with your mum. I'll get a chap out to sort the window as well. I've used him on my place, and he's kosher.'

I could have hugged him. 'Thanks, Jim. I really appreciate it.'

I did sit down, but then began feeling really sorry for myself, for the deeds I'd done, for my selfishness and my thoughtlessness.

Forcing back my tears, I murmured, 'Sorry, Mum. I just – it's all been a bit too much for me.'

Taking my hand, she patted it. 'There's no need to apologise, April, love. You've had a nasty shock, and you don't look at all well. Why don't we help you clear up the office once we've had our tea, and then you can get some rest?'

I nodded gratefully. 'Thanks, Mum.'

It was only as we placed my books back onto the bookshelves that I realised exactly what was missing. Some of my first editions, all numbered, all signed. We counted them. Fifteen books had gone.

'How they managed to get that lot down the street without the help of a car, I'll never know,' Jim murmured.

'Unless they had help,' I said, thoughtfully.

'You mean – like two people?'

'Yes.'

'Quite possibly. And that would explain how they got through the window so easily. One could have helped the other one up.'

'I'll ring the police and let them know,' I said.

Just then, Ralph and Pam popped round to see how I was. I gave them tea and biscuits too, and we all chatted in the kitchen.

'I noticed a couple of bowls out the back last night while I was checking the place,' said Ralph. 'They're not for Marmalade, are they?'

'Marmalade?' I asked, puzzled.

'The ginger cat. I put food out for him as well.'

'Do you?' said Pam. 'I didn't know that. Since when?'

'I just leave him a tin of tuna, down near the shed. That's okay, isn't it?'

'Well – yes. But you do know he belongs to Frances, don't you? And Martha on the other side feeds him? And probably a few others, by the looks of it.'

'What?' I said, shocked.

She smiled. 'It's true.'

Ralph roared with laughter. 'You're joking, Pam. He'll be costing us a fortune in tuna as well.'

'So when do you buy this tuna, then?' she asked. 'I didn't know about it, that's for sure.'

'I don't. I found a load at the back of the cupboard – the stuff we got when Jacksons closed down, remember? Well, we never use it and it was running out of date, so I took it down to the shed. I've nearly run out, as it happens, so I was planning on stocking up again.'

Sipping her tea thoughtfully, Mum shook her head. 'Well. Would you believe that?'

'That's such a brilliant story,' I said. 'What a boy.'

'No wonder he's such a big chap,' said Pam. 'So what happens now?'

Ralph shrugged. 'Well, we can't exactly starve the poor thing, can we?'

*

That afternoon, the window guy, Daz, came over to replace the window fastening. He was local from Bradwell, so was fine about calling out on the spur of the moment. Gratefully, I paid him a huge tip and accepted his business card for future reference.

Then I got down to some work. It's the only thing that does the trick when I have something on my mind. I can switch off, totally. And I can become the person I'm writing about, whether it be a man or woman, a dog or a cow.

Admittedly, it's not very often you come across dogs and cows in chick-lit. But this was the problem. I was becoming bored of writing love stories. I really needed to extend my writing repertoire. All this investigative work had whet my appetite for something bigger than just boy meets girl.

I needed to chat to Sandy.

But not today.

Today was a day of licking my wounds, of working and working, until the anger, the disappointment, the upset, had worked their way through my system.

I lit candles, soy candles, rose-scented candles; my office looked like the church at Christmas.

Then I sat down and I typed.

I used to believe in love. In the power of love, love at first sight, love everlasting, love 'til death do us part. Not any more ...

Such sad words. But they were true. Because they were written from the heart. I'd had enough. Enough of the hurt. Enough of sleepless nights. Enough of tears that came so hard I could no longer breathe.

I was feeling decidedly sorry for myself. And Mavis sitting on my desk, her big eyes staring at me, the gift card still attached to her leg, was not helping.

I just had to end it.

31

Undecided, she pushes the letter back inside the bedside drawer. But as she does so, she finds another one, further back, tucked neatly into place beneath a pair of black ten denier stockings ...

32

Millerstone, Derbyshire

THURSDAY morning. Delaying the inevitable, I decided to take Dash for a long, leisurely walk. And Chatsworth was the place to do it. So, pulling on my padded coat, hat and gloves, I locked the house, set the alarm, and drove out. The Christmas Market was on, so the roads were busy, but I was determined to get some fresh air and exercise. I needed to think.

You see, Colin was due to fly home the following night, and I'd decided to come clean and tell him everything. The whole truth. I just couldn't lie. But I needed to develop my strategy – I needed to tell him in a way that caused the least offence. If that was at all possible.

A scattering of snow had settled on the grass around Chatsworth, and delicate lights hung across the trees, lighting the scene beautifully. But I wasn't in the mood for Christmas, not any more. I'd done the most stupid, stupid thing, and now I had to suffer the consequences.

So Dash and I walked. Down towards the river and along. We could see the lights of the market in the distance, and the rows upon rows of parked cars. Other people getting on with their lives, enjoying their families, having something to look forward to.

Me? I was just dreading that weekend.

But as I walked, my head cleared and I began to accept the inevitable. Yes, I'd been stupid, and yes, I needed to sort my life out. But it wasn't the end of the world. After all, I'd been here before, hadn't I? I just needed to pull myself together and make a new life for myself. Probably with someone else.

The grass was crunchy beneath my boots. I caught my foot on a clump and tripped over, pulling at Dash's lead to steady myself. And suddenly glimpses of that awful night in November came rushing back to me. The dead man on the ground. Dash sniffing at the body. The blood.

Such a lot had happened since then.

But I still couldn't work out what had happened to Lucas and Felix. My usually excellent deduction skills had deserted me. Had Fliss borrowed from Felix and then he wanted it back? Had he owed Lucas money? Did he kill Lucas, then commit suicide by drinking or drowning, or both?

But what about Katie, Lucas's wife? Did she know her beloved husband was having an affair? But if she did, she wouldn't have killed him, would she? She'd just have taken him through the divorce courts, surely?

And what about the other guys in Lucas's car dealership? Who were they, and what had happened there?

I needed to ring Sean, check out the details. DI Jasper may have left the case, but that didn't mean I had to. No. I was going to put all my energy into sorting this out. After all, I would no longer have to fly to Brussels every other weekend. And it would help my newfound career as a crime author. Although I still needed to ring Sandy about that one.

My walk was wonderful, exhilarating, and I called in at Edensor for coffee and cake afterwards. And water for Dash, of course.

So I drove back home, more content than when I'd left, and rang Sean.

'I'm on my way to do a report,' he said. 'Can I get back to you?'

'I just need the name of that car dealership – you know – the one Lucas was involved in?'

'Oh, wait on.'

I waited.

'The other guy is a Carl Smith,' he said. 'They're called Smith-Hanssen Motors, and they're out Gleadless way. Why? What are you up to?'

'Carl Smith! I know him!' I exclaimed. 'He's the guy who ran into my car. Bloody idiot.'

'Is he? Well, that is a coincidence. You think he knew you were on the case?'

I shook my head. 'No. I don't. Definitely not.' But then I did begin to wonder. 'At least, I don't think so. Although it was all a bit weird.'

'Be careful, April. Don't get too involved.'

'By the way, have you heard about the stash of ecstasy they've found out near Monyash? Toni told me about it on Tuesday. I was just wondering if it might have something to do with Felix.'

'Interesting. But no, I've not heard anything. I'll try and find out, though.'

*

I spent the afternoon on my manuscript's third draft. It was all coming together nicely, and I knew Sandy would be pleased. But all the while, my mind kept returning to the case. Two dead men, and nothing to say what had happened and why.

It's funny how things turn out though, looking back. I'd agreed to send the receipt for my car repairs to this Carl Smith and hadn't yet had time to do it. But what better excuse for paying him a visit?

I picked up my phone, googled his number, and called.

A guy picked up with a quick 'Hello? Smith-Hanssen Motors.'

'Is that Mr Smith?'

'Yes?'

'Hi – it's April Stanislavski here – the owner of the car you ran into?'

'Oh – yeah.'

'I'm just wondering if you're free at all today. I'm in the area this afternoon and thought I'd drop off the receipt for my repairs. If that's okay?'

'Yes, love. I'm here all day – it's fine.'

'Okay. Thanks. I'll see you later, then.'

What now, I wondered, as I rang off? How on earth do I introduce the subject of weird dealings, of cars being sold and no money being paid? I decided to call round when it was dark, so he wouldn't keep me standing at the door, so I could possibly see his books, or just get a feel for the kind of person he was.

But first I needed to ring Sandy.

'Sandy? It's April here.'

'Darling. How are you?'

'I'm fine, thanks. And you?'

'Only fine, my darling? You need to come visit us in London, come for a chat, go for coffee. You sound tired.'

Tears threatened, but I blinked them away. 'I am tired, but I'll be okay. I've had a lot on just lately. But hey, I've finished my manuscript.'

'That is marvellous news, April. Well done. So if you send it on down, we'll proof it and get it on its way.'

'Don't forget to let me have final say, though.'

'But of course, of course. As usual. We'll ping it back to you as soon as.'

I smiled. 'Thanks, Sandy.'

'But you must come and visit. Promise?'

'I will, I promise. And yes, I could do with some time off – you're right.'

She laughed. 'I'm always right. Aren't I?'

I smiled. 'Yes, Sandy – you usually are.'

'So let me know when you're coming to see me, and I'll leave some time in my diary. It will be just lovely to see you. Take care, and have a wonderful Christmas, darling.'

'Thanks, Sandy. You too.'

Quickly, before I could change my mind and make even more alterations, I emailed my manuscript to her.

There, I thought. Done.

*

It was four o'clock and dark when I rang the doorbell to Carl Smith's house. It was a red-brick house, built like a semi, but joined onto a repair shop instead of another house. The entrance to the repair shop stood level with the front door of the house, and there was a small showroom on the other side with two newish cars on show. I'd called into the repair shop and showroom first, but there was no-one there when I called out, so I returned to the house and tried the doorbell.

Carl Smith, a small man with small, piggy eyes and a brown checked shirt, sleeves rolled up to show his thick, muscled arms, opened the door himself.

'April Stanislavski,' I said, offering my hand.

'Hi, love. Come in then,' he said, waving me inside and closing the door.

'I won't keep you long, Mr Smith. I just need to let you take copies of the receipts, if that's okay. My printer has broken, I'm afraid.'

It was a lie. My printer was in perfect working order, but I needed the chance to look around.

'No problem. Come on in.'

So I followed him through the hallway and kitchen to a door at the side of the house. This led into the repair shop, a dark, damp place. As he flicked on the long fluorescent light, I looked around. To the left, at the front of the building, was a wide roll-top door, open, and beside it a small pedestrian door, painted white. A pile of old tyres filled the far corner, and to the right of me was a dilapidated internal office with glass windows. At the centre of the repair shop sat an old Ford Focus, its left-hand passenger door missing. The place smelled of burnt oil and fresh paint.

'This way,' he said, leading me into the office.

Taking care not to brush my coat sleeves against the narrow door, I followed him in. The place was a mess, the cheap pine desk littered with bits of paper, dirty mugs, and scattered pens.

'Excuse the mess,' he said. 'I am tidying it up, but it's a work in progress.'

'It's fine, Mr Smith. Don't worry about it.'

I guessed any paperwork would either be on the desk or in one of the drawers. There was one drawer beneath the desk, and three in a small chest in the corner. An expensive-looking Epson printer sat on top.

'Here,' he said. 'Let me have the receipts and I'll take a couple of copies. Just in case the insurers lose them. You know what they're like, these places.'

I pulled a large envelope from my bag and passed it to him. 'Thank you. It's very good of you.'

There was a bit of a fuss because the ink on the first copy was too pale and he had to sort it out. Eventually, however, after taking two copies of each document, he passed the originals back to me.

But I took advantage of the distraction to look around. Other than the desk and chest of drawers, a chair sat against the wall, cradling a grubby cushion and an old green telephone. There was also a metal coat-stand, but no coats. An air freshener hung there instead, the pine scent making my nose wrinkle. Moving closer, I tried to check out the paperwork on the desk, but then decided something illegal wouldn't just be left lying around. No. It had to be in one of the drawers. Unless of course he kept that kind of thing in the house, which I doubted very much. He was married, wouldn't want his wife finding out about any dodgy goings-on, would he? Unless, of course, she was in on it.

But to determine anything at all, I needed more time.

Luckily, Carl's mobile rang just as I should have been leaving the premises.

'Just a minute,' he murmured, and walked back into the kitchen.

I could have taken this opportunity to search the drawers, but I didn't. It was too risky. So I waited, scanning the desk whilst trying my best to look bored. I noticed a letter-heading showing the dealership's opening hours. So Smith finished work at five. It was five to five now. A mad idea filled my head, and I hatched a plan.

The door to the kitchen was still open, as was the roll-top garage door. But the small door to the side of it was closed, a Yale lock giving access, and it was this that inspired me.

So I called out, 'Thank you, Mr Smith – I'll be off now.' Moving quickly, I turned the knob of the Yale lock to release the catch then stepped outside, beneath the roll-top door.

I'd parked up on the main road two streets away as the other parking spaces were for residents only. However, I had no intention of heading back to the car just yet. I was determined to find something to prove that Smith was dodgy. One dodgy dealing on its own was not going to put him into prison, and I was becoming more and more certain that he'd bumped into my car on purpose. But why?

The rush hour had begun. Although it's never just an hour, is it? But cars were streaming up and down the main road as I walked away from Smith-Hanssen's. The smell of diesel from the local Shell garage irritated my nostrils, but I called in anyway and bought coffee and a brownie. Retracing my steps, I found a small secluded area with trees and a bench, where I sat to eat and drink. I needed the calories.

Thirty minutes later, I picked up my bag, placed my phone on silent, and walked back. Smith-Hanssen's was closed for the night, but as I pushed against the small pedestrian door I found it still unlocked. Sighing with relief, I stepped inside. It was dark, and quiet. So I pulled my phone from my bag, shook it to bring on the torch, made my way around the Ford Focus, and entered the small office in the corner.

The desk drawer was full of paperwork. Letters, invoices, old receipt books. How on earth this guy managed to run a business, I had no idea. But I couldn't see anything untoward, so I moved to the chest of drawers. The top drawer had packs of printing paper, BIC pens, Tippex. The drawer beneath was nearly empty; just a few old magazines, some paperclips caught at the edges. The bottom drawer appeared to be the same, and I was just about to close it when the light from my torch caught something. A small plastic bag.

It had been taped to the back of the drawer. I tugged.

Just the feel of it told me what it was. Soft Powder. Drugs.

Pushing the bag inside my coat pocket, I closed the drawer and made to leave. But suddenly the door to the kitchen opened, flooding the repair shop with light. Shaking my phone to switch off the torch, I crouched down.

It was Smith. Whistling, he walked to the front of the repair shop, checked both doors, locked the Yale, turned round, and came right up to the office door.

Terrified, my legs began to shake.

Looking around the repair shop briefly, he turned the key in the lock of the office door, turned off the light, and returned to the house.

Tense, shocked, I managed to control my legs and stand up. Rushing to the door, I turned the handle. Locked.

Damn. I'd done it again.

This time, however, I had an advantage. I had my phone.

I texted Sean.

Bad news - locked inside Smith-Hanssen's repair shop. Good news – found drugs. Help me?

It took a whole eleven minutes for him to reply.

Not again? On my way.

By this time it was six thirty, and I realised I wouldn't be making rehearsal tonight. Alfie would not be pleased. And even if I managed to get there in time, which was unlikely, I wouldn't quite be in the mood to be playing Mrs Erlynne. So it wasn't going to happen. Not only that, but I was also becoming decidedly hungry.

I texted.

So sorry, Alfie, but can't make rehearsal tonight. Will explain when I see you. I promise to learn my lines. xx

I felt really bad. Poor Alfie. That was two rehearsals I'd be missing.

I hope it's a good excuse, my darling. The show must go on. See you Monday? Big hugs and keep smiling. Alfie xxx

I gradually stopped shaking and began to relax, knowing Sean was on his way. Even so, how he was supposed to get into the premises without alerting Smith to my presence, I had no idea.

I was soon to find out.

Just over forty minutes later, the banging started. On the door of the repair shop, and on the front door of the house.

'Police! Open up!'

Sitting on the cold floor of the office, I smiled. Good old Sean.

The following hour was a blur.

Smith must have let them in through his front door. His face as he switched on the repair shop light was a blank - until he saw me there. Then he knew.

Sean unlocked the door and pulled me out. 'You okay?'

I nodded. 'Yes. Fine.'

He grinned. 'At least it's not an old shed this time. I did say I'd keep you out of old sheds, didn't I?'

'Haha. Very funny.'

He quickly guided me outside. Lights from police cars flooded the street, and neighbours were spilling from their houses. DI Sellars took some details, reprimanded me for breaking and entering, then proceeded to get samples from, and photographs of, the drawer that had held the drugs. Cocaine, as it turned out.

Sean and I left them to it after that, each driving back in our own cars to my place.

I arrived home to find Dash fast asleep behind the door. I let him into the back garden and put on the kettle. Fifteen minutes later, Sean arrived with an Indian takeaway. Aubergine curry with a side of fragrant jasmine rice.

I pulled some chapatis from the cupboard, set the table and sat down.

'Thanks, Sean. It looks delicious.'

He tried some, smiled, but then put down his fork.

'Right. Tell me what happened. What the hell put the idea into your head to break and enter a car repair shop? You must be mad.'

I felt bad. 'I'm sorry.'

'So you should be. Anything could have happened. We don't know what type of guy this Carl Smith is yet. He could be our murderer, for all we know.'

I nearly choked on my rice. 'Sorry, Sean. I didn't think about that.'

He shook his head. 'Obviously. Well, it's done now. Just don't do it again. I thought you didn't want to be locked in a shed again?'

'It wasn't a shed,' I protested, 'and I didn't think he'd come back in and lock the door, did I?'

'Okay, okay, let's forget about it. Hopefully, something will come of it.'

We ate in companionable silence until, having made decaf coffee, we moved through to the lounge, where Dash was curled up on the sofa.

'So where are we with this investigation?' I asked. 'What has our friend Carl got to do with it?'

'I've no idea. But if he's into cocaine, chance is he's supplying it, too. So he might have sold the car on for nothing, or very little, as a way of paying Felix for his drug habit. Payment in lieu, so to speak.'

'An expensive habit, don't you think?'

'It is, April – highly expensive. They can charge what they like once you're hooked on the stuff.'

'So where does Lucas come into it?'

He rubbed his face thoughtfully. 'So what if Lucas was selling to both Carl and Felix? I mean, why was there a stash of ecstasy in Monyash? Maybe there was some kind of blunder and Felix wanted Lucas to discuss it, said it was urgent. So Lucas left the rehearsal still in costume, and they ended up arguing.'

I had a sudden thought. 'What about Fliss? What if she was involved in this drug-dealing, too?'

33

This letter, folded neatly inside an envelope, is written on proper writing paper, a pale watermark embedded into the sheet. Pulling it from the drawer, she reads ...

34

Millerstone, Derbyshire

EXHAUSTED, I slept in until ten o'clock that Friday morning. It had been a strange week, a week of endings, now I think about it, and it had taken its toll. I'd finished my manuscript, effectively ended my relationship with Colin, and got myself locked up – again – but I'd also put an end to Carl Smith's little game. Hopefully.

So I fell out of bed, let Dash into the garden, and made fresh coffee. Checking my phone, I found a text from Toni.

If you're around today, can I pop by? Not working til this aft. But lots of good things happening – just wanted to let you know. Hope you're okay? I'll bring cake xx

Dash was whining at the back door, so I let him back in and gave him some water.

'I'm going to take a shower now, Dash sweetie – won't be long. Then Auntie Toni is coming round with cake. So if you're a good boy, I'll take you out for a nice walk later.'

His huge brown eyes looked up at me, and I could swear he was saying, *I promise.*

So I left him to drink while I showered. Thirty minutes later, I was dressed in jeans and the pale pink sweatshirt I'd bought weeks ago, but never worn. It suited my skin and my hair, and I felt good. Colin would have loved it.

'A pity I have to dump him,' I murmured, tears filling my eyes as I surveyed myself in the mirror.

But just how am I supposed to do this thing, I thought? Do I just come straight out with it: *I slept with a complete stranger on Monday night, Colin?* Or do I say: *I slept with the producer of Look North on Monday - thought it would be good for my career?* Or even: *I thought you were sleeping with your ex-wife, so decided to cheat on you, too?*

No.

I knew what I'd have to do. I'd have to tell all, beg forgiveness, and when he threw me out, wallow in self-pity for months. Because, let's face it – that's usually what happens.

Dabbing at my tears, I put on Radio Two, made porridge and sat down to text Toni.

Need more than cake. But yes, come round. Now is fine. xx

I ate a few spoonsful of porridge, caught up on my emails, and emailed Sandy to arrange a date to discuss my desire to write crime fiction. Yet all the while I was feeling more and more unhappy at the way my life was turning out. Again.

Why did I do it? Why could I never be happy with the status quo?

I couldn't do the usual thing of blaming my parents for my inability to keep a relationship going. Theirs was the perfect marriage. And I couldn't say Colin wasn't right for me. He was lovely.

So what was it?

Maybe that tiny little spark of mistrust? That little bit of my brain that thought he was cheating on me? Because other men had? Because I just didn't trust men? Or was it because I didn't think I was good enough, so they were bound to cheat on me at some point?

Sighing heavily, I stood up, emptied the rest of my porridge into the bin, placed my bowl and spoon inside the dishwasher, and called to Dash.

'Come on, Dash. Outside.'

I needed air.

I played with Dash for ten minutes, throwing his squeaky toy, a brown monkey, to the end of the garden, near the compost bin. He'd run for it, never catch it, then pick it up and carry it back to me. It was fun, and laughing made me feel so much better. Who needs a man when you have a dog for company?

Me, I thought miserably.

Just then, Toni appeared from around the side of the house.

'April!'

Happily, I picked up Dash's monkey and we went inside. Radio Two were playing *We Are Never Ever Getting Back Together* by Taylor Swift. I turned off the radio.

So I made more coffee and placed the two pieces of chocolate fudge cake Toni had brought onto plates.

'From the deli,' she said, stuffing some into her mouth. 'I've had it before. It's to die for.'

I grinned. 'I thought you were on a diet, missus.'

'Ah, but Mike loves me just the way I am. He says so. No more dieting.'

'So it's definitely back on, then?'

She nodded. 'Yep.'

'How on earth do you do it, Toni? I've completely messed up every relationship I've ever had.'

'No, you haven't. You're just particular, that's all, and you can never make your mind up. Anyway, you've not told me what Colin said yet.'

I blushed hotly. 'I – I've not told him.'

'What? You are joking. So when *are* you going to tell him?'

'Tonight. Once I've picked him up from the airport.'

'Right. So you're going to drag the poor man all the way from Brussels - which must cost a fortune, by the way - pick him up, bring him home. And then you're going to tell him you're dumping him?'

I felt terrible. Was that really me she was describing?

'What sort of person are you?' she continued.

'Shit, Toni. I'm the sort of person who can't keep a relationship going for more than two minutes, then wonders why on earth she bothers.'

'You know why you bother. You don't want to be on your own, do you?'

I picked at my cake. 'If I'm honest, I don't really know. Maybe that's the problem. Maybe I quite like living on my own, but I also like going out and having a good time – and that usually involves having a man around.'

'So you don't like the sex part, then?'

I grinned. 'I didn't say that, did I? But you don't have to actually live with someone to have sex.'

'Obviously, my girl. So it looks to me like you're scared of commitment, April Stanislavski.'

'That's actually a male-dominated trait.'

'It may be. It's true though, isn't it?'

I couldn't deny it.

When I actually thought about it later, I had to admit that yes, I was scared of someone moving in and taking over my life. I was scared of actually having to look after someone. I was terrified I'd have to make time for them when my life was so full already. How I'd managed to incorporate Dash into my life, I had no idea. Probably because I was the one in the driving seat and he was the passenger.

I smiled at Toni. 'This cake is so delicious. Thanks, Toni.'

She tilted her head to one side. 'You've not answered my question.'

'Okay, yes, I probably am scared of commitment. So shoot me.'

'You need to sort yourself out, April. See a counsellor or something. Or you're going to be like this forever, never settling down, and never meeting the right man.'

'But Colin is the right man,' I insisted.

'As I've already said, he can't be or you wouldn't have slept with Todd.'

'Shhh!' I replied, embarrassed. 'Walls have ears.'

'Seriously, April, you can't keep going from one man to another. None of us is getting any younger.'

I sighed deeply. 'Sorry, Toni. I just keep messing things up, don't I?'

'Let's talk about something more uplifting, shall we? The reason I came over, in fact.'

'Go on then. You want more coffee?'

She nodded and I took her cup.

'Okay,' she said. 'So we've hit sixteen thousand likes and had loads of people donating. It's up to half a million already. I actually think we've touched a spot. Parents, all worried about their kids going off to uni next year. It's bloody fantastic, April.'

I poured the coffee. 'That's brilliant news. In fact, it's the best I've heard all week.'

*

I took Dash for his walk as promised. We walked down to the village, along Sheffield Road, past Toad's Mouth Rock and up. Just before turning left at the bend near Fox House, I instead turned right, towards the Longshaw Estate. Situated within the Peak Park, this estate consists of moorland, woodland, and some farms. And there's a café that does extremely good, freshly-baked scones, dripping with butter. So we sat outside on a bench with coffee and a scone (and water for Dash) before setting off again, back into Millerstone and home.

Dash curled up in front of the fire and fell fast asleep, while I made a meal of lentil stew with paprika and left it to cook in the kitchen. I too curled up in the lounge, but with a couple of magazines. Even though my walk and the fresh air had lifted my spirits, however, I was still feeling decidedly anxious and upset.

How could I have done it? How could I have cheated on Colin? What on earth was I thinking?

Do I subconsciously sabotage all my relationships, especially the ones that look like they're going somewhere? Do I actually have a problem, as Toni suggested? How on earth could I tell Colin I'd slept with a complete stranger?

What the hell had I done?

Sadly I removed Mavis, with her big accusing eyes, from my desk, and hid her at the back of my wardrobe. Then at seven o'clock I set off for Manchester Airport. Winnats Pass looked so beautiful in the moonlight it actually caused a lump in my throat, and I realised just how wonderful this Christmas would have been, if only I'd been able to commit. Soft tears rolled down my cheeks.

I parked up inside Terminal 2 and left Dash in the car while I went to find Colin. All the while my stomach felt heavy and sad.

'April ...'

He ran to me and we kissed and hugged as usual, and we held hands, as usual, and made our way back to the car.

I took his case and placed it inside the boot. It was the least I could do.

He smiled. 'It's good to see you. Long time, no see - or it feels like it.'

'Come on,' I said, 'let's get home.'

I drove this time, allowing Colin to rest. He looked exhausted, with all the extra work he'd been putting in. So we chatted about his work and my work; the fact I'd finished my latest manuscript and emailed it. And the incident in the garage. He agreed with Sean that I was stupid to have gone there in the first place, let alone break in afterwards.

'You could have got the receipt copied at the Post Office and posted it, you know. Or just scanned and emailed it.'

'No, Colin. I lied to him. There was actually nothing wrong with my printer. I went there because I needed to see the place. The guy's dodgy. I knew it even before I found the cocaine.'

'So you go into a building with a dodgy man, a suspect in a murder case, and not only that, but you bloody well go back there, and break in?'

He looked genuinely angry, and my stomach lurched. Maybe he really did love me. Maybe I was only imagining the affair with his ex. Me and my bloody imagination. Again.

'At least he'll be charged with something now,' I said. 'They've got some evidence.'

He turned to me. 'Don't do it again, April. Please.'

I couldn't answer, the lump in my throat way too big.

We were heading down Winnats Pass in second gear, and carefully. Then we entered Castleton, its Christmas trees standing guard along the pavements, heavy with lights and adorned with angels.

'So what are we doing this weekend?' he asked.

'It's so beautiful,' I murmured, pushing up into third.

'April?'

'I thought we could go to the school's Christmas fayre, if you like? Carol singers and all that? Festive.'

He nodded. 'Okay. Yes. That would be nice.'

The closer we got to Millerstone, the more my heart began to thump. And by the time I pulled up outside the house, I felt physically sick. I just couldn't tell him. I couldn't hurt him.

'A nice glass of wine, I think,' he said, pulling his case from the boot.

I unlocked the door, encouraged Dash inside, and switched off the alarm.

'There's a bottle of merlot on the side,' I called.

'Sounds just about right.'

'Come on, Dash,' I murmured. 'Let's get you to bed.'

After splashing drinking water all over the kitchen floor, he was as good as gold, nestling into his basket and nodding straight off.

I placed the lentil stew onto the gas to heat up, set the timer, and poured merlot into two glasses. Colin had settled himself in the lounge.

'Here,' I said, passing him a glass.

Placing my own glass onto the coffee table, I stoked the log burner effortlessly, bringing it back to life and adding a wonderful glow to the room.

Eventually, I sat down beside Colin, my heart in my mouth.

He pulled me to him. 'I've missed you, darling.'

We kissed as if we'd not seen each other in months. Passionately. All-consuming. Like two teenagers.

Breathless, we came up for air as Colin tugged at my top, a gypsy-style top in cotton with red embroidery. I remember it specifically as it ended up in a heap on the floor, and each time I washed it afterwards it was a potent reminder of my guilt. It's now in a charity shop.

Seconds later I, too, landed on the floor, along with my jeans and underwear. Colin's clothes soon followed.

Our lovemaking was particularly tender, loving, emotional.

I knew it would be the last time.

'I love you, April,' he whispered, afterwards.

I began to cry, softly.

'What's wrong, darling?' he asked, wiping my face.

But I couldn't say a word, just closed my eyes and pressed my body close to his.

So, tired but glowing, we lay there naked for a while, our arms around each another, the blazing fire keeping us warm.

'The timer's bleeping,' he said, suddenly.

'Shit.'

I jumped up, pulled on some clothes, ran into the kitchen and switched off the timer and gas. Catching myself in the mirror, I could see I was a complete mess. My tears had dried, but my face was stained with mascara and my skin was red and blotchy.

I ran through the door. 'Just popping upstairs,' I called.

In the bedroom, I freshened up and reapplied my makeup. But staring into the eyes of someone stained with guilt is not an easy task.

You shouldn't have let that happen. You should have told him. Straightaway. You fool.

I began to cry, again.

You complete and utter fool. Why?

Forcing myself to stop, I reapplied my makeup one more time, changed out of the errant top and jeans, and replaced them with a soft blue sweater and grey leggings. I needed comfort.

But as I made my way downstairs, I felt sick, so sick I didn't think I could face dinner at all. But I had to eat something.

I needed my strength for the morning.

I played BB King over dinner. It made for less conversation. We were too tired to talk anyway, and it was late. But I did get to thinking how easy it is to tell lies, to deceive people. So what if Lucas's wife, or even Gemma, had lied about his murder? Of course, I was feeling incredibly guilty about my own deception, but what if Katie and Gemma hadn't been brought up that way? What if they didn't have that guilt thing going on? They may have found it easy to deceive people.

So what if his wife had found out about the affair and had arranged to have Lucas killed by someone else? She had the money to do it, it would seem. What if she'd arranged to go to the US while he was being murdered? So she had the perfect alibi?

Or what if Gemma did know about the baby, even though she'd denied it? What if Lucas had said he couldn't leave his wife now she was pregnant, and Gemma, outraged and disappointed, arranged to have him killed while she was away in London? Again, the perfect alibi. What if?

35

Shocked, devastated, she places both letters back inside the drawer. So it's true ...

36

Millerstone, Derbyshire

OUR morning walk with Dash took us up Coggers Lane, along Long Causeway, down the Dale and along School Lane, back into Millerstone. It was a beautiful walk, but the wind was cold and our faces froze. Fortunately the local deli allows dogs, so we were able to dive in there to get warm and to buy cappuccino and cake. Spicy gingerbread with white icing, as it turned out.

We would have stayed for lunch, but Dash had to be left at home while we went to the Christmas Fayre. So we headed back, changed out of our walking trousers, fed Dash, fed ourselves with home-made carrot and coriander soup, parmesan and plenty of sourdough, and headed down to Millerstone Church of England school.

Professor Furness welcomed us in. A school governor and an asset when raising funds, he's a sweet man with twinkling eyes and a ready smile.

'April – it's lovely to see you again. Merry Christmas.'

'Thanks, Gerry, and Merry Christmas to you too. How's your beautiful wife?'

'She is as beautiful as ever - thank you. She's just helping out with the tea stall. There's some delicious cake if you'd like to try some.' He waved towards the main hall. 'Tea, coffee, and carol singers. As you'll no doubt hear. But have a lovely day, both of you.'

Silent Night echoed nostalgically through the corridor as we made our way further inside. Children's voices, shrill yet beautiful.

Innocent.

I swallowed hard to stop the tears.

'Right, let's grab a cuppa, then we'll look at the stalls,' said Colin as we pushed through the adoring parents to stand in the queue.

Catherine, the buxom and always smiling first year teacher, was serving cake from a long table covered in white cloth. We chose two pieces of home-made stollen and queued to the end of the table for tea, brewed in giant stainless-steel teapots. Colin paid, and we had to sit on very small chairs at a very small table in the corner.

The children were now singing *Away in a Manger*. Feeling Christmassy suddenly, I looked around.

Paintings of woodland animals filled the walls, some of them very good, others not so. But all were colourful and beautifully displayed, with the artist's name in big gold letters.

'Not quite appropriate for this time of year,' murmured Colin.

'What isn't?'

'I'd have thought there'd be Christmas pictures. You know – angels and things.'

I shrugged. 'Maybe they're left over from the summer. Maybe they haven't had time to replace them. Who knows?'

'Maybe they just like them?'

I looked into his smiling eyes. Such lovely eyes. Such a lovely man. How was I going to tell him?

Twenty minutes later, we left the hall and made our way upstairs to the classrooms. The smell of poster paint and play-doh hit me, and sudden memories filled my head. Jo's hair stretched back into a pony-tail, our satchels full of books and pencils and PE kit, our friends gathering round as we entered the school-gates. And Dad waving from the van as he drove away.

Life was so simple then. So uncomplicated. Where had I gone wrong?

On an impulse, I pulled at Colin's arm.

'Let's go to Cornwall. Now.'

His stunned face said it all; he thought I'd gone mad. 'What?'

'I need to be in St Ives. We can stay over. I'll drive.'

'But what about work?'

'You can arrange another flight as we drive. I'll pay.'

He stared at me. 'April – are you alright?'

Tears threatened, but I blinked them away and shook my head. 'No. No - I'm not alright.'

Taking hold of my hand, he pulled me back down the stairs and outside. We stood just outside the school gates, away from the entrance and from Professor Furness, who was still organising the queues.

'For god's sake - what is it, April? You're worrying me.'

'I just need to get away, even if it's just for one night. Please, Colin ...'

He looked at me carefully, and then he nodded. 'Okay, okay. Let's do it.'

We practically ran up the hill and home. I packed some clothes, a washbag and makeup, while Colin repacked his case. We let Dash into the garden for a wee, then bundled him and our cases into the Mini.

After setting the alarm, we left home at exactly one o'clock and headed out, towards Chesterfield. The journey took seven hours, on the dot.

*

Pulling up outside the Nirvana, a five star hotel I'd used once before, I heaved an enormous sigh. The sea air filled my veins, my blood flowing in time with the waves.

We let Dash have another wee before booking ourselves in. They had plenty of space, as I knew they would at that time of year, so we took ourselves along to our room on the ground floor and threw our cases onto the bed. To enable us to let Dash out whenever necessary, we'd booked a room with a wide patio door that led into the garden, its tall Scots pine trees forming a barrier between us and the road. It was lovely. Serene. Calming.

It was a beautiful room, too. Shabby chic with a silver chaise longue and muted grey furniture. I sat down on the bed, a huge affair, covered in a vintage cotton bedspread with a floral design weaved into the fabric, all white and clean and refreshing.

Colin looked round in amazement. 'Wow - April - this is lovely.'

'Expenses,' I said. 'Come on, let's get something to eat. I'm starving.'

We left Dash in the room with biscuits and a bowl of water while we walked along the Digey onto Fore Street. I found the small restaurant I'd used before, pushed open the door, and led the way downstairs to the cellar. It's a small place, intimate, with amazing food and individual service. I asked for a table for two, and the waitress showed us to one in the corner with a glowing church candle at the centre. It was ideal.

I knew we'd have a lovely meal together. And I knew we'd go for a romantic walk along the beach afterwards.

But at the same time, I was dreading it.

Colin and I both ordered the Thai-spiced chickpea stew with toasted almonds, and a side of lime and coriander cous cous. We chose an expensive Sauvignon Blanc, and a bowl of green olives to munch on while we waited for the main course.

'So, come on then. What's all this about?' asked Colin.

I sipped my wine. 'What's all what about?'

He waved an olive around. 'This. Coming down here for one day. It's not as if you can stay on, either, is it? You're driving me to Bristol first thing Monday morning, and we've got your mum's wedding on Saturday.'

I took hold of his hand. 'Colin, can we just have a nice meal, and discuss all this later? Please?'

He looked down, those lovely lashes creating a pale shadow on his cheeks. 'Okay. But I am seriously worried, April. How could I not be? This is crazy …'

'I'm sorry. I – I've got a problem and I need to get my head around it. Just give me time. Let's just enjoy this evening.'

He pulled his hand away. 'How am I supposed to enjoy this evening with that hanging over me? You're not being fair.'

I felt really bad. But I couldn't discuss it now, couldn't tell him what I'd done, couldn't admit to being the most idiotic and selfish person in the entire world.

I picked up the bottle of Sauvignon Blanc and topped up our glasses. 'There. That's how you enjoy it. You get pissed. We both get pissed.'

He grinned. 'April. You're mad.'

He took his glass, clinked it against mine, and drank.

*

Coloured lights greeted us as we stepped onto the pavement outside, our fingers icy cold while we hurriedly fastened our coats. I'd taken my grey fake fur, anticipating the weather, and a huge scarf in pink. Now I snuggled deep down into it, the cold wind not the only thing causing me to shiver.

We returned to the hotel briefly to check on Dash, fast asleep on the bed. Then we let ourselves out and walked along Fore Street onto Porthmeor Road. But I really needed to walk on the sand, so I pulled at Colin's arm, tumbled down the steps with him, then laughed and giggled as he tried to climb back up again.

'April, no - it's eleven o'clock …'

I laughed. 'And your point is?'

'Stop - I need to take my shoes off.'

Sitting onto the bottom step, he pulled at his shoes and socks, then tucked the socks inside his shoes. Much too intoxicated after two bottles of wine, I followed suit, then rolled up my jeans.

Colin stood up. 'Now what?'

I ran off. 'We paddle …'

'No. April - it'll be freezing.'

The waves lapped gently against the sand, with the occasional spurt as one was caught by the wind. Wobbling slightly, my arms outstretched, I placed one foot into the water.

'You're right,' I called. 'It is. It's bloody freezing.'

I would have placed both feet in, but he came up behind me to pull me back.

'No. Not a good idea.'

Turning round, I buried myself into him. Tears sprang from nowhere.

He hugged me tight. 'What? Come on, April, you need to tell me now. I need to know.'

So we sat on the beach, the wall of the surfboard-hire shop behind us and the sand beneath us. The wind was really biting now, but we huddled together, pulling our coats over our knees and beneath our toes to protect them from the wet sand.

And I talked.

I told him I'd been drinking, I was so drunk I couldn't even remember most of what happened. But I did remember going up to my room. I did remember waking up in the morning beside him. I did remember how awful I felt, how sick, and how I knew I would never, ever cheat on anyone ever again.

I began to cry. I cried and cried and cried, more tears than I'd ever shed in my life, other than when my dad died.

He didn't hug me, he didn't stop me, he just sat there, mute. We'd both been hugging our knees with our arms, but now his hung limply by his side, inert, traumatised, while soft tears rolled down his face.

Finally, I stood up and brushed the sand off my coat.

'It's fine if you want to stay in a different room,' I said. 'I understand. I'll pay the extra. But can we please go back now? I'm frozen.'

But he just sat there. Shocked. Eventually, he wiped his face and stood up.

'Come on,' he said. 'Let's go.'

*

He slept on the chaise longue, wrapped in the bedspread I'd been admiring earlier. Why I imagined it would all end differently, I don't know. Possibly that's why I went to Cornwall. Subconsciously, I must have thought *how could anyone not forgive someone in such a beautiful place?*

But he didn't. He didn't forgive me.

We dressed and then ate breakfast in silence.

Returning to our room, he packed his bag, picked it up, and turned to me.

'Why?'

Sitting on the bed in tears, I shrugged. 'I don't know, Colin. But I'm so, so sorry.'

'You just didn't love me enough, did you? It was your way out, wasn't it?'

I shook my head vehemently. 'No. No, it wasn't. I - I thought you were cheating on me. I thought you were with - with Natasha ...'

'Bye, April.'

He left.

He just left.

Turning onto my stomach, I cried and cried and cried. Until there were no tears left.

I fell asleep. I must have been asleep for an hour when Dash woke me up, whining to go outside.

Pulling myself from my daze, I got up, slid open the patio door, and let him out. The fresh air seeped into my lungs and I took a deep breath, breathing it in, the air and the salt and the sea.

I stepped outside, fully aware of the fact that I looked a mess. But I needed to feel the air around me, the cold wind blowing through me. I just needed to feel something. Anything.

Dash found a stick beneath the trees and brought it to me. Laughing at his wonderful naivety, I threw it back towards the trees. This time he caught it before it landed, and then time and again he caught it. As if he'd just been teasing me before.

'Dash, you're crazy - I love you,' I called, bursting into tears.

Rushing up to me, he nuzzled into my knees and I bent down to stroke him.

'Come on, sweetie, let's grab my coat, then go for a walk.'

After making myself look presentable, I fastened on Dash's lead and we walked along the seafront to the harbour. But I suddenly needed coffee. There were many cafés along the harbour road, but Fat Apples Coffee House looked so cosy and inviting with its stone walls and petite windows that I pushed open the door. A young girl stood behind the counter, the few tables in front of her devoid of customers.

'Do you allow dogs?' I asked.

She smiled. 'As long as it doesn't poop, we do.'

I laughed. 'He doesn't. He's a good dog, aren't you, Dash?'

The scent of fresh coffee was overwhelming and I breathed it in. Removing my coat and scarf, I allowed the warmth of the place to seep into me as I sat down and rubbed my frozen fingers.

'What can I get you?' asked the girl.

'Cappuccino, please. Large. And cake. What cake do you have?'

'They're here on the counter. You want to come and take a look?'

Fastening Dash's lead to the chair, I went up. There was zesty lemon drizzle, chocolate fudge, Victoria sponge, and salted caramel cake. They all looked delicious, and I was so hungry after all that crying, and being unable to eat breakfast.

So I chose the chocolate fudge cake. Of course I did.

'Small or large piece?' she asked.

'Large, please - very large. In fact, that piece there, with the chocolate curl on top.'

She grinned. 'No probs. You go and sit down.'

'Thanks.'

So I spent the next hour on my phone, on Facebook and Twitter and Instagram; all of them, in fact, whilst drinking coffee and eating cake. A message came through from Toni, then one from Sean.

Toni wanted to know if I could meet for coffee some time. I texted back:

Can I let you know? In St Ives at the mo. Me and Colin have split up. xx

Her reply was immediate.

What? You've told him? OMG April! What you gonna do now? When are you back? If you need to talk, ring me. Take care. xxx

I didn't feel like talking, not then. So I just replied.

Thanks, Toni. Speak soon. xxx

Then Sean texted, with news of the murder case.

Smith been arrested for more questioning. DI Jasper back on the case as the girl's turned up (ran off to France with the boyfriend - shoulda guessed). DIF wants to meet up?

A week ago, I would have jumped at the chance, been over the moon, overexcited. But now I wasn't so sure. I was tired. I needed a break. I needed to get away. Further away. Then a nagging little voice inside my head said, *but you want to write crime fiction, don't you? How will you do that unless you get out there and do it?*

So I texted back.

Wow! Exciting! When does she want to meet?

He took a while to reply, so I continued with my social media apps, then checked Amazon to see how my books were doing. There were some excellent reviews. So I could at least do something right, I thought. Maybe I should stick with the chick-lit?

My phone pinged.

She can make Wednesday, 2 o'clock? The station?

After some consideration, I replied.

Okay. I'm in St Ives at the mo – will come home Tuesday.

His reply was immediate.

I thought you were getting all ready for your mum's wedding? Why are you in St Ives?

Sighing loudly, I texted.

It's a long story, Sean. Will chat when I see you.

His reply was so sweet I nearly burst into tears all over again.

Hope you're okay, April. Take care. x

Giving the girl a five pound tip, I paid for my food and drink and left. I needed to walk.

*

Dash walked ahead of me as I left the harbour and headed for Porthminster Beach. I paused to admire the view. The cold wind of the morning was becoming stormy, so I wrapped my scarf around my face and peeked out from above it. Out at sea, the wind seemed to twist the waves back on themselves, churning them in and out, up and down. And despite the cold, I was mesmerised, I couldn't stop watching. There was such a beauty to them. But Dash was becoming impatient, so I continued, past the leisure centre and on, up the path and over the footbridge that crosses the railway line. There's a steep path here, and even though I'd no idea where I was heading, I took it. At the top I found a wooden bench and sat down gratefully. The wind was moaning fiercely now, forcing the berries off the holly bushes and sending them flying. Then small shards of ice began to fall to the ground, and I realised it was time to head back.

Dinner at the hotel was very good - root vegetable tatin with candied nuts & blue cheese -and I restricted myself to just the one glass of Beaujolais. I didn't fancy dessert, but asked for a bar of dark chocolate to take back to my room. Bless them - I actually think they sent someone round the block to the local supermarket, because the waiter returned ten minutes later with two bars of Green and Black's. My favourite.

It was then just a matter of getting some beauty sleep, and going through yet another dreadful day.

37

The second letter has the date as its heading. Friday 23rd November. She checks the local headlines on her phone. The day before Lucas Hanssen was killed. The other letter, the shabby one, must have been written the day after he was killed …

38

St Ives, Cornwall

IT took a few seconds after opening my eyes, but as soon as I remembered what had happened and the awful stunned, shocked look on Colin's face, my stomach tumbled. And it wasn't all the chocolate I'd eaten.

My arm was dangling from the bed, so of course Dash came up to lick my hand. I stroked him. He was soft and warm and comforting.

'Come on, let's open the door and let you out.'

But first I had to check my phone. No messages. Not one. Not one single one.

Sadly, I climbed out of bed and pulled back the heavy brocade curtains. Then I smiled. It was like a tableau, a winter tableau, the kind you see on a Christmas movie. Pine trees heavy with snow, the lawn crisp and white, the snow deep and untouched. I slid open the door. It was eerily quiet, no cars driving by, as if I was in the middle of a long silent dream.

Dash ran out, relieved himself against a tree, shook his nose in disgust, then came back inside. I laughed out loud.

'Mad dog.'

I only had my slippers on, but I couldn't resist placing one foot outside the door. I needed to feel the crunch of the snow, to see my imprint there, to know that I could just be crazy and walk through the snow in my pyjamas if I wanted to.

But I didn't. Sliding the door closed, I washed and dressed, fed Dash, and went along to the hotel restaurant for breakfast. I'd put on my old Selfridges jumper over a thermal vest and tee-shirt. Pale pink, tunic-length and pure cashmere, it made me feel warm and loved and cosy. I teamed it with tan joggers in a heavy cotton, and leather boots. I hadn't planned for snow, obviously, so that was a bit of a problem. But I'd think of something.

*

Breakfast was veggie, cooked with sautéed mushrooms and tomatoes. I sat and read while I ate. The book was a recent publication, a comedy, and just what I needed. I'd read up to page 52 and it was beginning to get really interesting. In fact, I was so engrossed it took me an hour to finish breakfast, including the three cups of tea I accepted from the waitress. She must have thought I'd never leave.

Back in the room , I kicked off my boots, lay on the bed and continued reading. I needed to immerse myself. Completely.

Then Mum rang.

'We've just been over. Where are you – out shopping, love?'

I groaned silently. 'No. I'm in St Ives, Mum.'

She practically screamed down the phone. 'What?'

'Sorry, I should have let you know. I'll be home again tomorrow, though - I won't be long. Are you okay?'

'I'm fine. I just wanted to arrange Thursday, really – my hen do. But what are you doing in St Ives, April?'

She sounded upset, so I didn't go into full detail - not over the phone.

'I just fancied a break, that's all. But look, I need to go, Mum. I'll explain everything once I'm home. Love you.'

'Okay, love, so long as you're alright. Love you, too.'

Suddenly, I needed to get out. So I forced myself from the bed, stretched out, put on thick socks, boots and coat, fastened on Dash's lead, and left.

The snow was beautiful, even though Dash hated it. But I think he sensed my change of mood, so he put up with it. We walked up to what's known as The Island, briefly admired the view of the sea, and turned back again. But all the while my mind was spinning. I felt as if my life was on hold suddenly, and all it needed was for something to happen to make me change direction, change course, change everything. Completely.

The shoe shop on Fore Street had placed a row of wellington boots outside, all of them at the most ridiculous prices and obviously taking full advantage of the weather. Nevertheless, I was interested. Anything to save my precious Russell and Bromleys. So I bought some bottle-green wellies and placed my wet leather boots inside the empty carrier bag. Then I carried on along Fore Street, turned left, and came upon The Wheelhouse, a small restaurant opposite the harbour. Seeing they accepted dogs, I decided to give it a try. Pushing open the door, however, my first thought was *Colin would love this*. Sepia pictures of sailors, and ships at sea. Crafted models of boats and lighthouses and anchors, all set high on the walls. And an old fishing net draped over the counter, intertwined with seashells and glass buoys. Colin *would* have loved it.

I chose a table near the counter and sat down, encouraging Dash to sit beneath the table and fastening his lead to the back of my chair. A young waitress appeared immediately and took my order of Bartlett pear salad and walnut bread, with a large pot of tea.

I'd begun to remove my coat and scarf when I felt someone staring at me. Turning, I found myself staring back. The woman was slim with a dark bob and deep brown eyes.

I smiled at her. 'Hi, Bethany. How are you?'

Picking up her coat and bag, she came over. 'How lovely to see you. What are you doing in St Ives? You should have called me.'

This lady was none other than Bethany Thomson, a freelance dress designer, and the owner of the cottage I rent when I escape to St Ives for proofreading. It's called Beachcomber, it's on a street called the Digey, and I just love it, with its worn stone steps and its bright blue door. Bethany, in her mid-fifties, was divorced with a son away at Oxford. After his father left, she'd never really bothered with men again. I don't quite know what happened to their relationship, but on this particular day I could certainly see her point.

I patted the chair beside me. 'Come on, sit down. Have you eaten?'

'Well, yes. I was just about to leave, but then I saw you sitting here.'

'Have you time for a drink? A tea? Coffee?'

She nodded. 'Okay, yes. I wouldn't mind an espresso – thanks. How are you doing, anyway?'

Waving at the waitress, I ordered a coffee. 'I'm fine, thank you. Actually no, I'm not fine, but that's another story. But it's good to see you. So what are you doing here?'

'Checking on the cottage. I've had the decorators in, so I've just been to make sure they've done a good job and to pay up. It looks nice.'

I grinned. 'It would look nice if you never ever decorated it again.'

We go back a long way, Bethany and I. She took a risk the first time I rented the cottage, because she could only give me a stay of five days, she said. And I'd have to put up with cobwebs and dust until the cleaners could arrive and spring-clean. They'd need two days, she said, then after that she had holidaymakers arriving. But I proved my worth by staying the week I'd intended, sending the cleaners away, and doing the job for her during the evenings. I did a good job, too, and she let me off the two days' rent. We've been friends ever since.

'So how are you?' I asked.

'I'm well, I'm fine. Getting by. I just thought I'd get this sorted while it's winter and no-one's visiting.'

I sighed heavily. 'Actually, it's quite nice being here with no holidaymakers around. Peaceful.'

She sat back. 'So come on, then. What's going on with you?'

Sudden tears filled my eyes. 'Oh, relationship problems. You know – the usual.'

'Oh, love, you're not very good at this kind of thing, are you?' She smiled. 'But I've told you before – you *can* live without them.'

'I know. I'm sorry. I'm a bit of a mess.'

'Where are you staying?' she asked.

'The Nirvana.'

'Are you here for the week?'

'No, I'm leaving tomorrow. I've got a meeting with a Detective Inspector Jasper.'

She looked at me, wide-eyed. 'You're joking. So what have you been up to?'

I grinned. 'Nothing. I'm actually assisting in a murder case. I helped with one last year, and I helped catch the perpetrator, as they call them. So DI Jasper has asked me to help out with this one.'

'Wow, April, how interesting. So what made you become involved in all that?'

'Through an old friend – he was involved in the investigation. He works for the local paper, and needed help from someone who lives in the area. Someone with insider knowledge, I suppose.'

She grinned. 'Look, this all sounds really interesting, but why not come and stay at my place tonight, then we can have a proper catch-up? I'll cook lasagne. Are you still veggie?'

I nodded. 'Okay, thanks. That would be lovely. Are you okay with dogs?'

*

It was sleeting as I left The Wheelhouse, and very cold, so I pulled up my scarf and walked quickly. I wanted to do some shopping before the day ended, but first I took Dash back to the Nirvana for his afternoon nap. Relieved to be in the warmth again, he licked my hand gratefully. So I dried his fur, gave him biscuits and a drink, and allowed him to curl up on the bed.

I stroked his head. 'There you go, sweetie. All nice and warm now. You have a nice sleep and I'll be back before you know it.'

Leaving my leather boots in the room to dry, I returned to Fore Street in my wellies and browsed through the shops. Christmas carols filled the air, coloured bulbs lit the way, and the few people about were full of the Christmas spirit, laughing and jolly, and brimming with shopping bags.

I bought a few things to cheer myself up; a fisherman's sweater in blue and ivory, a Radley shopper in red with *You Got This* in large letters (I hadn't got this, but it kind of helped), and some silver earrings in the shape of a reindeer. I also bought a twenty quid bottle of prosecco to take round to Bethany's, and a tartan coat for Dash.

By five o'clock I was ready for home. So I returned to the hotel, ordered room service – hot chocolate and toasted teacake – set my alarm, and fell asleep on the bed.

An hour later, nicely refreshed, I showered, changed, packed my case, paid my bill, and left.

The drive to Penzance seemed to take ages, but only because I drove so carefully; the snow was freezing over, and the roads were treacherous. But as I drove, my mind was churning.

I realised with a start that Colin hadn't even denied sleeping with Natasha. When I gave that as the excuse for my cheating on him, he never said anything, never denied it. He could have done. He could have said, *April - no - you're the only one for me - you must know that,* which is what he'd said before. But no, this time he didn't say a thing. Not one word.

I shivered inexplicably. So I was right. So subconsciously, I must have known he was cheating on me. Subconsciously, I must have slept with Todd to give me the excuse I needed to get out of the relationship.

Angrily, choking back tears, I gripped the steering wheel, turned onto Bethany's drive, and pulled up behind her car. But I had to sit for a few minutes, breathing deeply, calming myself, before opening the door.

Bastard.

*

Bethany's apartment was small but beautifully proportioned. On the top floor of an old terraced property, it overlooked Mounts Bay, supposed to be one of the loveliest bays in Cornwall. The apartment itself was full of trinkets collected on Bethany's travels – India, Nepal, New Zealand, Hawaii, and many others. But tonight I wasn't interested in her holidays. Tonight I was more interested in having a lovely evening with great company, numbing my mind with good food and wine, and forgetting all about Colin and Todd.

The lasagne was delicious, and afterwards we sat in front of her roaring log fire and talked. We'd moved on from the prosecco to a bottle of Beaujolais, which helped wash down the fresh fruit trifle and the box of rather expensive chocolates that appeared from Bethany's kitchen. And we talked. About everything – men, women, property, money, cars. Eventually, however, we got onto the subject of the Chatsworth murders.

'So we have a few suspects, really,' I said. 'There's Fliss, Felix's sister, for a start. She owed Felix money and couldn't afford to pay it back. Now it's possible Felix borrowed it from Lucas as he's a financial adviser. But also, Lucas and this other guy called Carl sold Felix a car a few months ago, and no money changed hands. So there's a definite link there, but we need to find out what happened to the money. Of course, Felix could have been involved in some kind of dodgy dealing, allowing him to earn enough to be able to lend thousands to his sister without borrowing from Lucas.' I stared at Bethany through a haze of alcohol. 'This is top secret, highly confidential. You do realise that?'

She grinned. 'Of course, April, not a problem. It's not like I have anyone to tell, is it?'

I shook my head. 'No, I suppose not.'

'So go on then - who else could it be? I'm intrigued.'

I had to think about that one. 'Okay - possible culprits. So there's Fliss and Felix, then there's Carl Smith, who's a real dodgeball. He and Lucas Hanssen own a motor dealership in Sheffield. When the police found a V5 document in Felix's car, they traced it back to Smith-Hanssen's. They bought the car in part-exchange and sold it onto Felix, but for some reason no money changed hands. So either they are very, very good friends and they let him have it for nothing, or the money has been hidden in some way – possibly through some kind of money-laundering. Bearing in mind the car's worth over twenty thousand quid. Oh - and Carl Smith's into drugs - I found some hidden in a drawer.'

Bethany leaned forward with interest. 'Gosh, you do lead an exciting life. Money-laundering? Drugs?'

I nodded. 'Then of course there's Gemma, Lucas's lover. And his wife, who's now pregnant with his child. They both had very good motives.'

'Especially if he told his lover he was leaving her because his wife was pregnant.'

'Or if his wife found out about the lover.'

'No. If she's pregnant, I doubt she'd have killed him – the child would need a father. I think she'd be more likely to kill the lover.'

I laughed. 'True.'

'So we have the lover, the wife, and three men who are involved in some kind of financial jiggery-pokery?'

'Yes.'

'Anyone else?'

'Not that I can think of. Of course, it could just have been a random attack. But I don't think so. I'm usually quite good at picking up on clues and stuff.'

'Are you sure about that? Your head's all over the place at the minute.'

'You're right. And I really should stop drinking this stuff.' I waved my glass around.

She smiled. 'What? You're going tee-total?'

'No chance of that. But I should cut down a bit. It's obviously not good for me.'

'If you mean because it releases your inhibitions, then that can be a good thing. Maybe you and Colin just weren't suited.'

'No, I think we were. Genuinely. I'm just not the faithful type.'

'Scared of commitment.'

'My friend Toni said exactly the same thing.'

She looked suddenly thoughtful. 'You don't think Felix killed Lucas, then drank himself to death on purpose – a kind of suicide?'

I was stunned. 'What makes you say that?'

'It would explain both deaths, wouldn't it? I mean, they happened within the same week, close to each other, so they must be related in some way.'

'I suppose it would be weird if they were completely unrelated. We've been working on the assumption that maybe someone forced Felix to drink that much. But that wouldn't be easy, would it? He was a big man, by all accounts.'

Helping herself to more wine, Bethany nodded. 'Exactly. So if we assume there was some kind of battle between them - over money or something - and it got nasty, and Felix killed Lucas, then he might have felt incredibly guilty, got pissed, and fallen into the river. Or he did it on purpose.'

'Okay?'

'Just surmising, of course. I mean, was there an actual suicide note?'

'No. But you may have a point. We just need some kind of evidence, don't we?'

'Like a fingerprint, or DNA?'

'Exactly. As I said, I'm meeting up with the police on Wednesday. Let's see what they have to say on the matter.'

She looked suddenly thoughtful. 'April?'

'Yes?'

'Are you sure you're not in the wrong job?'

'Why?'

'You face just lights up when you're discussing this case.'

'Does it? Well, it certainly gets the old adrenaline going. But no, I love my work. Although I am thinking about writing crime fiction at some point.'

'Ooh. Lovely.'

'I just need to discuss it with Sandy, my agent.' Smiling, I reached for the nearly empty bottle. 'And on that note - more wine, I think.'

39

But why were the letters written by hand, rather than texted or emailed? No-one writes letters these days. Did they write because a text or an email can be so easily traced?

40

St Ives, Cornwall

THE sun was out and the snow was melting, so there were no excuses. I had to drive back home. Bethany and I had talked well into the night, the conversation made easy by our long friendship, Bethany's good food, and of course the wine. And our conclusion regarding the Chatsworth murders? That Felix killed Lucas, got drunk, and fell into the river. Why he killed Lucas was a matter we had yet to discover. But our conclusion regarding my relationship with Colin? That I was a fool, that I really shouldn't drink so much (said Bethany with a third glass of Beaujolais in her hand), and that I really should learn to trust the men in my life.

Still no messages, no texts, no missed calls. So that was it, then.

So with fried eggs, veggie sausages, hash browns, mushrooms, tomatoes and a slice of buttered toast inside me, I packed, took Dash for a quick walk around the block, and climbed into the car.

Pushing a flask of tea into my hands, Bethany hugged me. 'Take care, and let me know once you're home.'

'I will. And thank you – it's been lovely to catch up.'

'It has. But I've got you booked in at the cottage for the end of January, haven't I?'

I nodded. 'My proofreading, yes.'

'So I'll see you then. Drive carefully now.'

I did drive carefully – all the way along the A30 to St Ives. I wasn't quite ready for home just yet. With it being December, I found it easy to find a parking spot at the railway station. So I put some money into the meter, pulled out my sunglasses, and helped Dash from the car.

I needed sea air. I needed to shed some tears. I needed some kind of closure.

Seagulls screeched overhead as I walked along the road to Porthmeor Beach, to the scene of my confession. Sitting down upon the sand, I snuggled against the wall, the one just beneath the surfboard-hire shop, the one Colin and I had sat against. And I watched the waves. For ages and ages. Their gentle swish, swish, sound was so calming, so soothing.

Then, pulling Dash towards me, I began to cry.

Self-recrimination is a wonderful thing sometimes. You really can't blame anyone else for what you've done; you can only blame yourself. And if you only have yourself to blame, then there's absolutely nothing you can do about it, except to decide it will never happen again.

I really was getting too old for one-night stands, anyway. They don't suit an older woman, even if she does still wear Gucci and Chanel, and high heels and cute pyjama shorts.

No. I needed to settle down, to start behaving myself, to stop acting like the characters in my novels.

But aren't they my inspiration, I thought? If I didn't act like them, how would I know how they feel? How would I have known what heartbreak feels like, how wonderful it is to be in love, to have someone adore you so much he'd spend a fortune on flying to Brussels and back alternate weekends, just to see you?

Oh, God ...

That set me off again, and I really couldn't stop. Luckily, the cold wind made sure the beach was deserted.

Until, eventually, I did. I did stop.

There were no tears left to cry.

So I picked myself up, dusted off the sand, and went in search of a loo. I needed to make myself presentable before I went in search of lunch. I was suddenly hungry again.

*

The drive home took me along the M5, through Exeter and Bristol, then on and on until I hit

Nottingham. Pulling in at the Trowell Services, I ordered coffee and a veggie burger. It was dark by this time, Dash was fast asleep on the back seat, and I was exhausted.

Checking my phone while I drank my coffee, I found a text from Sandy.

Did you know your first editions are up for sale - the signed ones? If you needed money, you should have said. Are you okay, darling? xx

My heart missed a beat. What the hell was going on? Whoever had stolen my books knew their worth, that was for sure. I texted back.

They were stolen from my house last week. And yes, I'm fine – just been to St Ives on a whim. Where did you see them? xx

Her reply was quick and to the point. Sandy never did like texting.

London dealer, local. Peter C Rare Books. You need to tell the police. xx

Will do. Thanks, Sandy. xx

So I rang Sheffield Police, spoke to the constable on the desk, and told him everything. He agreed to pass on the information.

My late night had begun to take its toll, so I took a quick half hour nap in the passenger seat. It did me good, and I drove the rest of the way much refreshed.

Driving through Millerstone brought me back to reality, however. To the fact that I was on my own again, that I wasn't getting any younger, that I would be hard put to find someone as loving and as kind as Colin. Miserably, I drove through deep puddles, past the Christmas trees and coloured lights of the village, and home.

The sky was dark tonight, the rainclouds were gathering in, and the moon was well hidden. So as I pulled onto the driveway, the house and garden were dark and quiet. But at least there were no neighbours out to greet me this time. Climbing out of the car, I pulled my case from the boot and released Dash from his rear seat.

I pulled on his collar. 'Come on, sweetie.'

Opening the front door, I rushed to unset the alarm.

But as the piercing noise subsided, I sensed a movement behind me. As if someone had followed me into the house. I turned, but before I could completely turn, a hand was placed over my mouth from behind. I screamed, but it became a tiny squeak.

'Quiet,' said the intruder.

A man.

Again, I tried to scream, but couldn't. So instead I opened my mouth wide and brought my teeth down hard upon his fingers.

'Fucking woman. Not a good idea,' he warned, pulling his hand away and placing it around my throat, forcing my head back.

Panicking now, my heart racing, I lifted my right leg and kicked back. But he dodged it. So, wriggling as hard as I could, I punched back with both elbows, then each of my feet, until finally he had to let go.

My first thought was to run to the front door, to get away. But I could hear Dash cowering in the corner, moaning, unsure of what was happening.

'Dash,' I called, 'come here, sweetie.'

He came up to me, fearful and unsure, so I bent to stroke him, intending to pull him away as I ran.

But my assailant kicked out with his foot, pushing Dash away and making him yelp. Then, pulling him roughly by his collar, he forced him into the lounge and shut the door.

'Don't you dare do that,' I screamed. 'He's just an innocent …'

'Fucking dog,' he muttered.

My eyes had by now adjusted to the darkness, and I realised who it was. I'd thought I could smell oil.

Carl Smith.

'You!' I said. 'You!'

Grabbing hold of my shoulders, he pushed me through the hallway and into the kitchen. Forcing me onto a chair, he stood back, closed the door, and switched on the lights.

Anger rushed through me and I stood up, throwing myself at him. 'How dare you …'

But he knocked me back, pushing me to the floor. Tears filled my eyes as pain from my right arm ran up, across my shoulder, and into my neck. Sitting up, I screamed loudly.

'Help!'

Someone had to hear me.

But there was only Dash to hear. I could hear him barking and yelping at the lounge door, scratching to get out.

'Dash,' I cried, trying to stand up.

But Smith pushed me back down again. 'Stay there, woman.'

So I lay there, helpless, in tears, yet angry as hell.

'What do you want?' I asked.

Calmly, as if I'd just invited him in for coffee, he sat down at my kitchen table.

'What I want, Miss Stanislavski, or whatever you call yourself, is for you to keep your nose out of my business.'

Outraged, I turned towards him. 'Like that's going to happen.'

He smirked, mercilessly. 'So you thought you'd get away with breaking into my premises, did you?'

'So you thought you'd get away with buying cocaine and fiddling the books, I assume?' I retorted.

He stood up, his body heaving with indignity. 'So it *was* you!'

So I had him. If I carried on, he might just let something slip.

'What was me?'

But I could hear Dash becoming more and more agitated. My head throbbing by now, I knew I had to do something. But what?

'If that dog doesn't shut up ...' he began, turning to the door.

'Just let him in here. He'll be quiet if he's with me,' I pleaded.

'What, and risk it biting me? You really do take me for a fool, don't you?'

I shook my head, but I didn't reply. Seemingly calmer now, he returned to sit at the table.

'So what is it you want from me, exactly?' I asked, rubbing my injured shoulder.

'I want to know what you know. I want to know what you've told the police.'

'Is all this because they took you in for questioning?'

Agitated at this, he ignored me and began to search through the wall cupboards. 'Ah – biscuits. Good.' Pulling out my pack of unopened ginger biscuits, he returned to the table and sat down. 'Yes. The questioning ...' He tore open the paper and ate one in silence. 'It'd go just right with a cup of tea, would this.'

I nodded towards the kettle. 'The kettle's there - help yourself - it's fine.'

He filled the kettle and switched it on. 'Teabags?'

Again, I nodded towards the box of Clippers on the side. 'There.'

He sniggered. 'Organic. Posh. I'd make you one, but you'd probably throw it at me.'

'I'm fine.'

Dash by this point had begun to squeal loudly. It seemed that every time I spoke he became more and more agitated. Tears sprang to my eyes at the thought of how he must be feeling, but I turned away quickly so Smith couldn't see. He was too busy with his tea and biscuits, anyway.

Realising this, I took the opportunity to slide myself towards the door.

Inch by inch by inch. Slowly. Imperceptibly.

He turned suddenly. 'So what I need to know is this. What made you come and raid my garage? What did you think you were doing? I only ran into your fucking car, there was no need to come and rob me.'

'I was looking for evidence.'

He walked across to me, the biscuits in his hand. 'Evidence for what? What do you think I've been doing?' Pulling out a second biscuit, he came over and crushed it onto my head forcibly. I boiled with rage as crumbs fell to the floor. 'Fucking women.'

But I resisted taking the bait. 'It's not what *I* think you've been doing. It's what the police think you've been doing. And they'll know it's you if any harm comes to me.'

'Oh. Will they, now?' Sitting cross-legged in front of me, his dirty oil-soaked trousers on my kitchen floor, he glared at me with his piggy eyes. 'And how will they do that, then? DNA? Hah – you're joking. They'd have to find your body first.'

I began to tremble. I knew he was only trying to scare me, but I couldn't help it. First my hands trembled, then all down my back. But I swallowed down my fear, sat up as best I could, and screamed again. Loudly.

'Help!'

Jumping up, he put his hands around my throat. 'You stop that right now, or …'

I stopped.

Just then, the kettle clicked off behind him, making him turn. Releasing me, he went back to his tea-making while I sat there, my mind racing. My bag, with my phone inside it, was on the floor behind me. I'd dropped it when he pushed me into the kitchen. Even if I couldn't reach the door, I decided, I could reach that. So I began inching backwards again. The movement sent waves of pain along my arm and shoulder, but I knew I had to do it.

He turned. 'You got sugar somewhere?'

I stayed stock-still. 'In the cupboard. Over there.' I pointed with my head towards the baking cupboard. 'And the spoons are in that drawer, near the kettle.'

Carrying a mug in his hand, he found a spoon and walked over to the cupboard. Holding my breath, I inched further and further away.

But suddenly, there was an explosion of noise, the door was forced open, and in came Ralph, followed by Dash.

'April?'

Running towards me, he yanked me off the floor and held me close, Dash jumping around excitedly.

I was so shocked I only glimpsed Smith scuttling past. The mug he'd been holding was in pieces on the floor, the teabag swimming in hot water.

In pain, I held onto Ralph and sobbed and sobbed. Embarrassed, he patted my back as if I were a child. 'There, there, love. Let's get you sat down, then I'll call for Pam.'

But she was coming through the door as he spoke.

'Oh my god, what's happened? Who was that just rushed out the door?'

'Don't ask.' I rubbed at my shoulder.

'Come on, love, let's get you sat down.' Easing me gently onto a chair, she checked me over. 'Now then – where does it hurt?'

*

I pulled out the treats tin for Dash. He so deserved them. If it hadn't been for his whining and barking, Ralph would never have checked the house. As it was, he was taking his evening walk when he heard Dash barking loudly. So, seeing my Mini parked on the drive, he peered through the window and questioned why the tree lights weren't on, and why the curtains weren't closed if Dash and I were home. And then he saw my key still in the lock.

Ralph rang the police and they came to take a statement. He and Pam stayed with me until they arrived, and stayed with me even after they'd gone. I opened a bottle of Merlot – for our nerves – and Pam applied arnica gel to my bruises. There was nothing broken, thank goodness, so I just took some paracetamol for the pain.

Then I texted Bethany. She'd asked me to let her know once I was home, so I did. I would normally have rung, but I just couldn't face telling her about the assault. Not yet. It would have opened a floodgate I wasn't quite ready to handle. So I texted.

Hi Bethany. Home safe. Thank you for a fab evening. See you in January. Dash says hello. And Merry Christmas! xx

Her reply was short and sweet; it was late, after all.

Glad you're home. Lovely to see you. Merry Christmas and Happy, Happy New Year! xx

'Do you want us to stay with you? I can bring some blankets?' asked Pam, kindly.

But I shook my head. 'No - thank you - I'll be fine. You've been wonderful for staying with me this long, but I've got Dash here. And the police are on his trail now - he won't dare come back. I'll be fine, I promise.'

'Well, we're only next-door but one. So just ring me if you're unsure.'

I smiled. 'Thanks, Pam - you're very kind.'

'Eeh, but you've had a bit of a week, haven't you?' said Ralph. 'What with the break-in and everything?'

'Did they find out who it was?' Pam asked.

'No, not yet. But someone in London is advertising the books for sale – the ones that were stolen. I've let the police know.'

'Goodness. That didn't take long, did it?'

'They obviously know what they're doing. Signed first editions can fetch a pretty penny,' said Ralph.

Pam stood up to carry her glass to the sink. 'We'll be getting off then - it's way past my bedtime. But I'll leave my phone switched on, so if you need us, you ring.'

'Thanks, Pam. I don't know what I'd have done if you …'

She hugged me. 'Now don't. I'm just glad we were here to help.'

After they'd gone, I passed through each room in turn. I checked the locks on every window and on each exterior door. I pulled every curtain across and left lights on in two of the bedrooms. So it didn't look as if I was there on my own. By the time I'd finished, my hands were shaking.

I opened another bottle of the Merlot, poured myself a glass, and carried it into the study. Then I did what I really needed to do.

I wrote.

The play I'd begun weeks ago, the two-parter, was just waiting to be finished.

So I put a match to my candles, wrapped my blue cardigan around my shoulders, and I wrote.

The ending came to me in a flash.

The director's wife's revenge is perfect. She writes her own play, a true story about the director of a professional theatre company who hires prostitutes and brings them back to the theatre after rehearsal. The script exactly mirrors her husband's misdemeanours, even using his real name. It takes her a while, but once it's finished, she prints a copy and leaves it on her husband's desk in an envelope. That weekend, he deigns to read it. She threatens to send it to the local radio company; they're always crying out for scripts. Unless, of course, he confesses all, and agrees to a divorce that allows her to keep everything. He refuses, and in doing so reveals that he only married her for her money. She says she knew that, but then she only married him because she wanted children. She also tells him that all her property, which is still in her name, has just been put into trust for them. So he won't get a penny. Et cetera, et cetera.

It was three o'clock by the time I'd finished.

My mind was now exhausted enough to sleep, so I blew out the candles, woke up Dash, and climbed up the stairs to bed.

41

The first letter was written by Lucas. Says he wants to end their relationship. Says his wife is expecting a baby. Says there's no way he can leave Katie now. Says he's really sorry …

42

Millerstone, Derbyshire

THE trees were beautiful, the dusting of snow on their bare branches giving them a painterly look. And the sky was a deep blue, not a cloud anywhere. My walk would have been heavenly, if only I'd felt at peace. But I didn't. I didn't feel at peace. I was in a state of shock. From Carl Smith's little episode. From ending it with Colin. And from not hearing a word from him. Not one word.

I'd been running late that morning after my ridiculously busy night, so I'd thrown on joggers and a sweater over my pyjamas (getting to be a habit), slung on my coat, and chased Dash up Coggers Lane. It was bitterly cold, so I'd pulled my scarf up over my face and walked as quickly as I dared on the icy surface.

But my head was spinning. I felt totally bereft, my throat tight and my stomach the same. Not even

Dash could lift my mood. I allowed him to race ahead, but he'd turn back now and then to make sure I was still there.

Back home, I fed Dash and put out food for Marmalade. Then I turned on the radio to fill the kitchen with music and chat while I stirred at my porridge. I needed the noise - the house seemed much too quiet otherwise. There was a sense of dread about the place, as if Smith had left behind this awful, evil mark. I had no idea what he'd have done if Ralph hadn't intervened, and my mind spun with thoughts of it.

He could have killed me.

My overactive imagination never helps in these circumstances, and I had to stop myself from overthinking, which is not easy. So, to the sound of *Driving Home for Christmas*, I determined to redecorate the kitchen come the New Year. Fresh colours, pale blues and greys – that's what was needed. And the blue Italian tiling from Messina I'd had fitted a couple of years ago would blend in nicely.

*

I wore my old tweed jacket and hat to drive to Sheffield police station. The jacket is one I bought in Paris many years ago, so it feels comforting, like an old friend. I found it at the back of a small boutique, just off rue Gabrielle in Montmartre. The place was choc-a-bloc with British tweed, all imported from London. Jackets, trousers, waistcoats, suits, hats and gloves, even bedroom slippers. I must have spent over an hour in there, but I left with *the* most amazing jacket. Turquoise, narrow lapels, three large wooden buttons in rose pink, and a pink silk lining to match. It cost nearly five hundred euros, but was it worth it. And I've worn it so much now that it really is an old friend. But the hat is a pink Baker Boy cap that's not so old. Of course, I had to have it because it matches the buttons on the jacket perfectly.

Anyway, I digress. As usual.

So I drove out of Millerstone towards Toad's Mouth Rock, then up to Fox House, where I turned left to drive into Sheffield. The trees either side of me were coated in a frosty white; you could tell which way the snow had been blowing. But they looked pure and simple, and somehow rejuvenating. And as I parked up near the police station, I did feel slightly better. My mood was lifting, possibly because I was doing something positive, something meaningful. I was helping out.

The station, a huge red brick building, was busy as I walked into the reception area. But Sean was there waiting for me, and after receiving ID badges from the sergeant on Reception, we walked through to DI Jasper's room. She welcomed us in with coffee and biscuits, and we stood before a long table with chairs either side, unoccupied except for two men.

'I'd just like to introduce you all,' she said. 'This is DCI Tom Watkins, who's heading the investigation.'

Indicating a tall, middle-aged guy, clean shaven with a balding head, she then introduced another, this one in his thirties, blonde, skinny and enthusiastic-looking. 'And this is DI Charlie Sellars. Guys, this is April Stanislavski and Sean McGuire. Sean's senior crime reporter for the Sheffield Star and April is a writer, but also Sean's partner-in-crime, so to speak. They've been helping with the case, and I'm here to fill everyone in, to ensure we're all working from the same page.' She sat down at this point, and we both followed suit.

DCI Watkins checked the notes on his open laptop before proceeding. 'First of all – I'm very pleased to meet you both. And I hope once we've put our heads together, we can successfully bring this case to a close.'

'So, if we can begin with Forensics,' said DI Jasper, sipping her coffee.

Nodding, he again checked his notes. 'Okay. So we have Lucas Hanssen, a financial adviser. Business is doing well. His wife's a locum pharmacist, now pregnant with their first child. On the night of the murder she was in New York attending a seminar covering immunisation and its side effects - we checked it out. She was due to fly home the following Thursday, but after hearing of Hanssen's death she cut short her visit.' Pausing, he checked his notes again. 'Now, Hanssen also had a lover. But his wife has no idea and we'd prefer to keep it that way for the time being. The lover, Gemma Jameson, was also away the night of his murder – in London with a girlfriend. We've checked out her story too, and there's CCTV showing them at the Piccadilly Theatre - they went to a show on the Saturday night.'

'So there's no woman scorned, as far as we can tell,' murmured DI Jasper.

'Correct. Now Hanssen, like Jameson, was into amateur dramatics – that's where they met,' continued DCI Watkins. 'He was rehearsing with Cavendish Amateur Dramatics at Chatsworth House the night he was killed. Forensics have time of death as between nine and ten pm. The weapon used was a stainless steel paring knife, the type you'd find in any kitchen. We found it near the murder scene, but there were no fingerprints. So - premeditated or not?'

'It was a cold evening,' I suggested. 'They could just have been wearing gloves.'

He nodded. 'Possibly. Now, the angle of entry would suggest the knife was pushed in from below. So possibly someone smaller than Hanssen, or someone who'd fallen over and came at him from that position. Which leads us to two suspects, both of whom had a possible axe to grind.'

Cupping my coffee mug in my hands, I leaned forward with interest.

'First of all, there's Carl Smith.'

My stomach churned suddenly.

Here, DI Jasper picked up the baton. 'He's currently in custody after forcing his way into April's house yesterday. We shall charge him with unlawful entry and assault, but not just yet. The fact is we have more against him than he knows, so we need to interview him in regard to the murder of Hanssen. We know already there was some kind of deal going on between Smith, Hanssen and another guy, Felix Porter-Bentley, who was head forester at Chatsworth House. Porter-Bentley was also found dead, the same week as Hanssen, and both within a mile of each other.'

DCI Watkins continued. 'So Hanssen and Smith were joint owners of a car dealership in Sheffield. They sold a Mitsubishi Shogun to Porter-Bentley in October, and should have charged over twenty thousand pounds for it. He part-exchanged his previous car, which was worth around eight thousand, so he would have owed them roughly twelve thousand pounds. But CID have trawled through bank accounts left right and centre, and we've been unable to trace any money changing hands. Now Smith's defence is that Porter-Bentley was going to pay them for the car in November, but never did. He said Porter-Bentley then told them he was having problems getting the money together and would have to defer payment for another two months. But again, there's no trace of him trying to borrow the money – we've searched everywhere.'

He sipped his coffee. 'Now if Porter-Bentley did owe Smith and Hanssen money for the car, and there was some kind of disagreement between him and Hanssen, then there may have been a fight of some kind. Another explanation, of course, may be that Hanssen or Smith already owed Porter-Bentley money for something, and the car was given as payment in lieu of cash.'

I turned to Sean to see what he thought of the idea, but he was listening intently.

DI Sellars leaned forward to gain our attention. 'So – we know Hanssen sold cocaine to his fancy friends, because one of the amdram group confessed to buying from him. But we don't know who supplied him. Now it's just possible, given Porter-Bentley's links with the US – he grew up there - and the fact that trace elements of coke were found in his body, that he was the one who bought and sold the stuff, but we're still checking that out. So far the FBI have traced a couple of bank accounts in the names of Porter-Bentley's ex-wife and his daughter. Both of which they apparently know nothing about. But there's a guy out there called Garcia, a long-time pal of Porter-Bentley's and a known drug dealer. The FBI have been onto him for a while, but they've been sitting back waiting to catch the bigger fish. But it's looking like Porter-Bentley has been using these fake bank accounts, and maybe others, to clean the money he sent to friend Garcia.'

DI Jasper interjected. 'So what if Hanssen buys cocaine from Porter-Bentley and sells it on, covering his tracks with some kind of investment portfolio? Then what if he's owed money by someone who's suddenly unable to pay? And what if Porter-Bentley needs this money to pay his supplier Garcia, and Hanssen can't get it for him? Now that one time he was able to give Porter-Bentley a car in lieu of the money, but what if there's another time, and he's unable to cough up?'

'Also,' said DCI Watkins, 'there's the possibility that Porter-Bentley knew about Hanssen's extra-marital shenanigans and threatened to blackmail him if he didn't pay up. There's always potential for blackmail when you're hiding dirty little secrets like that.'

DI Sellars nodded in agreement. 'So Hanssen leaves the rehearsal without getting changed first, because he's been threatened and needs to stop Porter-Bentley in his tracks.'

'But he doesn't have the money,' said Sean, 'says it's going to be a while. So it gets nasty, and Felix pulls out the knife he'd brought just to threaten him. But then it gets out of hand.'

DCI Watkins nodded. 'You've got it.'

'So what happens now?' I asked.

'We still have some GPS tracking to do, but it shouldn't be too long before we get some results. Hanssen actually had two phones - he used a pay-as-you-go to speak to the lover. But we have them both and are working on them as we speak.'

'What about Felicity Porter-Bentley? Is she involved at all?' I asked.

'Only as far as the loan her brother gave her,' said DI Jasper. 'He lent her a hundred thousand two years ago, on the understanding she paid him back at five hundred a month. But she was struggling, the business not doing well, and then in June she stopped paying.'

'She did say she'd moved out of her flat to save money, and that Felix was happy to wait until she was back on her feet,' I said.

She nodded. 'That's true. But it's a large chunk of money. What if Felix had borrowed it from Lucas and was paying interest on it? Then couldn't pay it back because Fliss stopped paying? If that's the case, there's always the possibility that Lucas bought drugs from Felix, but refused to pay up because he already owed him on the loan. There are a lot of ifs and buts here, but it's definitely looking like there was potential for disagreement over money.'

'So we're checking GPS,' said DCI Watkins. 'We're checking out Porter-Bentley with the FBI, and we're looking further into the affairs of Smith and his shady car dealership.'

'When do we get to find out?' I asked.

He looked hopeful. 'I'm hoping by tomorrow or Friday. I'd like to get this case wrapped up before Christmas.'

*

Sean and I left the station together, our heads full of what-ifs and what-abouts. The air was icy cold and I pulled my jacket close.

'Come on, let's grab a coffee or something before we head home,' said Sean, taking my arm. 'You looked dead miserable in there.'

I didn't need asking twice, and we headed towards the Library Café, a favourite of Sean's. It's smart, intellectual, with clean lines, modern in orange and black, and has good food.

'Cappuccino?' he asked.

I nodded. 'Yes, please.'

'Chocolate fudge cake?'

I grinned. 'You know me far too well, Sean McGuire.'

So, a few minutes later, he returned with the coffee and cake. Both were irresistible, and I breathed in deeply at the rich scent of freshly ground beans.

'Thank you, Sean.'

'My pleasure. So – come on – tell Uncle Sean all about it. What were you doing in the middle of St Ives the week before your mum's wedding?'

I hesitated, could barely say the words. Then I said, 'Colin and I have split up.'

He looked shocked. 'Oh, April, I am sorry. So what happened?'

I looked at him carefully. Could I trust him not to judge me, not to think me cheap and tarty and utterly deplorable?

I decided I could.

'I cheated on him, Sean. A one-night stand. A complete mistake.'

His face seemed to curve in on itself. I think he was actually trying not to cry.

'Oh, April, what the hell ...'

Blinking back my own tears, I looked away. 'I know.'

'And there's no way back?'

I shook my head. 'No. It's over.'

'You want to talk about it?'

I shook my head. 'No. Not really. But thanks.'

He patted my hand. 'Come on, eat up and we'll go for a walk – get some air, make you feel a bit better.'

So we walked through the streets of Sheffield in the dark. The Salvation Army Band was singing *Joy to the World* in glorious tones of silver and gold outside the Town Hall. Huge coloured bulbs hung from the sky, and the aroma of spices drifted from market stalls specially set up for Christmas. People stopped and bought from huge plates of paella and curry and chicken stew, and small children ran about, too excited to stand still. A rush of warmth surged through my heart, and I did, finally, begin to feel better.

'Sorry, Sean,' I murmured, as we stood in the queue of a fudge stall.

'For what?'

'For being a miserable cow.'

'Never a miserable cow, April – just an unsettled angel.'

I laughed. 'Hah! I'm no angel, that's for sure.'

'You could be if you tried hard enough. You just don't know what it is you want.'

I pecked him on the cheek. 'You're so sweet – you know that?'

He grinned. 'Come on, let's not bother with fudge. It's bad for us, anyway. Let's get back home. I imagine you've got work to do, and so have I. Newspaper articles don't write themselves.'

*

And so it was that I drove home, opened the door, and found Dash fast asleep in his basket. Opening his eyes, he looked up at me mournfully.

'Poor Dash. Sorry I've left you so long, sweetie. It was only meant to be a couple of hours. Come on then, let's go for a quick walk.'

Removing my lovely jacket and hat, I replaced them with my blue duffle coat and scarf. It was too dark to walk up to Stanage, so we walked down the hill into the village. Some of the local children were walking along, carrying torches and small buckets ready to go carol-singing. I pulled some pound coins from my pocket and threw them into the bucket.

'Thank you,' one of them shouted. 'Merry Christmas.'

I threw him a big smile. 'And to you. Have a good one.'

I walked as far as School Lane and then turned back. The village looked beautiful from here, the Christmas tree lights hanging like diamonds, the life-size Nativity scene lit up in the distance. People of the village assemble here every Christmas Eve to sing carols and to listen to the words of the local priests. The Catholic, the Methodist, and the Parish churches all come together as one. It's a wonderful service, a magical start to the celebrations, and we attend every year – me, Mum, Jo, Joe and the girls. And now, I thought, Jim would be joining us.

Sighing deeply, I smiled to myself. There was life after this. There had to be life after this.

Just then, my phone pinged.

Hi April. I hope you are well. Just to let you know I've read your very first novel. Any chance you'd be interested in writing the screenplay? Would love for it to be a film. Please say yes.

Love, Todd xx

43

The second letter was written by Felix. Says he still loves her, could have given her everything. Marriage, children, everything. Says he can't live without her. And now she's done what she has done, how can he?

44

Millerstone, Derbyshire

TODAY was so cold that even Marmalade ventured into the kitchen. Dash wasn't too sure about him at first, but begrudgingly allowed him to curl up beneath the radiator. Poor thing. I think he'd been out all night. I fed him a pouch of chicken-flavoured Whiskas and left him to sleep while I ate my porridge. Afterwards, Dash and I wrapped up (he was loving his tartan coat) and went for our usual walk, even though I couldn't set the intruder alarm. We didn't intend taking a long walk and besides, not even a burglar would work on a day like today.

The sun was shining, despite the cold wind, and I found by the time I returned home I had much more energy than when I'd set off. I'd been awake since five, the howling wind and my ghastly thoughts both conspiring against me, so it was good to have that new energy.

Marmalade had formed a small puddle on the kitchen floor while we were out, but it couldn't be helped. I just mopped it up and told him not to do it again. He was such a lovely cat, though. Heavy with fur, but with gorgeous golden eyes that looked at you as if you didn't know what on earth you were doing. And sometimes I don't. Obviously.

So after checking my emails, I set to and made lunch for us all. Dash had tuna and gravy (he loves it, honestly), Marmalade had a saucer of milk, and I had an omelette of eggs, red pepper, spring onion and Stilton. Delicious.

The doorbell rang then, and I took delivery of a magnum of champagne from Sandy. She sends the same every Christmas and every birthday, for all of her clients. But that put me in the mood for Christmas suddenly. So I rushed upstairs and pulled out the bags of presents I'd bought that inauspicious day in Leeds.

Stoking up the fire in the lounge, I switched on the telly. Amazon Prime had *Love Actually* available, so I sat and watched as I wrapped. So there I was, kneeling on the lounge floor in front of a roaring fire, wrapping my gifts in brown wrapping paper, with a big smile on my face. Never underestimate the power of a rom-com. I used rubber stamps and an ink pad to cover the gifts in Christmas trees, snowmen, baubles, and angels. There was perfume for Jo, Vicky and Toni, shirts for Rebecca and Daisy, fragrance for Joe and Sean, the lemon cashmere for

Mum, and finally the sweater and fragrance for Colin. Just in case.

I stamped each present carefully, in neat rows, so it looked professional. A neatly-tied satin ribbon in red held a name tag that I'd cut from the previous year's cards, and there I had it – environmentally-friendly parcels. I was feeling warm and cosy by this time, and slightly optimistic. After all, Colin wasn't the type to just leave it like that. Was he? Surely he'd want to sit down and talk, because that was the kind of man he was. He liked to discuss things, get them out in the open. Didn't he?

I piled up the presents beneath the tree and stretched out my legs from their kneeling position. Dash stretched and yawned, and I went to stroke him.

'Come on, then, sweetie. A nice cup of tea.'

The kitchen was now cold and unfriendly, and Marmalade was mewing at the door trying to get out. I let him out with a 'Take care now, Marmie', and put the kettle on. I just fancied settling down with a good book, because I needed to take my mind off Todd's offer. It was an amazing opportunity and would secure my career for years, but it was a tough decision and one I needed to spend time over.

Then my phone rang. It was Sean.

'Can I pop over? We have a decision on the case, and I thought you'd want to know.'

'That's brilliant, Sean. Yes, it's fine. But why can't you tell me now?'

'Thought I'd come and see you. I've bought you a present.'

I grinned. 'That's nice. I've got one for you, too.'

'Thank you - that's very kind of you. Would four o'clock be okay? I've got a few things to catch up on before I finish for Christmas.'

'No problem. But I'm out tonight, so it can't take too long.'

'I'll see you later, then.'

The mention of presents panicked me, as I realised suddenly that I hadn't ordered flowers for Sandy. I send them every Christmas, but usually I'm so much more organised. Quickly, I went online and ordered lilies to be delivered the following day. I had to pay the most ridiculous price for postage, having left it until the last minute, but at least it was done and I could relax and wait for the kettle to boil.

I studied my kitchen. Boring brown tiles on the floor, an even more boring white sink, and murky cream wallpaper. I'd never updated it since moving in, other than the wall tiles, which had been pretty desperate, if I'm honest. I'd only got around to doing the bathroom the previous year, but it was now a delightful palette of bright sunshine yellow (my new roll-top bath, painted in Farrow and Ball), white tiles, and grey limestone on the floor. It has old-fashioned silver taps, the kind you find in Parisian hotels, and I absolutely love it.

But the kitchen was in definite need of an update, whether or not Smith had left his mark. So before

Sean arrived, I rang Bob Prendergast, my local DIY guy.

His kind, weather-beaten face popped round the back door ten minutes later.

'Here, I've brought you some mince pies,' he said. 'Linda's just made them, fresh out the oven.' He handed me a battered old tin depicting Duchy of Cornwall shortbread.

'Thank you, Bob, that's very kind of you. How's Linda doing?'

He came to sit at the table while I made tea for us both. 'Oh, she gets on with it, you know. And the medication helps a lot.'

Bob had been a member of the Village Players for years, helping with the set and the lighting. That's how I got to know him. But he left when his wife became ill. Linda has MS, and for a while she was housebound. But with this new medication she manages to get out and about, and life is nearly back to normal for them.

Bob and I chatted for a while, each taking a mince pie to eat with our tea. He gave me a final quote for renovating the kitchen and I accepted. I don't need to shop around when it comes to Bob's quotes. He's always very reasonable, and anyway I like to help out.

So we decided on pale greys and soft blues, with grey marble worktops and a grey granite sink. The floor was to have marble tiles, polished and white. Clean and fresh and bright, and no expense spared.

'There,' said Bob, putting away his pen and paper. 'We're done.'

'Thanks for coming over, Bob. It was a spur of the moment decision, but you've been really helpful.'

'Well, it's that house I did recently, you know. Up the Dale. Very posh it is. Beautiful. Same colours as you're wanting, so we might as well do the same, don't you think?'

I smiled. 'And why not?'

'Better get back, then. That tree won't be decorating itself.'

'Well, have a lovely Christmas, Bob, and give my love to Linda.'

He nodded. 'You too, April. Merry Christmas.'

*

Sean and I sat in the lounge. I'd made decaf coffee and we munched our way through Linda's mince pies.

'Nice pastry,' said Sean. 'Thank you.'

'I didn't make them. It's Bob Prendergast's wife from the village - he's just been here to price up a new kitchen for me and he brought them round. But yes, she's an excellent cook.'

'Pastry not too thick. Just how I like them.'

'So, come on then,' I said. 'What's been happening?'

He took a sip of coffee. 'Right. So we've had the GPS results from Lucas's phones, but they found no unusual activity of any kind. And it would appear that Felix's phone was switched off on the Saturday, or had run out of battery, so there's no joy there. But he's well-known around Chatsworth and Baslow, so the police have been able to trace his whereabouts anyway. He was definitely at the Wheatsheaf in Baslow until nine o'clock on the night of Lucas's death and we have no idea of his tracks after that, but he definitely left at nine.'

'That's not telling us a lot,' I moaned.

'Ah - but - they've also found some fibre on Lucas's jacket, the one he was wearing when he died. It's miniscule, but they've traced it back to a green knitted jumper.'

'Oh – that's more like it.'

'They haven't been able to trace it, but Felix's workmates say he used to wear one around the estate a lot, that it was an old favourite. So maybe he got blood on it or something, and destroyed it. But we can assume from this that Felix and Lucas met while Lucas was still in costume. And the only way that could happen ...'

'Is if he met him that night.'

'Exactly.'

'Okay. So we think there was some kind of a fight.'

He nodded. 'Over drugs or money. Or both.'

'So what happened to Felix after that, do we know?'

'He must have charged up his phone, because we have GPS again from the Sunday afternoon. He was at home on the Sunday, and appeared to be working on the Monday as normal. Went to the pub for one pint, as usual – we checked with the landlord. Drove around the estate, as usual. The only unusual thing was on the Tuesday, presumably after news leaked out about Lucas.'

'What was that?'

'He didn't go into work. Apparently, he never, ever missed work - was very conscientious - didn't even ring in on this occasion. From the GPS, it looks as if he stayed home in Baslow until lunchtime, visited the local Spar - we think to get booze - then walked around Chatsworth for a while, ending up in the river.'

'So, he heard about Lucas's body being found, knew we'd catch up with him eventually, couldn't face the consequences, so decided to do the deed.'

He shrugged his shoulders. 'Unless he just got pissed, didn't actually mean to fall into the river. It could have been an accident.'

'I suppose. So what happens now?'

'DI Jasper is in conference as we speak. They're currently of the opinion that Felix killed Lucas in a fight, and then died either by committing suicide, or through accidental death caused by alcohol consumption. Anyway, they've released his body. It's the funeral tomorrow.'

'Just before Christmas as well. Poor Fliss. Is she still around, do you know?'

He nodded. 'She's organising the cremation.'

'So sad.'

'He's not actually that nice a character, April. He does have form, you know.'

I was surprised, after the way Fliss had described him. 'What?'

'Over in the States. He was charged twice with Aggravated Assault and Battery. It's never stuck though, because people were too scared to testify. Apparently, the laws in Wyoming can be quite lax, and they tended to treat his little paddies as a mere squabble between friends.'

'Bloody hell.'

'That drugs haul in Monyash was found in an old lockup, by the way. But it's nothing to do with Lucas or Felix. It was rented out by someone entirely different, nothing to do with this case.'

'Crikey. We have no idea, do we, of what's going on right beneath our noses? But Sheffield police have done amazingly well, and in so short a time.'

'It's all a bit late now, though – the murderer is dead. And you helped too, you know. You uncovered quite a case when you found Lucas Hanssen.'

'I did, didn't I? But it was Dash who found him. Wasn't it, Dash?'

Hearing his name, Dash came running up. 'Good boy, aren't you?' I turned to Sean. 'So will there still be a prosecution of some kind?'

'I'm not too sure. I suppose there's no point in prosecuting someone posthumously – the idea of prosecution is to act as a deterrent. Besides, it's a waste of public money. Obviously, the FBI will look further into this Garcia guy in the US, but other than that, that's it. We've got the killer.'

'And what about Smith? What's happening with him?

His face hardened. 'He's still in custody. He's going to be done for - hopefully - drug-trafficking, money-laundering, tax evasion, unlawful entry, assault, prostitution, aiding and abetting - you want me to go on?'

A shiver ran through me. 'To think he's been here. In my kitchen.'

'He'll be locked up for quite a while, I'd say. You certainly won't be seeing him again.'

I smiled. 'That's just what I wanted to hear, Sean. So, another case ticked off the list. In that case, it's Christmas pressie time.'

He jumped up. 'Of course, yes.' Pulling a small package from his jacket pocket, he passed it to me. 'Here you go. Merry Christmas, April.'

I just love small packages; they always contain the best presents. However, I did feel slightly embarrassed. I'd only bought Sean some smellies.

'Go on – open it then,' he insisted.

So I undid the perfect red wrapping paper and pulled out the box. Lifting the lid, I found a pair of earrings. They were made of enamel, and they were beautiful. Deep blue ovals, with an ivory-white elephant on each one, its eyes old and wise, its trunk curled high into the air.

I blinked back sudden tears. 'Oh – Sean.'

'Hey, I didn't mean to make you cry. I just saw them and they reminded me of our last case. Yes?'

I nodded. 'Yes. Thank you. They're beautiful.'

Our previous case had involved a burglary victim called Dr Jani. We had to call at her house and she'd had the most beautiful silk rug hanging above her mantelpiece. It had displayed just such an elephant and we loved it so much that Sean and I, individually and without knowing about the other, bought similar rugs for our own homes. Mine still hangs above my bed.

Removing my silver earrings, I placed the new ones through my earlobes and checked them in the mirror. They were perfect.

I pecked Sean on the cheek. 'Thanks, Sean. I love them.'

He beamed. 'My pleasure, partner-in-crime.'

I laughed at that. 'DI Jasper does have a strange turn of phrase sometimes.'

Stretching my arm beneath the sofa, I pulled out my present for Sean.

'Merry Christmas, Sean.'

*

Pulling up outside Mum's house, I glanced at the clock. Six-thirty. I'd just made it. Dinner after Sean left had been a quick penne pasta with tomato sauce from a jar. Then I'd showered and changed into smart navy trousers, a Gucci silk blouse in pink, and pink heels. All set for Mum's hen night at Sheffield's

Crucible Theatre. We were going to watch My Fair Lady, a favourite of hers, then finish off with a couple of drinks at the Flying Toad. I couldn't wait. I was so ready for a fun night out after the trials of the past two weeks.

I knocked at the door to find Mum in her crimson dress and shoes, a brown faux fur thrown over the top. She was so excited she could barely speak. But Jo made up for her, chattering on about Christmas and the girls, and the presents she'd bought.

'Nice outfit, April,' she said, eventually.

I grinned. 'Thank you. I try my best. You look lovely, too.'

'Oh, I bought this last year for that gardening exhibition I did in Kensington.'

'Ooh. Kensington. Posh.'

'Come on, you two - I'm so excited,' cried Mum, taking hold of my arm. 'I just can't wait to hear all those beautiful songs.'

'You're all set for Saturday, then?' I asked.

'You try holding her back,' said Jo. 'I've not seen her so happy in years.'

'Wish I could say the same for you, April, my darling,' murmured Mum. 'You look like you've found a penny and lost a pound.'

I sighed heavily. 'I'll tell you all about it tomorrow, Mum.'

We climbed into the car and I pushed into first gear.

'No,' she said, patting me on the knee. 'I want you to tell me now, or I'll be worrying all evening and it'll spoil it.'

So I told them. About Todd, and about Colin, and about how I just couldn't hold down a relationship, even if it was with the most perfect man on earth.

'You need some kind of counselling, love,' said Mum.

'You definitely need your head looking at,' said Jo, from the back seat.

'Thanks, Jo.'

'No probs. But seriously, why would you jump into bed with someone you've only just met?'

'I was drunk, Jo. And yes, it was a mistake. And yes, I'm really sorry.'

'It's not like you're ever going to see him again. You live here, he works in Leeds, and he lives in London.'

'Actually, that's where you're wrong,' I said.

'What?'

'I might see him again. He's asked if I want to make one of my books into a film.'

'Wow.'

'That's very nice, dear,' said Mum. 'But I hope you've turned him down.'

I changed gear as we climbed the hill towards Surprise View. 'I haven't replied yet. I can't decide.'

'It's a fab opportunity, though,' said Jo. 'Which book?'

'The first one - *Love in the Valley*. And if it's successful, who knows?'

'Sounds like you're talking yourself into it,' she said.

'I suppose I am,' I replied.

'Rubbish title. You'd have to change it.'

45

Tears fill her eyes. Is it really her daughter, her very own daughter? She'd had no idea Amber was dating someone called Felix. She had stayed out overnight occasionally, and there was that big green jumper she wore that obviously belonged to a man. But she'd never interfered, never asked questions. After all, Amber was twenty-three now, a grownup, a young woman. So did she date Felix, then finish with him for Lucas? And did she really, really kill Lucas because he wouldn't leave his pregnant wife? How could she? Her own daughter? How on earth could she?

And if she did actually kill him, did she then confess all to Felix, causing him to commit suicide? What a terribly sorry state of affairs ...

46

Millerstone, Derbyshire
CHATSWORTH House was closed for Christmas. No cars, no coaches, no visitors. Just peace and quiet. I parked in my usual place, put on my walking boots, cashmere scarf and gloves, pulled Dash from the car, and walked.

Bobbles of ice littered the ground around us, the grass stiff and frozen, the mud rutted and hard. Undeterred, Dash raced on, pulling at his lead excitedly.

'Calm down, Dash,' I cried. 'Not easy, walking on this ...'

He did slow down, and we carried on towards the river and Chatsworth House, the Cascade creating a beautifully picturesque backdrop. But the sky was grey, heavy with snow, and I prayed it wouldn't arrive before tomorrow - Mum and Jim's wedding day.

And as I walked, I thought about Todd's offer. Should I accept it? Should I even renew our friendship, if that's what it was? Or should I accept it, but keep the whole thing on a strict business footing? How *would* it all end?

We walked for half an hour until I was warm and breathless and nicely refreshed. I needed to get home - I had things to do before Mum's big day.

As for Todd, I would accept his offer, but keep it professional. After all, he was miles away, so there was no way we could have a romantic liaison if we wanted one.

And as for Colin - well, not a word, not a sound. It was breaking my heart, but I'd cheated on him and that was that. No-one could blame him for leaving me.

But Christmas was going to be a miserable affair this year. We'd been planning to spend it at his place, but now it looked like I'd be staying over at Jo's with the girls. It would be fun, yes, but not quite the same. Although it would be fun reminiscing, something Jo was always good at. She'd be going on about how Dad would insist on making Christmas dinner, even though he never quite cooked the potatoes correctly, according to Mum. But it did mean Mum could spend Christmas morning with us, eating chocolates and watching films on the telly. Then every so often we'd call Dad through to open another present. They weren't amazing presents, we weren't rich, but they never failed to delight. Warm gloves and hats, tiny bottles of sweets, and tins of toffee with embossed pictures on the front that made you run your fingers over them time and time again. Then of course there'd be presents from Gramps and Grandma, Nannie and Grandad. Hand-knitted sweaters or dresses, and huge chunks of chocolate and packets of jelly babies. They would all call round after lunch to celebrate with a glass of sherry and a chocolate from the Roses tin ...

But I digress. As usual.

Dash stopped for a wee beside a beautiful oak, and I took the opportunity to check my phone. Sean had texted.

Police found stash of cocaine in remote shed in grounds of Chatsworth. Shed used solely by Felix for work. And you were right – Fliss was buying from him. He'd leave it with her friend in Aberystwyth, and she'd pick up. So they never had to meet ...

Stupid girl, I thought. Why? Why do people put such horrendous substances into their bodies? I'd felt kind of sorry for her. She'd seemed so unloved, struggling along, penniless. Practically homeless.

Maybe that's why she puts that awful stuff into her body, I thought. Maybe it takes away the pain.

I could have done with something similar myself.

I texted back.

Thanks for letting me know. I'm in Chatsworth now, walking Dash. Such a beautiful, peaceful place. Who'd have thought?

So I headed home, showered and changed, fed the cat and the dog, then myself. Mine was much more appetising than theirs, of course. You can't beat a good organic jacket with baked beans, melted cheese, and salad with splashings of French Dressing. Superb. For pudding, I made frothy coffee with a splash of Cointreau. Well, it was Christmas.

So, with a little Dutch courage inside me, I texted Todd.

Hi Todd. Thank you for the offer - that would be amazing - I'd love to write the screenplay. I need to check with my agent Sandy, but I'm sure she'll be happy to go along with it. So I'll be in touch in the New Year. Merry Christmas. April x

I had a hair appointment to keep. Toni was going to tidy it up for me, ready for Mum's wedding. Plus, I was going to have my nails done.

A pampering day. Just what I needed.

So I left Dash with a bowl of water and walked down to the village, the wind dry and ice-cold. Reaching Toni's place, I pushed open the door to be greeted with *We wish you a Merry Christmas!* sung loudly by Toni and Mandy.

Mandy ushered me inside and sat me down with a glass of Bailey's and an After Eight chocolate.

'Thanks, Mandy. Wow, this is the way to do it.'

'After Eights. Smooth, slim, and dark,' said Toni. 'Just how I like my men.'

I laughed. 'Don't talk about men. I've had just about enough of men.'

'Sorry, April. You've not heard from him, then?'

I shook my head. 'No.'

She put the glass of Bailey's into my hand. 'Here – drink up. There's plenty more.'

I left two hours later, not that it took that long, but more because I needed the company. And I did feel so much brighter. My hair had been washed and dried, and Toni had fastened it up with a French Plait along the front. It looked lovely, and for once I didn't need to go home and wash it. Afterwards, Mandy had manicured my nails and painted them with shocking pink gel varnish. I could not wait to get all dressed up in the morning and attend my mother's wedding.

Inside the house, I found Dash whining and sniffing at the back door. I opened it gingerly, but it was only Marmalade, mewing to come in from the cold and the dark. So I allowed him inside, gave him a bowlful of Whiskas, and watched as he curled up beneath the warm radiator.

I grinned. 'Looks like we have a friend, Dash. I'm surprised at you.'

He looked up at me as if to say 'Huh!', stretched out his legs and lay down upon his bed.

Leaving them both to sleep, I made tea and carried it through to the lounge. Kneeling on the floor, I busied myself, wrapping the wedding presents I'd bought online weeks ago.

Le Creuset in coastal blue. The casserole, the frying pan, the saucepan set, and the rectangular roasting dish. Mum would love it, and I knew Jim would, too. His kitchen was soft grey with a marble worktop, and the coastal blue would set it off beautifully. So I wrapped each item in turn, using starry silver paper and bows of silver satin. Then I wrote the card, wishing them every happiness and a wonderful future together. I carried them through to the lounge and placed them on the dresser, all ready to go.

My phone pinged at that point, but it was only Bob Prendergast.

Hi April. Are you around for the next half hour? I just need to take some measurements – won't be long. There's a sale on at the showroom right after Christmas.

I replied.

Home all evening, Bob. I'll leave the front door unlocked so you can come in that way. I'll be in the kitchen – the tatty one that needs a remake ...

I was hungry, it was six-thirty, so I busied myself making veggie spag bol. The radio was blaring loudly with *I Want It All* by Queen (I remember it well as I thought it was appropriate at the time), although I still heard the front door slam.

'Hi, Bob,' I called.

But it wasn't Bob.

It was Fliss Porter-Bentley.

I went to greet her. 'Fliss. Hi, how are you?'

'Hi there, April.'

She looked drunk, or high, her pupils dilated, her fingers fiddling with her handbag haphazardly. Her long skirt and short cotton jacket, both black, looked out of place for this time of year, and I remembered she'd just attended her brother's funeral. Unsure of how to address this new Fliss, I turned off the gas and sat at the table, encouraging her to do the same. I thought it might calm her.

'Come on, take a seat and I'll make us some tea.'

But she stood by the doorway, blocking it with her body.

'No. It's okay. I just want to talk.'

'That's fine, fine. So what is it you'd like to talk about?'

All the time, I was watching the door behind her. Bob would be walking in at any moment. Maybe I should text him, tell him not to come over?

'About Felix, of course. About my Felix. My brother.'

Her voice teetered on the edge of hysteria. I stood up to fill the kettle, anyway, while I wondered what on earth to do.

'Are you sure you don't want tea?' I asked.

'This fucking British obsession with tea,' she cried, wiping her nose with the back of her hand. 'I'll never fucking understand it. What have you done with your hair, anyway? You going somewhere special? Looks ridiculous, all done up like that.'

Furtively, I picked up my phone from beside the cooker.

'I'll take that as a no, then, shall I?' I said, texting Bob as I spoke.

Get police.

'What you fucking doing? Give that to me!' Fliss grabbed the phone and threw it to the floor. 'Stupid woman!'

My legs began to shake, I couldn't control them. Instead, I realised, I had to take control of the situation.

'What is it you want, Fliss, exactly?'

She mimicked me in a silly little girl voice. *'What is it you want, Fliss, exactly?'*

I sat down, suddenly exhausted. 'Don't. Please.'

'What is it I want? What I want is a fucking apology. What I want is to know what the hell you were doing poking around in the grass, looking for dead bodies.'

'I wasn't. I wasn't *looking* for dead bodies. I was out walking my dog and he found the dead body. I didn't do it on purpose. Why on earth would I do that?'

She moved towards the cooker and leaned back against it, her hands a little calmer now. She rubbed at her eyes. 'So why didn't you just leave him there? Why did you have to go ringing the cops and telling everyone? What's the matter with you?'

'Because that's what you do, Fliss. You tell the police when you find a dead body. It has to be reported. What would you expect me to do?'

'I expected you to leave him. I expected you to just walk away.'

A sudden thought hit me, and I felt sick. I hardly dared ask the question, but knew I had to. Because it was just possible Fliss had seen Felix that night, had borrowed his jumper, and then killed Lucas for some reason.

'It wasn't you, was it?'

'Was what me?'

Terrified of her reaction, I tried a gentler tone. 'Fliss? Did you kill Lucas?'

Throwing back her head, she laughed crazily. 'What? What? You think I killed him? You think I killed Lucas Hanssen? You really are stupid, aren't you?'

I shook my head, doing my best to appear calm. 'No. I'm not. I just don't understand why you're so upset, that's all.'

She stared at me, her eyes wild, insane. 'Because, Miss Stanislavski, you made my Felix kill himself. There's no way he would knife somebody – no way. But no, you had to tell the police he killed Lucas. So my Felix went and drank himself to death. And now he's gone. He's dead. And don't think you're gonna get away with it, either. I'll make you pay, one way or another. I've already sold your books – nice little collection you had there. Made me a few dollars, they did. I rang Pete, my old buddy from London. Turns out you've got quite a reputation, April Stanislavski. A pity you made my Felix commit suicide.'

My throat constricted. I'd obviously had her wrong all this time. 'What? No. No, I didn't make him kill himself. That's a ridiculous thing to say.'

'Yes. You did.' Grabbing a knife from the block on the side, she nursed it between her hands. 'And now you're gonna tell me why.'

'Look – Fliss – you're going about this the wrong way. I only told the police about Lucas. I never for one minute suggested Felix killed him. I didn't even know Felix, and I'm sorry he's dead. I feel for you, really I do. I have a sister, and I can't imagine ever losing her. It must be devastating.'

Her face crumpled and the tears began. 'Yeah.'

'But this isn't the answer, Fliss. You could end up in trouble yourself, and how would that help?'

She stared at me defiantly. 'If I did kill you, no-one would know.'

My heart raced ferociously, and I stood up in an attempt to calm myself. Dash, sensing my alarm, growled deeply from his basket. Fliss moved towards him, the knife glinting beneath the overhead light.

'So you're the thing that found the body, are you? Maybe I should be getting rid of you instead.'

I stepped forward, standing between them. 'No. No, it wasn't him. The body was covered in leaves. The wind blew them off and we saw it, just lying there.'

I stared at her, still unsure. Standing there with the knife in her hand, she looked utterly capable of killing someone.

She could so easily have killed Lucas.

I felt cold suddenly.

Terrified.

'He was a good man, my brother,' she said. 'He'd have done anything for anyone, you know. That girl he was with – she used him. She used him and then she threw him away. Stupid fucking woman.'

I looked up. We never had traced Felix's girlfriend.

'What girl, Fliss? Who was he seeing?'

'Some hoity-toity type. I don't know her name or anything. But she sure welshed on the deal.'

'What do you mean? What deal?'

'He was gonna marry her.'

This was good, I realised. There was a story here. I could keep her talking until the police arrived. Assuming Bob had received my text.

I prayed Bob had received my text.

'Okay. So what happened?' I asked.

'She dumped him for someone else. Bitch.'

'Poor guy. So how long were they together?'

'Ages. He'd ring me sometimes, tell me how well he was treating her, how he bought her stuff - expensive stuff. But she took nearly all his dough. Fucking cow.' Angrily, she stared at me, the knife high in the air. 'Now get out of my way. This dog needs to go.'

Panicked, I rushed forward, grabbed both her wrists, and tried shaking the knife to the ground. At the same time, I tried my best to kick her.

But the commotion alerted Dash and he flew from his basket, sinking his teeth into Fliss's ankle. She screamed, pushed me away, and yanked Dash up by his collar, the knife all ready for action.

But Fliss hadn't reckoned on Marmalade, still there, snoozing beneath the radiator.

With his claws in the attack position, he threw himself into the air, scratching her face and clawing at her flimsy jacket as he fell to the floor. Dropping the knife, she covered her face with her hands and screamed.

'Bitch of a fucking cat - should be put down - let me get my hands ...'

The kitchen door opened with a thud.

'Police! Drop your weapons and stand very still.' It was PC Sonia, the girl who'd sat with me that night in Edensor.

I sat down. It was all I could do. My whole body trembled violently. Dash lay down on the floor beside me, watching me, guarding me. Marmalade just curled up beneath the radiator again, his job done.

PC Sonia and her male colleague charged Fliss with unlawful trespass and threatening behaviour, then bundled her away, amidst much shouting and blasphemy.

A few minutes later, Bob popped his head around the door, bringing with him another tin of mince pies. My wonderful neighbours, Ralph, Pam and Frances, arrived a few minutes after that. They'd seen the police arrive, and had then heard the commotion. They brought brandy round, and made hot tea, and we all sat there eating mince pies with the tea and the brandy. Then they made sure the house was safe and secure, and left for the night.

It was only after they'd gone that the tears came. Calming, therapeutic tears that allowed the fear and the tension to rise to the surface.

But one good thing would come out of this evening, I realised. I had to step up to the mark with the MAUD campaign. I had to use any influence I had to make people see. Drugs do awful things to lovely people. And if I could help prevent just one person from taking them when they first leave the safety of the family home, then I would have done a good thing.

I'd ring the papers after Christmas, I decided, and really get things moving.

So, after another tot of brandy and a whole bar of Green and Black's, I put down a bowl of tuna for Marmalade, and gave Dash some milk – his favourite, but only for special occasions. After all, they were the heroes of the hour. A dog and a cat. Who'd have thought it?

Then I climbed the stairs to bed. But not before I'd had a long soak in the bath, with strawberry bubbles up to my neck.

47

Pulling both letters from the drawer, she carries them down to the kitchen, walks into the garden, away from the chicken shed, and sets them alight. She watches as orange scraps of parchment fly through the cold night air ...

48

Millerstone, Derbyshire

MUM'S wedding day. Without Colin. I awoke with a heaviness that was hard to shake. I didn't want to move, didn't want to put my feet to the floor. I just wanted to hide.

But then I had a good talk with myself.

Get up, get under that shower, put on some slap, and get yourself dressed. Today is going to be a good day, a happy day.

However, I was just putting my feet to the floor when my phone rang. Reaching out sleepily, I pulled it towards me.

It was Sandy.

'Hello?' I murmured.

'April, darling, how are you?' There was a pause, then, 'have I woken you up, darling?'

'No, it's fine, Sandy. I need to get up, anyway - it's Mum's wedding day today. But it's lovely to hear from you. Merry Christmas, and thank you so much for the champagne.'

'Oh no, you deserve it. And thank you for the lilies - which is why I'm ringing. They arrived first thing this morning, and they are so beautiful.'

Forcing myself awake, I sat up and pulled the duvet around me. Dash came bounding in and jumped onto the bed.

'It's my pleasure, Sandy. Actually, did you ever get my email about meeting up in January?'

'I did, yes – sorry – been busy. It's just – I'm going to be away most of January. Is it very urgent?'

'No, but it is important. It's about changing my genre.'

There was a slight hesitation before, 'In what way, darling?'

She sounded upset, so I softened the news a little. 'I've been thinking about writing crime fiction. It wouldn't be to replace the romance, it would be more in addition to it. You know, the heroine becomes involved with the killer, or the lover becomes involved in vice, or something. I just thought it might be more interesting, more gripping.'

There was another pause, and then a huge, audible sigh. 'Oh no, April, darling. No, no, no. Not at all. It wouldn't do. Your name, it's synonymous with romance, love, relationships. No, people wouldn't like it. Not at all.'

There was nothing more to say, so I said nothing.

'Sorry, darling, but you know how amazingly well we've done in building up your reputation. And it's taken years. This is not the time to tear it all down.'

Disappointment flew to my throat, and I had to swallow hard. I really wanted this.

'No - it's fine, Sandy. I just feel I need a change, that's all. I'd love to do something a bit more adventurous.'

'Look - okay. Why don't you come and visit after I get back from Mauritius, and bring me an example, an idea or two? We can take a look at it.'

'Okay. Thanks, Sandy – I appreciate it. But there's another thing.'

'Yes?'

'I've recently been in touch with someone, a TV producer. He's asked if I'd like to make *Love in the Valley* into a film, wants to know if I'd be happy to write the screenplay. What do you think?'

'Now you're talking, darling. Well, well, that is excellent news. We'd have to check out the contract, of course, but yes - why not? So how did you get to meet this guy?'

I felt myself blush. 'Oh, it's a long story. But it was after a TV interview I did in support of my friend's campaign against drugs.'

'But that's really lovely, darling. And it's all such good publicity, isn't it? So is there anything we can help with at all, in the way of funding?'

My heart warmed to her. She always does like to help. 'No, not currently. But if there is anything, I'll let you know. Thanks, Sandy.'

'Did you ever hear anything about those books that were stolen, by the way?'

'It's funny you should ask that. I only found out last night. It was actually someone I've had dealings with before. She'd been to the house and must have seen them here.'

'Gosh, what a world, darling. What a world. But listen, don't worry about them. You're going to write plenty more, and the shelves will be completely full again, we'll make sure of it. So put your feet up and have a wonderful Christmas. And enjoy the champagne.'

'Thanks, Sandy. You too. And have a fab holiday.'

'The manuscript's looking amazing, by the way. You really are very talented.'

I was feeling tired, low, dispirited, and Sandy's words brought tears to my eyes. I wiped them away. But I couldn't wipe away the sound of my voice, thick with emotion.

'Thanks, Sandy. I appreciate it.'

'Hey, honey, are you okay? What on earth is wrong?'

'Oh, man trouble, the usual. Sorry ...'

'I should've guessed when you went rushing off to St Ives, *just on a whim*. Men - they're really not worth it. But listen, honey, do you remember when you were going through your divorce, and I sent you those little cards I got on a yoga retreat, way back?'

'Yes?'

'Do you still have them?'

I nodded. 'I know exactly where they are.'

'Then dig them out, darling, and read them again. And bless you.'

I did dig them out. After breakfast. I'd kept them all those years, hidden inside a small white shoebox beneath the bed - my memories box. Tucked beneath a pile of old letters and some old photographs, I found them. Two small cards, brightly-coloured, with words that never fail to inspire me, always manage to ease the pain. I sat down on the bed, the cards on my lap, the shoebox beside me, and I read them.

I can release the past. And forgive everyone. I am free to move into new glorious experience.

Life supports me. Life created me to be fulfilled. Life is always there at every turn. I am safe.

The ivory-white elephant hanging on the wall smiled down upon me, and I cried bitter tears.

But it was cathartic, the crying. Afterwards, it all felt so much better. I didn't have time to wallow in self-pity, anyway. I had a wedding to get ready for.

*

But first, there was a drive to the village, with joggers and a coat thrown over my pyjamas. I needed to get wine and chocolates for everyone – at least, the people who'd been there for me when I needed them. Bob Prendergast and my wonderful neighbours. So I chose three bottles of the best red wine they had. Cabernet Sauvignon, four years old (delicious). And three boxes of Green and Black's gift boxes containing milk chocolate pieces with sea salt (also delicious). I then bought a dozen pouches of Whiskas (the tuna one), a small blue cat collar, and some biscuits for Dash.

Then I drove home, ate a quick bowl of cereal, wrapped the chocolates in brown paper with red satin ribbons, and took them round. First, there was Ralph and Pam. Marmalade was there in the kitchen, lapping at a saucer of milk, so I placed the collar around his neck and said thank you.

'Hero of the hour, that one,' said Ralph, still in his chenille dressing gown. 'But he thinks he's a gypsy, travelling from house to house like he does. Then of course, when Frances goes looking for him, he's disappeared - not a hide, nor a hair to be seen. The elusive pimpernel.'

'You want a cuppa, love?' asked Pam.

I shook my head. 'No thanks, Pam. I have some more errands to do before the wedding.'

'Well, thanks so much for the chocolates and wine. But you shouldn't have. We were just concerned about you, that's all.'

'I know, but you were there when I needed you. If you hadn't come round when you did, twice, I dread to think of the state I'd be in. Thank you so much. And Happy Christmas.'

'And the same to you.' She hugged me. 'And enjoy the wedding, love. I'm sure your mum will be very happy. Jim Allsop's a lovely fella.'

'Thanks, Pam.'

I called on Frances next. Still in her nightie, she was a little embarrassed at the early hour, so I just pushed my gifts through the open door and gave her my sincere thanks.

'Marmalade is next door at Ralph's, in case you're looking for him.'

'Oh, that cat – what's he like? Thanks, pet, I'll pop round when I'm dressed.'

I grinned. 'He'll have gone by then.'

She shook her head. 'Oh, no, he knows which side his bread's buttered on. It's Christmastime - we've got ham and turkey in the house. He'll be turning up for sure.'

So I said my goodbyes and went home. I could call at Bob's on the way to the wedding, but first I needed to take Dash for his walk.

So we did the usual, up to Stanage Edge, then back down again. The sky above the hills was grey, heavy with snow, and I prayed it would hold off until much later.

So then it was time to get myself ready.

I had a strawberry-flavoured bubble bath with music by BB King playing in the background, and a face pack made of papaya and rose petals. Half an hour later, I was so relaxed I was practically comatose. So then I made fresh coffee and toasted teacake, and sat in my dressing gown in the kitchen with Dash.

'Well, what a week,' I said, stroking his head. 'This time last week we were in St Ives.'

He looked up at me, his eyes appealing, his nose wet and shiny.

'Don't worry. I'm not leaving you here by yourself all day. I've got a little surprise.' Reaching inside my handbag, I pulled out a small red ribbon and fastened it to his collar in a bow. 'There. You shall go to the ball.'

Upstairs, my hair only needed a little titivation with the curling irons, but it looked lovely once I'd finished. Then I spent ages on my makeup. Concealer, powder, eyeshadow. Getting it just so. But the pièce de résistance was the hat, of course. Putting it on brought back painful memories of my trip to Leeds, but I resisted letting it get me down. What's done is done, I said to myself, bravely.

So, dressed in pink chiffon and cashmere, I checked myself in the mirror and went on my way. Bob lives not far from the railway station, so I called round with my gifts, leaving Dash in the car.

'The wedding today, is it?' he asked, smiling at my outfit. 'I'd forgotten.'

'It is, so I can't stay long. But I've got a little something for you. Just to say thank you for rescuing me last night.' I pushed the wine and chocolates into his hands.

But he waved me away. 'I only called the police, you know. I didn't actually rescue you.'

'No, Bob. I dread to think what would've happened if you hadn't called them, and I'm really grateful. So thank you.'

'Okay. Well, it's very kind of you, and Merry Christmas. You look like a box of treats, by the way.'

I smiled. 'Thanks Bob, and Merry Christmas to you too. Give my love to Linda, and I'll see you soon.'

*

The parish church in Millerstone dates from the 14th century. It's beautiful, high on a hill, surrounded by green grass and calm tranquillity. I parked in the village to leave space in the car park and walked up the hill. The bells were ringing out as Dash and I approached. They told their tale loud and clear. My mum was getting married.

Jo and Joe were there waiting for us, and we stood for a moment before entering the church.

'The girls are so excited,' said Jo.

'I bet they look beautiful,' I replied.

'They've been at Mum's since ten. They'll be starving by now.'

'Jim will have made sure they're fed, don't worry. He won't want the bridesmaids misbehaving because they're hungry.'

'Ooh, I'm getting butterflies, it's all so exciting,' she said, rubbing her stomach.

I couldn't quite believe it myself. My mum. Getting married. A year ago, she'd been so depressed, so miserable, living on her own with no-one but the dog for company. But she would never have moved in with me - she liked her independence too much. Bless her.

Maybe that's where I get it from, I thought. The independence gene, that's what it was. But she'd managed to be happy with Dad for all those years. How did she do it? Just bite her tongue? Take a deep breath? And now, she's with someone else; she's with Jim. But I'm older now, I can see more. Jim seems to encourage her independence, not stifle it. But then Colin never stifled mine, either. It was just me. Scared of commitment.

'Come on,' said Jo, taking my arm. 'We need to go inside.'

*

Mum looked beautiful. So extremely happy, so wonderfully relaxed. And the girls were all well-behaved, even when the photographer kept us hanging around in the cold. Their dresses were lovely, in a gorgeous rose pink, with silver sequins that caught the light whenever they moved. It really couldn't have been a more beautiful day.

The reception was held at the Ashbourne Hotel, so I dropped Dash off at home before walking down and finding my place on the top table. It was a small affair, the reception, made up of family and close friends. The décor was exceptional, with rose pink gauze everywhere, and white candles and pink roses on the tables. Jim's best man was his brother Ken, whose speech was sometimes witty, sometimes sad, but always entertaining. Then Jim himself, used to public speaking, proceeded to enliven us with tales of their courtship, and particularly Mum's driving lessons, a complete disaster. She punched him with her clutch bag as he sat back down, amid howls of laughter.

'Obviously a match made in heaven,' said the guy sitting beside me.

I had no idea who he was, other than that he was related to Jim. They had the same surname, gleaned from the place card in front of him. So I just smiled and turned back to watch the speeches.

'Sorry,' he said. 'I should introduce myself. I'm Jim's nephew, Ken's son. You're Judy's daughter?'

I nodded. 'I am, yes. Pleased to meet you.'

So his name was Timothy Allsop and he was a freelance animator living near Chester. The creative talent had continued down through the generations, obviously. He was divorced, with a son still at school, and he was very charming - also a genetic trait, obviously.

'That's the good thing about being freelance,' he said. 'I can live wherever I like.'

'Me too. I write novels, so it really doesn't matter where I write. I could be living on a bus.'

'So where *do* you live?' he asked.

'Just up the road, actually.'

'Not far to stagger home, then. I'm staying here at the hotel. Uncle Jim and your mum are staying too, but they've got the bridal suite, of course.'

Timothy and I talked about quite a lot that afternoon. He was charming, as I've already said, and fun, and easy to be with. And I was having a wonderful time.

Halfway through the evening, however, Sean rang. I'd had a couple or three glasses of champagne by then, but I heard him out.

'DI Jasper just rang, so I hope you don't mind me calling. I'm off after today until January, so I thought you'd want to know.'

I excused myself from the table and walked out to Reception. 'It's fine, Sean. Fire away.'

'Okay. So the police have finally managed to get hold of the other amdram guys, the ones who were busy set-building when we interviewed. It transpires that our friend Lucas had offered to help with painting the set that night, but he spilt paint all over himself. So he had to get changed and wash it off before it dried. His jeans and tee-shirt are still there now, apparently. They've been clearing the place out for Christmas and that's what's jogged their memory. So the only clean clothes Lucas had available were the ones he wore on stage – the dress shirt and the trousers.'

'Bloody hell, Sean. That's incredible. Why didn't I think of that? We should have thought of that.'

'Are you drunk, April?' he asked, accusingly.

'Hey, if you can't get drunk at your own mother's wedding, when can you get drunk?'

He laughed. 'You're having a good time, then?'

'I most certainly am, yes, an amazing time. So come on then, what do they think happened after that?'

'They think he got changed, and was heading back to the rehearsal when he was called out. We can't find any calls on his phone, so we must assume someone called to see him – either between the rehearsal room and the theatre, or when he'd popped outside for some reason.'

'I know he smoked, so maybe he went out to light a cigarette?'

'Exactly. So along comes Felix, says we need to talk, so they walk to Edensor trying to sort stuff out, but then it gets into a fight.'

'Blithering idiots.' I was sobering up quickly. 'So have we discovered what the fight was about?'

'No. That's the missing piece of the jigsaw. But as they were involved in drug-dealing and money-laundering and god knows what else, it could have been anything.'

'No doubt the truth will out.'

'No doubt.'

'So what's happened to Fliss? Has she been arrested?'

'No. But you poor thing, April - DI Jasper has just told me what happened. No, they've let her off with a caution, seeing as she'd just been to her brother's funeral and was high as a kite. She's on her way home now.'

'Let's hope Felix has left her all his money.'

'You mean all the money he made illegally?'

'He did work for a living. There must be something.'

'You know what, April - you're a soft touch.'

'I'm not, not really. I just feel for her. She lost her parents and her home at such a young age, and now she's lost her brother. She's also a drug user, and that can't be easy for anyone. That's why I'm going to help Toni with this campaign. Big time.'

'Good girl. But I think for now you should go back and just enjoy the party. Have a good time, April, and Merry Christmas.'

'Merry Christmas, Sean.'

I popped to the loo to powder my nose, and was just heading back to the party when I received a text.

Hi, April. Merry Christmas. I hope the wedding went well. Look, I've been doing a lot of thinking and maybe you were right about me and Natasha. Maybe we were getting a bit too close for comfort. So can we talk? Please? I still love you. Colin. xxx

I didn't reply. I couldn't reply. There was nothing to say in my reply. So my overactive imagination hadn't been that overactive, after all.

Damn him, I thought. He can bloody well go back to bloody Belgium, and bloody well stay there.

*

I drank many glasses of champagne that night. I danced with everyone - Jo and the girls, and Joe, and Jim and Ken, and Mum.

Then Timothy asked me to dance, and we smooched until midnight, to music that took me back to the heady days of my youth, to music that will never, ever grow old. We danced and we danced, until my feet ached so much I decided I should collect my things, say goodnight to everyone, and make my way home.

And that's when the trouble started.

Because, as I glanced outside, I realised there was six inches of snow on the ground. And there was I, still in my three inch Jimmy Choos ...

49

Three days later, Christmas Day
And so the evidence has been destroyed. Forever.

But what else could she have done? Really?

She, the mother, the protector, carries the organic bronze turkey, crisp and succulent and all ready for carving, into the dining room. Her family sit there, patiently waiting. George and Gemma. And Amber.

Placing the turkey onto the table, she smiles ...

THE END

Acknowledgements

I finished writing this novel during the COVID19 Lockdown. Such an awful time for so many people.
So I'm dedicating this book to all the people who helped us out, who lifted our spirits, who kept us strong.
The NHS, the shopkeepers, the postal workers, the van drivers. Everyone. And my wonderful family and friends.
Thank you.

Thank you, too, to my proof readers Liz, Graham and Michaela. Also to Daniel and Benji for their IT expertise. Small pieces of this book must be credited to each and every one of you.
Thank you so much.

I do hope you've enjoyed *Murder on Her Doorstep*.

If you have - the best way to thank an author for writing a book you've enjoyed is to leave an honest review.

Click here: https://www.amazon.co.uk/MURDER-DOORSTEP-Stanislavski-Murder-Mystery/product-reviews/B08CPLDDY3/

to post your review of *Murder on Her Doorstep*.

Alexandra Jordan is the author of the Benjamin Bradstock Tales: *Snowflakes and Apple Blossom, Seasalt and Midnight Brandy,* and *Stardust and Vanilla Spice.* She has also written *One Tiny Mistake* and *Murder on Her Doorstep, the April Stanislavski Murder Mysteries.*

Snowflakes and Apple Blossom was shortlisted for the Writers' Village International Novel Award 2014. *Seasalt and Midnight Brandy* has been serialised on BBC Radio.

Alex practises yoga, walks, reads, eats chocolate, and treads the boards of the amateur stage. She lives in the Peak District with her husband and twin boys. Find her on Facebook, Twitter@Alexjord18, and Instagram. Please visit https://alexjordan1.wixsite.com/author to leave an email address for updates on Alexandra's new publications. Thank you.

Printed in Great Britain
by Amazon